The Faerie Ring

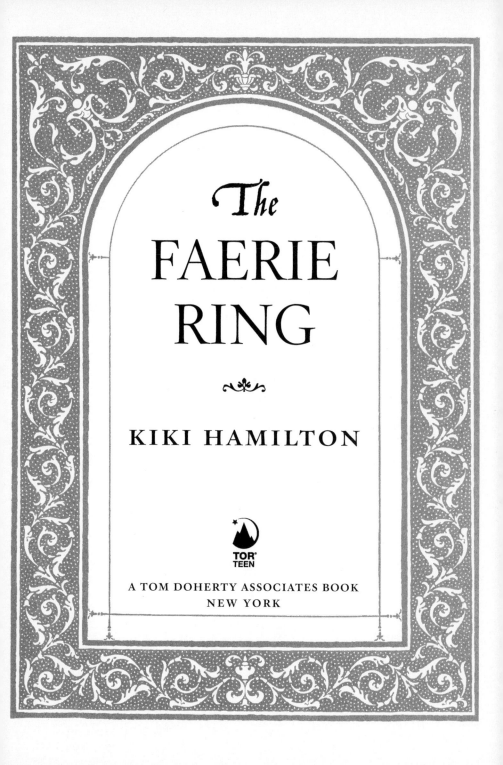

The

FAERIE
RING

◈

KIKI HAMILTON

TOR®
TEEN

A TOM DOHERTY ASSOCIATES BOOK
NEW YORK

THE FAERIE RING

Copyright © 2011 by Karen Hamilton

Map by Jon Lansberg

A Tor Teen Book
Published by Tom Doherty Associates, LLC
175 Fifth Avenue
New York, NY 10010

www.tor-forge.com

Tor® is a registered trademark of Tom Doherty Associates, LLC.

ISBN 978-0-7653-2722-2

First Edition: October 2011

Printed in the United States of America

0 9 8 7 6 5 4 3 2 1

For my daughter, Carly, who taught me
that love truly has no limits

❧ AND ☙

For all of us who see the shadows move
and know there's something more

Key to Pronunciation and Meaning of Irish Words

(With thanks to irishgaelictranslator.com)

An fáinne sí (un FAWN-yeh shee):
The faerie ring

Na síochána, aontaímid
(nuh SHEE-uh-khaw-nuh, EEN-tee-mij):
For the sake of peace, we agree

Grá do dhuine básmhar
(graw duh GGWIN-yeh BAWSS-wur):
Love for a mortal person

Óinseach (OWN-shukh):
Fool/idiot (for a female)

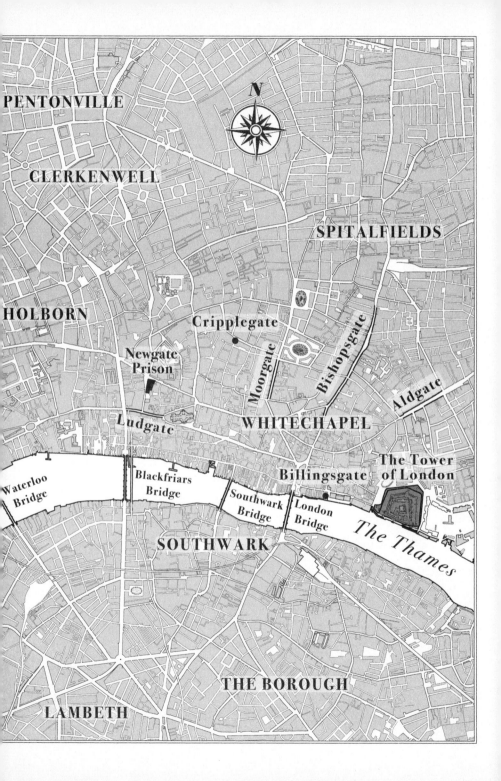

The Faerie Ring

Chapter One

Y OU wouldn't be here pickin' pockets, would you?"
Tiki jumped as the dark figure loomed over the corner where she sat, pretending to be half-asleep. Thick, black hair hung low over the figure's forehead, shadowing his eyes. The glittery light of the pub illuminated his face as he leaned toward her, and the fear that bubbled in her stomach dissipated as she recognized him.

"Rieker." Tiki spoke in a low voice. "What are you doing here?" His timing couldn't be worse. "Are you following me again?" She'd identified her mark and was just waiting for the right moment to make her move.

"Me follow you?" Rieker gave an arrogant snort. "Now why would I do that?" He jingled the coins in his pocket as if to taunt her. "I've been workin' the World's End for a few months now." He leaned an elbow on the plank table, a mug of ale clutched in his hand. "Maybe *you're* followin' *me*." He looked her up and down with a mocking gaze. "Because I'd swear I've never seen your pretty face in here before."

Tiki forced an insincere smile. "Maybe you weren't looking hard enough." She tugged the bill of her cap down to hide her features. Dressed in breeches and a man's over-size jacket, Tiki was perfectly disguised—no one but Rieker would have known she was a sixteen-year-old girl. And even he hadn't known until two months ago.

She'd spotted him coming out of a clockmaker's shop in King's Cross with both hands shoved into the pockets of his tattered black coat. The cautious way he'd glanced around had made her wonder what he'd nicked. Curious, she'd followed him.

Rieker was a thief who had made a name for himself throughout the slums of London. Stories about him stretched from Bishopsgate in the East End, to Charing Cross in the heart of the City, all the way to King's Cross here in the North End.

As if the weight of her stare had tapped him on the shoulder, Rieker had glanced back at her. Before she could react, his gaze had skipped from her face to something behind her. Without a word, he'd turned and run. Instinct had made Tiki run, too. That's when the bobby had shouted at them to stop.

Fear had fueled her feet, for she didn't know the nooks and crannies of King's Cross well enough to be confident of escape. She'd followed Rieker until he'd dashed through an archway, rounded a corner, and simply disappeared. Tiki had slowed in surprise. The bobby had just latched on to the back of her loose jacket when she'd spotted Rieker motioning to her from a narrow corridor.

With a jerk, she'd slipped her arms from the sleeves— revealing long braided hair and a shape that couldn't belong to a boy—and raced into the shadows of the brick hallway. She'd never forget the look on Rieker's face that day.

"What are you doing up north here in Camden Town?" Rieker's voice brought her back to the present. "Bit far from Charing Cross, aren't you?"

"Maybe." Tiki kept her tone even. "But the biggest pub in all of London is worth the trip."

Rieker pulled one of the chairs away from the table, the wooden legs scraping against the floor. "Are you here alone?"

Tiki put out a hand to block him. "Don't sit down—you're not staying. And it's none of your business who I'm with or where I go." Irritated, she turned back toward the crowd. Where was her mark?

A smoky cloud hung in the room above the motley crew of sailors, chandlers, coal porters, and dustmen who filled the pub. She recognized Bilby the rat catcher, and Mr. Bonfield the costermonger from up round Covent Garden Market, but where was MacGregor?

For weeks she'd been watching the big, ruddy Scotsman, following him in the evenings from pub to pub. He owned clothing shops in Seven Dials and Petticoat Lane and loved to drink his profits, especially on a Friday night. When he drank he got careless. Tiki's fingers itched in anticipation. It was hardly a challenge for someone of her skills, but she had grown to dislike his swaggering and the way he bullied the barmaids. It would be a pleasure to lighten his pockets. Had she missed her chance?

"Last call!" The bartender's voice cut across the noise of the room. "Drink up, fellers, pub's closin'." The World's End had a packed house tonight. The wooden plank floor of the pub was slick with spilled ale, and the rich, yeasty smell of beer hung thick in the air.

A row of sailors sat shoulder to shoulder along the wooden bar, hunched over their drinks. Big mirrors lined the walls, etched with the names of ales or whiskeys, reflecting the bright lights in the room as well as the cloud of tobacco smoke. Barmaids and prostitutes, their skirts partially tucked up in their waistbands, worked their way through the crowd smiling and joking with the customers. The tinkling notes of a piano were a backdrop to the cacophony of accents that clashed above it all.

Tiki's eyes stopped on the silhouette of a tall man with a large, bulbous nose.

There he was.

A meaty-looking fellow with shoulders like a bull underneath his worn brown jacket, MacGregor looked in fine form tonight. Red-faced, he was belting out a raunchy tune as he waved his mug of ale in time to the song.

Rieker followed Tiki's gaze. "No. Not MacGregor."

Tiki let out an impatient breath. "Why in bloody hell not? I've been watching him half the night." She started to slide out of her chair, but Rieker's hand clamped down on her wrist, pinning her to the table.

"He's too drunk," he warned. "If he catches you, there'll be no mercy."

"Take your hand off me," she gritted through clenched teeth. Tiki yanked away and shot out of her chair. Fiona might chatter on about how handsome Rieker was with his tall, rugged build and elusive air, but Tiki found him insufferable.

The corners of Rieker's mouth quirked, his smoky eyes dancing.

"Just like a kitten pretending to be a lion," he said. "Except I don't think your claws are sharp enough to hurt anyone, little kitten."

Tiki reacted without thinking. She jabbed her finger into his chest.

"Listen to me, Rieker. I'm not your 'kitten' or anybody

else's. I'll do what I please, and I'll thank you to leave me the hell alone."

Fast as a cat, he grabbed her arm. A look Tiki couldn't decipher crossed his face. "What's this?" he asked, holding up her wrist.

Rieker's grip was so tight that her fingers began to tingle. Tiki winced, swallowing a gasp.

"Rieker, stop it. You're hurting me."

His grip loosened, but he didn't let go. "Tiki, where did you get this mark?"

Rieker's strange reaction made Tiki glance down at her arm where her birthmark was exposed. Delicate lines twisted and turned like a tangle of vines, dark against her pale skin.

Rieker's gaze was incredulous, searching, as if trying to see into her very thoughts. She couldn't help but notice how long his dark lashes were, framing his smoky eyes. A strange nervousness started to flutter in the pit of her stomach when MacGregor's drunken bellow for more ale cut through the noise in the pub and broke the spell.

"I. Said. Let *go!*" With a great surge, Tiki jerked her arm back, sending Rieker's mug of ale directly into the face of a nearby sailor. The stunned man shook his head, his bleary eyes searching the crowd for the culprit.

Tiki turned just in time to see the sailor drop his head and plow his shoulders into an innocent chimney sweep. Still covered in coal dust, the chimney sweep went flying backward into the crowd. Mayhem broke loose as sailors and tradesmen shoved back with fists and feet.

Tiki stepped away from the table and slid sideways through the crowd, head down so the bill of her cap shadowed her face. Usually she wouldn't take such a risk on her last pick of the night, but she wanted to prove Rieker wrong.

"Tiki, wait," Rieker called after her.

Tiki glanced back, but Rieker was stuck in the crowd, unable to stop her. She smiled to herself in satisfaction. She could handle MacGregor. Plus, a few more coins to line her pockets would certainly warm the long, cold ride home to the abandoned clockmaker's shop adjoining Charing Cross.

Tiki took a deep breath as she neared her mark, dodging the arms and legs swinging wildly around her. MacGregor was engrossed in the brawl, red-faced and hollering encouragement in a hoarse roar. His face shone with excitement, a large bead of sweat hanging from the tip of a nose that had seen more than a few fights.

She slithered close and slipped her hand into his pocket. Just as she'd hoped, MacGregor was carrying a load of money. She pinched several of the coins together and started to pull her hand free.

The big man jerked around and squinted his red-rimmed eyes in her direction.

"Wot you be about, boy?" he growled.

"N-nuthin', guv'nor," Tiki stammered. She tried to back away but was hemmed in by the mass of bodies.

"Wot you got in your hand?" He snatched for her with a big, meaty paw. "Show me."

Tiki slapped her hands together to mask the sound of the coins dropping and held her palms up, wiggling her fingers to distract him as the coins slid down her sleeve. "Nuthin', sir, I swear."

There was another surge in the crowd, and a large man, dressed like a coal porter, collided with MacGregor. The man's black hat flew off as MacGregor's glass of ale hit the wooden floor with a resounding crash.

This was trouble.

MacGregor roared with rage. Tiki swung her right elbow back as hard as she could, hitting a soft belly.

"Umphf," a voice gasped as her elbow made contact. "What the bloody hell?" The man behind her stepped back, opening a small space in the crowd. In a blink, Tiki darted through the gap.

"Come back 'ere, you little thief," MacGregor yelled.

Tiki cut her way through the crowd. She reached the heavy plank entry door and yanked it open just enough to slip out into the chill winter air. Her breath came in short gasps, her chest heaving with exertion. Where could she hide? She only had a moment before MacGregor would catch her.

In the distance, the brisk clip-clop of a lone carriage working its way up the cobblestone lane echoed in the cool night air. *Blast.* It was so late that there were few cabs about, and this coach was headed in the wrong direction.

She took a step toward the street, peering right and left, looking for any other means of escape. Behind her, the pub door creaked open.

"Where is he?" a thick voice cried.

Tiki's breath caught in her throat. It was MacGregor. She pushed away from the building and ran. The carriage was just turning the corner onto the lane.

"You there," MacGregor cried. "Stop!"

Tiki darted out of the shadows and raced toward the back of the carriage. With a burst of speed, she placed a hand on one of the rear struts and jumped lightly onto the boot where the luggage was usually stored. Wedging herself into the corner of the little shelf situated behind the wheel box, she watched as MacGregor lumbered down the cobblestone lane, his head swiveling back and forth in confusion.

"Where'd he go?" he bellowed.

Behind him, just exiting the pub, Tiki recognized Rieker's tall silhouette before the carriage creaked around a corner, and the pub disappeared from view. "And that's how you pick MacGregor's pocket," she whispered.

Tiki repositioned herself on the small shelf with a tired sigh, settling in for the ride back to Charing Cross. She fingered the solid weight of the coins she had stashed in her pocket and pressed her lips together in a small, satisfied smile. There would be enough to pay the muffin man and to buy a chunk of cheddar big enough for all of them.

Tiki thought of how excited the others would be. Food had been scarce lately. Shamus and Fiona had been giving part of their portions to the younger ones, Toots and Clara, and even with that, four-year-old Clara was painfully thin. Tiki tried not to think of the persistent cough that had been racking the child lately. Maybe she could find some milk for Clara to soak her bread in as well.

Wrapping her arms tight around her knees to ward off the chill, Tiki eyed the black swirls on her wrist and wondered again about Rieker's strange reaction to her mark. She usually made an effort to keep her wrist covered, not wanting to draw attention to the odd birthmark. When she was younger, her mum had teased her and told her she'd been marked by faeries. Her mother's whispered words came back to her now: *They're around us. Pay attention and you'll see them.*

A pang of longing twisted inside at the memory of her

mum. She pushed the painful thoughts away. She had more important things to think about now, like finding enough food to fill their stomachs each day. Tiki leaned her head back and closed her eyes, listening to the staccato rhythm of the horse's hooves echoing in the night.

Chapter Two

TIKI jolted awake. The carriage had come to a stop.
She leaned forward to peer around the edge of the cab and stared in confusion at the orbs of lamplight glowing through the thick mist. She could make out the dim shapes of other carriages forming a queue. Snorts and the shuffling clack of horse's hooves were oddly muffled by the dense fog. To her left, through the shadows, the walls of a great mansion loomed. To her right, she could see the dim light of the streetlamps through the over-hanging trees. Where was she? It was impossible to tell through the blanket of fog.

She tightened her grip on a strut as the carriage jerked forward.

"Bring her this way," a man cried in the distance.

Through the fog, she could see the outline of the large building. Tall columns stretched along the front of the façade. The bare limbs of several elm trees stretched in a row toward the entry. She had to get away. Taking a deep breath, Tiki jumped from the back of the carriage and ran for the shadows that surrounded the trees. Bark was rough on her fingers as she leaned against one of the trees. After a moment, she pushed off and raced toward the side of the building.

Tiki heaved a sigh of relief as she slumped against the rough stone. Of all the idiotic things to do, how could she have fallen asleep on the boot?

Her stomach gave a loud growl. She hadn't eaten since afternoon, and that biscuit had been hard enough to crack her teeth. Clara and Toots would be starving unless Shamus or Fiona had been able to pick a pocket or snitch some fruit from a costermonger's stall today. But the costermongers guarded their fruit and vegetable carts well, carrying a long switch to swat the hands of hungry children who might think to steal from them.

A twinge snaked its way through Tiki's chest. It had to be close to midnight. She usually returned home around the supper hour, as the crowds were too thin to safely pick a pocket. Clara liked to wait up for her return each day. Was the little girl clutching Doggie, her sawdust-filled rag doll, wondering where she was right now?

Tiki peered toward a swath of light that cut across the dark yard. A side door was stretched wide open, as if beckoning her. The aroma of roasting meat was tempting. Tiki's stomach gave another growl, louder this time.

She hesitated. The coins she had snitched tonight were heavy in her pocket, but the muffin man who worked near Charing Cross was long gone for the day, and the shops were closed. The children would be so hungry. Did she dare try to find some food before she started for home again?

She inched closer. She couldn't resist the fragrant smells of baking bread and roasting beef. As Tiki stepped through the doorway, the heat from the coal-burning fires of the kitchen enveloped her like a warm blanket. The room bustled with activity. A red-faced, round-bellied woman, clearly in charge, brandished a butcher knife as she barked orders at the kitchen maids.

Tiki ducked into a dim alcove stacked with bags of flour and stayed tight to the wall as she peered around the corner. Her eyes grew wide at the staggering amounts of food being prepared. Soups and sauces were stirred over the fire. Some sort of meat, venison or beef, dripped juices onto the open flames. Nearby, pots full of peas and carrots waited to be steamed, and there was an entire table full of bread. Loaves and loaves of fresh-baked bread.

Tiki's mouth watered as she eyed the bounty. What she would give to take even a few loaves and a good hunk of beef home to the others. At seventeen, Shamus was grown, but he'd become so thin and tall that his wrists and ankles stuck out from his ragged clothes as if he'd pulled on ten-year-old Toots's trousers by mistake. And fifteen-year-old Fiona's pretty face had become angular and sunken.

"Turn that spit before the meat chars and I have to char your backside." The cook whacked at the meat on the cutting board. "An' you, young miss . . ." The cook pointed her knife at a girl who stood stirring a large pot. "Don't let me catch you daydreamin' again."

Tiki eyed a round block of cheddar on a nearby table that was surrounded by a number of smaller chunks of cheese, just waiting to be melted. She could snitch a few of the smaller hunks and a couple of loaves, and no one would be the wiser.

A movement to her left caught her attention. A young boy watched her from the floor. He reminded her of a dormouse, his big eyes like two dark plums centered in the round pie plate of his face. She raised a finger to her lips.

He blinked at her and nodded that he understood she wanted him to be quiet. Could she take the chance?

"That bread has had time to cool," the cook bellowed. "Mary, start putting it in the bread baskets and store them against that wall. We need that table for the sweet-cakes."

It was now or never. Tiki made her way over to the table with the cheddar and crouched beside it. Watching the swirling skirts of the kitchen maids walking to and fro, she snaked a hand up over the edge of the table and grabbed blindly for a hunk of cheese. She slid the cheese into the oversize pocket of her jacket and on hands and knees worked her way over toward the table laden with loaves of bread.

She shot a quick glance back at the young boy. He was still watching her every move.

"Ellie," the cook yelled, "get me a bag of flour." The clank of pots and pans along with the rhythmic beat of chopping knives continued, as though the kitchen were a great machine, its gears and cogs in full motion.

Tiki crept along the floor, grateful for the shadows cast under the tables. Under the bread table, she paused, waiting for the right moment. Whoever lived here had so much food they'd never notice a few missing crusts. She thought of how Toots's freckled face would light up when she showed him the fresh cheddar.

One of the kitchen maids came over to the table where Tiki hid. Tiki held her breath as the girl shuffled the loaves of bread from the table to a basket. When the girl walked away, Tiki groped blindly over the edge of the table. She'd just latched on to a loaf when a scream split the air.

"Who's under there?"

Tiki bolted out from under the table. She caught a fleeting glimpse of the little boy, his eyes wide, his mouth open to form an O of surprise, as she flew by. As she ran for the door she'd come in, another kitchen maid stepped out of the alcove where Tiki had hidden earlier, a huge sack of flour clutched to her chest. A scream erupted from her throat and she froze in place, blocking the exit.

"Stop, you!" the cook bellowed. "Thief!"

Tiki darted toward another door, desperate to escape. A dim hallway stretched before her, and she flew as fast as her feet could move, unmindful of the clatter her boots made on the wooden floor. Shouts and shrieks followed her departure, and Tiki could hear the lumbering gait of the well-endowed cook. "Get back in the stables where you belong!" she yelled.

Tiki ran down a warren of dim corridors until she found a door slightly ajar. She slipped inside, closed it softly behind her, and pressed her forehead against the cool grain of the wood. She strained to hear any sounds of pursuit. Long moments ticked by as Tiki held her ear to the door. Nothing. She heaved a sigh of relief.

Thankful that she'd escaped for the moment, Tiki turned and gasped. She stood in a huge room with eight angled walls that formed an octagon. Every wall was filled with bookcases, every shelf filled with books. And if that weren't enough, a second set of bookshelves lined the walls above the first set, reaching all the way up to the large, arch-top windows far above her head.

Tiki's jaw sagged in disbelief as she tilted her head back and gazed up at the enormous number of books. Underneath her boots, plush carpet softened her steps. Tiki turned in a full circle, trying to take it all in. The sheer size of the room made her feel antlike and small.

A large desk sat in the center of the room, and on the far side there was a glass-paned door. A fire burned low in the grate, gas lamps lighting the interior of the room with a soft glow. A familiar longing tugged at her as she gazed at the shelves lining the walls.

An old memory rushed to mind, of her father sitting before the fire, a pipe clutched in one hand as he read stories from Dinah Craik's *The Fairy Book*. Scotty, her cocker spaniel, was asleep on Tiki's lap as she listened. Her mother sat in a nearby chair, her dark head bent over her fancy needlework. A lump filled her throat at the vivid recollection.

Drawn by an irresistible pull, Tiki moved to the nearest shelf and ran her fingers over the leather spines. She longed to pull open the pages and read the secrets kept inside. She moved deeper into the room. The great desk was exactly the same shape as the room, with four legs to support the eight-sided top. Nearby, an oversize book lay open on a stand, with a magnifying glass resting on its surface. Tiki picked up the circle of clear glass suspended by an ornately carved handle and peered at the map.

"I know it's here somewhere," a voice said from outside the glass-paned door. "I was looking at it earlier."

Tiki jumped in alarm as the door to the library swung inward. Still clutching the magnifying glass, she dove under the desk, her pulse drumming in her ears. The soft shuffle of boots on carpet moved in her direction.

"It's the only way you'll get him to believe you at this

point, Arthur," a second voice replied. The pages of a newspaper rustled overhead, alarmingly close to Tiki's hiding place.

"Ah, here it is." Arthur's voice was deep and pleasant.

"Have you found it, then?" The second voice was not as deep as the first and sounded younger.

"Yes, I've got the information right here," Arthur said. "Smithson will have to eat his words once he looks at these numbers. I'd wager this is Grace's best cricket season yet."

Tiki's heart beat a wild rhythm in her chest as she listened to their conversation, huddled under the massive desk. She couldn't possibly explain her presence in this room to these two young men, with bread and cheddar tucked in her pockets. They would know at a glance that she was nothing more than a thief.

"Probably should've upped the bet," the younger voice said. He snickered. "You know what they say, Arthur, build your wealth when opportunity knocks."

"Yes, Smithson owes me after the beating I took in cards the other night. Speaking of that, Leo," Arthur said, "I think Isabelle Cavendish considers *you* an opportunity."

Leo's voice answered just above her head, and Tiki jumped in surprise. She had to bite her lip not to gasp out loud when she spied the toes of two black boots only a few feet from her shoulder.

"At least Isabelle is interesting. And pretty. Doesn't she look breathtaking tonight? So many of these young women can hardly carry on a decent conversation, what with their incessant giggling and whatnot. Why is the female of the species so dreadfully boring, I wonder?"

Arthur laughed. "Maybe you should try talking about

something besides horses and hunting. What is it about Isabelle other than her appearance that you find so fascinating, then?"

Tiki heard a soft *pop!* and then the clink of crystal.

"She was asking me about one of Mother's rings tonight. You know the one." There was a pause and then a soft sigh. "I do love champagne."

"What ring?" Arthur sounded as though he had moved closer.

"The one Mother has hidden, with the red stone," Leo said. There was a rustling sound. "This one."

There was a long moment of silence. "Is that the ring of the truce?" Arthur's voice was hushed. "Where did you get that?"

"I took it from Mother's strongbox earlier today," Leo said.

"Does she know?"

Leo snorted. "What do you think I am, a complete fool?"

"What are you two doing down here?" The strident tone of an older woman interrupted their conversation.

"Oh, hello, Mother," Arthur replied smoothly. "Just came down to get the paper to show Charlie Smithson something." Papers rattled as if to emphasize his point.

"And Leo? What is your excuse?" The sound of skirts swishing moved closer. "You both belong upstairs in the ballroom with your guests. And what's that in your hand, Leo?"

"Just a glass of champagne, Mother," the younger voice replied. Something dropped down into the darkness underneath the desk. "I thought I'd take a break from the party." He took several steps away from the desk but remained close enough that Tiki could still spy the black heels of his boots. "I need a breather every once in a while from all the attention."

"Yes, well, the attention serves a purpose," the woman said. "There are alliances to be forged. Stop spending so much time with Isabelle Cavendish. You've known her all your life. Spend some time with that young duchess from Russia—what's her name? Maria?"

"Grand Duchess Maria Alexandrovna," Arthur said.

"Yes, that's the one."

"She looks like a horse," Leo said.

"Well, you love horses, so you should find her quite appealing." Fingers snapped. "Come along, then, both of you. Our guests expect to have the opportunity to see and talk with you tonight," the woman said, "and many have traveled a great distance to be here."

"Yes, we'll be right up," Arthur said. "I just wanted to—"

"Now." Her tone made it clear there would be no further negotiation.

There was a second of silence before the whisper of boots moved across the carpet.

"Brilliant idea, Mother." Leo's voice was light and pleasant. "Can we escort you upstairs?"

"Thank you, dear, that would be lovely. I plan to return to . . ." The woman's voice faded as they left the room and the door closed.

After several long minutes, Tiki released her breath and relaxed against the thick carpet.

That was close.

She eyed the item that Leo had tossed under the desk. Mesmerized by its beauty, Tiki reached for the ring. It was a burnished band of rich gold, capped by an intensely red stone the color of blood that almost seemed to beckon to her.

Tiki stared into the ruby red depths, turning the stone this way and that to catch the light. Something flickered, and her heart caught in her throat as she peered closer. Deep within the heart of the stone, flames burned.

She crawled out from under the desk and tilted the ring under a lamp. How could there be flames *inside* a ring? A tiny bit of writing inside the band caught Tiki's eye.

Na síochána, aontaímid: For the sake of peace, we agree.

Tiki murmured the words aloud to herself. She held the ring up again and watched the flames within the stone flicker and dance. It was breathtaking. She couldn't look away.

She slid the ring onto the third finger of her right hand, and her skin tingled as though warmed by the fire in the ring. She held her hand out to admire the beauty of the stone, the flames winking in its depths as if sending her a secret message.

Tiki gave a furtive glance around the room before sliding the ring off her finger and into her pocket.

"They'll probably never even notice the ring's gone missing," she whispered.

She had never stolen something just for herself before. She had only stolen to survive. But she had to have this ring.

A clock on one of the bookshelves chimed twelve times. Midnight. She needed to get back to Charing Cross. The others would be worried. She hurried to the back wall and eased the door open a crack to peer into the hallway. There was no one in sight.

She rushed down the dim corridor, keeping to her toes, trying to minimize the sound of her boots. As she wound her way through the maze of halls, the din from the kitchen became louder. Pans clanking and a gabble of voices talking: kitchen maids and the low tones of a man. Above it all, the shouts of the cook could be heard.

Tiki slowed as she approached the door. Stealthily she leaned forward and peered around the doorjamb. The cook and her helpers were busy chopping, stirring, steaming, kneading. A thin, balding man in a red coat leaned against the wall of the alcove that held the flour. His back partially blocked the door.

"A thief in the kitchens? Are you sure Cookie wasn't samplin' the wine again?" he said.

"Now don't you start in on that, Angus," the cook called over her shoulder from where she stood at the great stove. "I've heard just about enough out of you."

No one was looking in Tiki's direction. Now was her chance.

She hurried down the hall to the exterior door and skidded into the cold night. Without looking back, she dashed for the shadows under the trees. The fog had lifted and she could see carriages stretched in a queue around the corner, lined up to await the return of the partygoers. She didn't dare try to catch a ride from here.

Staying deep in the shadows, she ran across the street toward what looked to be a park and disappeared into the darkness. When she was a safe distance away, Tiki dug into the pocket of her trousers and pulled out the ring. By the light of the moon, she could see the flames embedded deep in the stone flicker and glow, like the embers of a fire.

A strange yearning pulled at her. She slid the band back on her finger, turning and twisting the ring to watch the play of light. It had to be worth a fortune. Could she take it home with her and fence it?

No. She didn't dare.

If caught with the ring in her possession, she'd be thrown into Newgate Prison to rot until the end of time. She needed some time to think, to plan.

Tiki ran alongside a lake until she came to the base of a stately old elm tree, its dark shadow looming over the other trees under the patchwork light of the cloud-shrouded moon.

She grabbed a branch and swung herself up on a limb. Perched in the crotch of the tree, she ran her hands over the spongy, moss-laden trunk until she found a rotted-out hole where an old branch had fallen away.

The ring would be safe here for a few days. No one would think to look in this old tree. She would leave it just until she made up her mind what she was going to do with the thing.

She tore a piece off the bottom of her ragged trousers and reluctantly pulled the ring from her finger. Tiki carefully wrapped it in the fabric. With tentative fingers, she reached into the hole and tucked the bundle into the crevice, then covered it with several chunks of moss.

Satisfied the ring was safely hidden, Tiki swung down from the branch and landed in the thicket. She brushed off her trousers and smiled to herself before turning to gaze back across the lake toward the grand mansion. Though the trees eclipsed part of her view, from this distance she could see the building lit up like Big Ben. Her smile faded as cold fingers wrapped around her heart. She recognized that familiar silhouette.

It was Buckingham Palace.

She recalled the names of the young men in the library. Leo . . . *Prince* Leopold? And *Prince* Arthur? And the older woman . . . *Mother* . . .

Oh, bloody hell. She'd just stolen the queen's ring.

Chapter Three

Tiki pushed aside the board hanging from a single nail and slipped into the abandoned clockmaker's shop that adjoined Charing Cross Station. The milky light from the railway station drifted in through the three arched windows that lined the common wall between the station and the room they called home. Positioned above their makeshift door, the windows let in just enough illumination that she could see the shadowy figures of her small family of orphans.

"Tiki!" Toots scrambled across the room and threw his arms around her. "We thought you'd been snatched by the bobbies."

"Or someone caught your hand in their pocket." Worry made Fiona's voice softer than usual. "An' hauled you away for good."

"Everything all right, Tiki?" Shamus stood, a tall, thin shadow in the dim light.

"Yes." Tiki wrapped her arms around Toots's thin shoulders. "I just hopped a boot and fell asleep."

"You fell asleep on the back of a carriage?" Fiona asked. She was snuggled in a pile of ragged blankets on one side of the small box stove, which gave off enough heat to keep the room bearable in winter, if they could find the coal to fill it. "In this weather? It's freezing out there."

"I was tired," Tiki replied.

A match sizzled to life as Shamus lit a candle. The small flame cast wavering shadows against the wall as the wick ignited. Shamus's blond hair glowed yellow in the candlelight.

Rumpled blankets and tattered pieces of clothing stretched on both sides of the box stove, divided into boys' and girls' sleeping areas. In the middle of the long room, an upturned crate covered with a plank of wood served as their table. Tiki made her way toward the two rickety chairs they'd scavenged from a burned-out flat in Drury Lane. "I'm home now, though, so let's eat." With a flourish she pulled the loaf of bread and chunk of cheddar from her pockets and placed them on the wooden surface.

"Cheddar," Toots cried. He skittered across the floor, nearly tripping in his hurry. "Where'd you get that, Teek?"

"Oh, had a bit of luck on my way home."

"I am so hungry." Fiona pushed aside her covers and joined Toots at the table. "We didn't have any luck today." She tore a chunk of the bread and shoved it in her mouth until her cheeks bulged.

"How's Clara?" Tiki asked. She freed her long, dark braid from her jacket and began to unweave the strands, anxious to massage the tension from the back of her head.

As if in response to her question, a deep gurgling cough rose from a small lump next to where Fiona had huddled. The cough ended in a raspy sigh.

Tiki turned toward the sound. "She sounds worse."

"Aye, she's been coughing a mite more," Shamus agreed.

Six months ago, Tiki had stumbled over the little girl curled up in a pile of trash on Craven Street outside

Charing Cross. Tiki had taken her home and cared for her, but for weeks she wasn't sure the little girl would live. In the ensuing months, Tiki had worked hard to nurse Clara back to health. Not more than four years old, the frail child had continued to improve until three weeks ago, when the cough had started again.

Tiki moved across the room, her eyes adjusting to the dim light. Deeply asleep, Clara clutched Doggie close to her face. A pang of love pierced Tiki's chest with such fierceness that it made her breath catch. She would need to find some medicine for Clara in the morning. She couldn't bear the thought of the little girl being so sick again.

Gently, she pulled a blanket up over Clara's shoulders, resting the backs of her fingers along the little child's soft cheek for a moment. She felt warm enough, but the congestion in her chest made her breathing labored.

Tiki sank into one of the chairs as Shamus tore off a hunk of cheese and sat on the floor beside her, one arm wrapped around his knees.

"I was so hungry," Toots said in between bites, "that my stomach was knockin' on my backbone. An' the bobbies were as thick as flies on fish today." Even in the dim shadows, his red hair seemed bright and his pale face was covered with freckles. He took a bite of bread, chewing with his mouth open. "That's why I thought they'd caught you. They were *everywhere*."

"And it was so bloody cold," Fiona said, "that Shamus made me stay home with Clara. And Mr. Binder wanted him to come in and talk about the bakery wagon today, so he and Toots only got to work the streets for a few hours. They came back and said the crowds were too light to even pick a pocket."

Tiki looked over at Shamus. "What did Mr. Binder want?"

Shamus shrugged. "Wanted to know if I could drive a carriage. Said maybe I could fill in when his regular driver doesn't show up."

Tiki smiled. "That would be wonderful, Shamus."

"Yeah, if he pays me."

"Is the pot empty again?" The pot was where they stored the extra coins they were able to steal. Their stash was hidden beneath a floorboard in the far corner of the room and was used for food on those days when they couldn't steal enough for a meal or pick a pocket.

"'Fraid so." Shamus nodded.

Tiki pulled out the coins that she'd collected at the World's End. They made a soft clinking noise as she laid them on the table, the silver, copper, and bronze gleaming in the light of the candle. "There was a pretty good crowd at the pub tonight, but I had a close call with MacGregor."

"You didn't try to pick MacGregor's pocket, did you?" Toots gasped.

"MacGregor is vicious when he drinks," Fiona said in a quiet voice. "I saw him beat a woman once."

"I didn't try." Tiki grinned proudly. "I did it." She held up two gold quid. "But he chased me out of the pub and I hopped a carriage that took the long way home. That's why I fell asleep." She nodded at the coins. "We can use some of this for food, but I'm going to go to the apothecary up in Leicester Square first thing in the morning and get something for Clara's cough. She doesn't sound very good."

"She waited a long time for you to come home, Teek." Fiona's brow furrowed in a worried expression. "But she was so tired she finally fell asleep."

"Well, that's what we all should be doing," Tiki said. "It's got to be close to two in the morning." She made a shooing motion with her hand. "Toots, get back to bed." Toots scrambled across the hard floor to his pile of blankets on the opposite side of the stove from where Fiona had been huddled. "We can talk in the morning."

Fiona followed the boy and crawled back into her own ragged pile of blankets, pulling them over her shoulders with a shiver. Tiki waited for Toots to settle in. It wasn't long before snores sounded from his corner of the room.

"I've done something," she said in a low voice.

"What is it this time?" Shamus asked. "Or should I ask *who*? Did you find another orphan to live with us?"

A year ago, she'd found Toots, thin as a rail, in Trafalgar Square. His mother had thrown him out of the house because she had too many other children to feed and care for. But even though he'd been starving, he'd offered to share half his apple with her. She'd brought him home to Charing Cross that day.

"And what if I did?" Tiki said. "I'm thankful every day that you and Fiona had it in your hearts to help me." After her parents' death, Tiki had been sent to live with her mother's sister, Aunt Trudy, and her aunt's banker husband. It had been only a matter of months before it became evident to Tiki that the well-to-do veneer of her uncle's position hid a dark side. Her skin crawled with fear as she thought of him watching her each night as he drank his whiskey. There was a look in his eyes that didn't need words to define. Even now she could hear the creak of the floorboards as his uneven footsteps staggered down the hallway, searching for her.

She had fled from their house for her own safety, intending to seek shelter with Mrs. Adelaide Bishop, a dear friend of her mother's. But upon her unannounced arrival on Mrs. Bishop's stoop, she'd learned the woman had also died of the fever two weeks prior.

Unsure of where to go, but knowing she had to hide from her uncle, Tiki had gone to King's Cross railway station. There, the small valise she had taken with her from her uncle's was stolen and she'd found herself with nothing. Then she'd met Fiona, who took Tiki to meet her cousin Shamus and showed her the hidden little room they shared in Charing Cross. They'd lived together ever since.

"But it's not a who this time." Tiki lowered her voice. "I took something."

"Oh." Shamus perked up. "Something good?"

Tiki nodded at Shamus through the dim light. "Yes, it's something completely brilliant if I don't get caught." She hesitated, then added, "This could be our way out of Charing Cross, Shamus. Into a real home."

He tilted his head at her, and Tiki could make out the frown on his face. "Blimey, Teek, what'd you do? Steal the crown jewels?" His teeth flashed as he grinned at his own joke.

"Next best thing," Tiki whispered. A thrill of excitement shot through her as she waited for his reaction. "Belongs to Queen Vic herself."

Shamus's brow drew down in a surprised frown. "Go on."

There was a rustle of cloth as Fiona wrapped a blanket around her shoulders and crept closer.

"I couldn't sleep," she whispered. She turned big eyes up to Tiki. "What'd you steal, Teek?"

Tiki recounted her tale of hitching a ride on the boot and waking up at an unknown mansion. "I didn't realize it at the time," she whispered, "but the blokes in the room with me were *Prince* Arthur and *Prince* Leo, and for a minute the queen herself was there." Tiki giggled and her voice danced with excitement now that she was out of danger. The story sounded fantastical even to her ears.

"So you took the ring?" Shamus asked. He spoke with a mixture of disbelief and awe. "And nobody saw you? Nobody knew you were there?"

"Well, a few maids and a little boy saw me snitch the bread, but nobody saw me take the ring." She grinned at him. "I was like a bloody ghost."

"We ate the queen's bread?" Fiona breathed.

"An' what'd you do with the ring?" Shamus said.

"I hid it. That way we'll be safe until we can figure out a way to sell the thing." She looked over at both of them through the flickering candlelight. "That is, if we can sell it without getting caught."

"I've heard Rieker talk of a bloke over in Cheapside who buys things," Shamus said.

Tiki grabbed his arm. "No. Not Rieker."

"Why not?" Fiona asked. "He's practically a legend. I heard he knows everyone." She gave Tiki a lopsided grin. "And he's handsome."

"I don't know . . . there's just something . . ." Tiki hesitated. "He's a bit dodgy. He's been around too much lately. He was even up at the World's End tonight. It's like he's following me." Her voice wavered with concern. "I'm afraid he wants part of our territory."

"The queen's ring," Shamus repeated with a dreamy air. "How much do you suppose the thing's worth?"

"I don't know," Tiki replied. "Maybe a hundred quid, eh? Enough to rent a nice flat over in Kensington and put some food in the cupboards, anyway." She nudged Shamus with her elbow and grinned. "We could pretend to be brothers and sisters. I could be a governess and Fi can be a seamstress. Toots will go to school and you could work for Mr. Binder. We'll be a family, just like we've always planned."

Tiki gazed around the familiar room as her words seemed to echo in her ears. They'd talked about leaving Charing Cross before, never really believing it could happen, but why couldn't their dream come true? She'd stolen something that would let them escape their daily struggle to survive. Now all she needed to do was sell the ring.

Chapter Four

T HE distant whistles and roar of the steam engines coming and going in the station woke Tiki the next morning. She shivered against the cool air and pulled her shabby blanket tighter, wishing for one more hour of sleep. The even breathing of Toots and Fiona as they slept was the only sound in the room until Clara's deep cough pulled her upright. Tiki shoved the blanket aside and hurried across the room in her worn nightgown to check on the little girl.

Shamus sat before the stove, poking at the burning coal through the small front door on the box with a long metal pole. He motioned to the kettle and raised his eyebrows at Tiki. "Do you want a cup?"

Tiki nodded at Shamus as she knelt and brushed the little girl's tangled blond curls from her forehead. "Hello, sleepyhead."

Clara stared up at Tiki with adoring eyes. "Tiki, you're home. I waited up for you." She reached up and held Tiki's hand with her tiny fingers, her eyes lingering on Tiki's wrist. "How come you have your mark covered up? I think it's pretty."

Toots pushed himself upright and yawned, stretching his hands high over his head. "You know why, Clara. It's because she doesn't like it. That's why she hides her wrist all the time."

"I don't either," Tiki said, even though Toots was right. "Mr. Potts was staring at it when I was in his bookstore yesterday and it made me uncomfortable." She didn't mention Rieker's strange reaction to her birthmark.

"That's because he thinks it's pretty, too," Clara said.

"Ol' Potts thinks *you're* pretty," Toots teased Tiki. "That's why he lets you read his books for free. He likes your green eyes. They remind him of the hills of Ireland," he said. "Heard him say it myself."

"No, he doesn't." Tiki glared at Toots. "He thinks I look like his dead daughter. That's why."

"*And* he thinks you're pretty," Clara cried. Her words ended in a coughing spasm, the congestion rattling in her chest.

"Why do you always want to go and read Potts' papers and books anyway?" Toots interrupted.

"Clara, sit up." Tiki put an arm behind the little girl's back to support her. "Maybe that will make it easier to breathe." She patted Clara gently on the back, waiting until the little girl drew a deep breath again before she answered Toots's question. "I like to read. I learn a lot by reading."

"Like what?" Toots shrugged off his blankets and moved toward the table, where he reached for a chunk of bread.

"Well, I read about faraway places. Like tropical islands that are surrounded with water as blue as the summer sky," Tiki replied. "And I learn about foreign lands where they make things, like silk for a lady's dress, from the thread of a worm."

"They can make a lady's dress from a worm?" Toots

asked. He shuffled closer to the stove and took the tea Shamus offered, taking a deep drink from the chipped cup.

"Oh, the most beautiful dresses in the world are made from silk," Fiona said. "And in every color. Like the rainbow."

"That's right." Tiki nodded. "There's lots of interesting things in books. And you get to meet people you might never know otherwise. Like in this one story, a little boy named Jack trades his cow for some magic beans and he grows a giant beanstalk all the way into the sky."

"And does it grow giant beans so they never run out of food?" Toots's eyes glowed.

"No." Tiki lowered her voice. "Jack *climbs* the beanstalk and finds a hen that can lay *golden* eggs."

"Golden eggs?" Clara's eyes got big.

"But the hen belongs to a giant. So Jack decides he's going to *steal* it." An image of the queen's ring popped into her head.

Toots laughed and nudged Shamus in the ribs. "He's a ruddy pickpocket just like us." He looked back at Tiki, his face alight with curiosity. "And what happens?"

"Yes, tell us, Tiki, what happens?" Clara's voice was high with excitement. "Did Jack get the golden hen?"

Tiki shrugged. "I can't really remember. Maybe we should read it together and see what happens." She grinned at Toots in a sly way. "Maybe *you* should read it to me."

"Oh, Tiki, that ain't right." Toots's face fell as he suddenly realized her ploy. "I don't want to learn to read."

"You need to learn to read. You don't know what you're missing." Tiki turned away to hide her smile. "I'll tell you the rest of the story tonight if you promise to practice your reading with me."

"Say yes, Toots." Clara turned pleading eyes on him. "Pleeeeeaaaase."

"I don't know," Toots grumbled. "Maybe." He walked across the room to his favorite perch and pressed his eye against the peephole.

Shamus poked at the meager amount of coal in their stove as Tiki went to warm her hands. He lifted up a tin kettle. "There's a bit of tea left, if you want. An' a little cheddar."

Tiki held her cup out. "Just a spot. I'm going to go up to the apothecary's over in Leicester Square this morning. You take Toots and see if you can find some bread or potatoes for today. If I have any money left, I'll get something from the muffin man and some apples from Mr. Albertson's cart up in the market at Covent Garden."

Shamus nodded. "I think Fiona better stay with Clara again, don't you?"

"Yes." Tiki rubbed her arms to try to warm up as she glanced toward the windows facing the railway station. A spill of light cast a watery beam across the long room. "What time do you think it is?"

"Almost ten."

She took a big gulp of her tea. "I better get going." She moved to the back of the room, pulled open one of the drawers built along the back wall, and lifted out a blue dress. "I'll need a few coins from the pot to pay Mr. Lloyd for Clara's medicine."

"All we've got is what you brought home last night."

An image of the ring hung in the back of her mind like a glittering star. Was it still safely hidden in the knot of the tree? A sudden desire to see the stone again, to hold the ring in her hand, burned inside. Did she dare go check?

She pushed the idea away and slipped behind the privacy screen—a blanket hung over a rope they'd set up in the far corner of the room—to change into the dress. "Then we need to work on getting a few more coins today, too." She wouldn't mention checking on the ring, she could do that on her own.

THE wind blew a gust of frosty breath down the lane as Tiki made her way out of Charing Cross Station. She cut across the Strand and headed toward Trafalgar Square. From there she could follow Charing Cross Road straight up to the apothecary's shop. She shivered in her dress and pulled her threadbare cloak tighter as she walked. The dress and cloak were all she had left from when she had run from her uncle's house. From the way the seams tugged at the bodice, she knew she wouldn't be able to wear the garment much longer.

The word *REWARD* scrawled in bright red on a hand-bill tacked to a nearby lamppost caught her eye. She moved closer to read the printed message.

IMPORTANT NOTICE
To the Tradesmen, Ratepayers and Inhabitants of London
particularly in the area of Buckingham Palace
REWARD!
£500
RING GONE MISSING
GOLD BAND CAPPED WITH FIRE-RED STONE
DISAPPEARED IN THE EVENING, FRIDAY, DECEMBER 8TH
If you have any information, contact
Captain Davis-Smith of the Royal Horse Guards

It was as though someone had poured the icy brown water of the Thames down her back.

Tiki reached a shaking hand up and tore the handbill free, staring at the paper in shock. For a second, the words faded away and she could see the flames flickering in the heart of the bloodred stone. Was the ring still safely hidden in the tree?

"There must be something fascinating on that page the way you're staring at it." Rieker's voice was a teasing whisper in her ear, his lips close enough that his breath warmed her skin.

Startled, Tiki loosened her grip on the handbill and a gust of wind yanked it free, sending the page sailing away. "Why are you sneaking up on me, Rieker? What do you want?"

He gave her a half-grin, his eyes dancing as though he were laughing at her. "I almost didn't recognize you. Why are you dressed like a girl today?"

"None of your business," Tiki snapped. "Are you here to give me more advice?"

Rieker's smoky eyes, framed with those ridiculously long lashes, were locked on her. "Are you ready to listen this time?"

Tiki bristled at the undercurrent of superiority in his voice. She would not give him the pleasure of seeing her irritation, so she turned to walk away.

Rieker stepped into her path. "I tried to tell you to leave MacGregor alone. You barely got away."

"But I did get away." She veered around him and hurried up the street.

"A bit of luck, there." He easily kept pace with her. "But you better listen now."

"No time." He would not intimidate her, she told herself, trying not to shiver.

He put an arm out to stop her. His voice was low and urgent. "You need to listen to me, Tiki."

Tiki jerked around and faced him. Purple shadows colored the skin under his eyes, and for a second she wondered where Rieker slept at night. Wherever it was, it didn't appear that he slept well. "Why? You and your gang take more risks than any of us."

He slipped a not-so-gentle hand under her elbow and steered her down the street past shop doorways and pubs, through the growing crowd of people on the street. No one gave them a second glance. "I'm just looking out for your well-being, Teek."

She didn't believe him for a second. Just who did Rieker think he was, anyway?

"I don't want your help."

Rieker's voice was soft in her ear. "But you've got something I want."

"I can't imagine what that would be." Tiki spoke with a bravado she didn't feel.

"I think maybe you can, my crafty little friend." Was that a note of respect in his voice? "Let's just be straight with one another. I followed you from the World's End last night." He left the words hanging, letting Tiki draw her own conclusions.

"And what of it?" Tiki jerked her arm free.

His lips tightened in a thin line. She could feel tension emanating from him. "I want the ring, Tiki."

She took a step back, her jaw dropping in surprise. How did Rieker know about the ring? He must be bluffing.

She lifted her chin and asked in an innocent voice, "What ring?"

His hand lashed out and grasped her arm before she could dart away. Rieker's tight grip slid over her small wrist, yanking her sleeve up to the elbow. His eyes locked on her mark.

"That's what I thought." His fingers dug into her skin.

"Let go of me." Tiki tried to wrench her arm loose, but he held tight.

"An fáinne sí," he said in a language she didn't recognize.

"What did you say?" She stopped pulling, her eyes steady on him now.

"The mark of the fey," he whispered. His intensity scared her. "I thought that's what I saw last night."

"The mark of the what?"

Rieker's eyes narrowed at her. "Who are you exactly, Tiki?" His fingers tightened on her wrist. "You're more than just a pickpocket, aren't you?" He studied her face until it felt as though he could see her every thought. "You speak too well—you've been educated. What's your secret?"

Memories flashed through her mind. Her mother and father smiling at her as they rode horses through Hyde Park on a sunny day. Their pale faces, drenched in sweat from the fever, dying within days of each other. Her aunt's tears at the funeral, a blurry image of her mother. Later, crouched alone in the darkness of a small cupboard, her knees clutched to her chest as she prayed that her uncle wouldn't find her.

Tiki clenched her teeth. "I'm nobody."

His gaze traced the contours of her face. "You don't know what you've done, Tiki," he said. "They're looking for the ring. Trust me when I tell you that you don't want them to find you first."

Tiki took a step back. "Then leave me alone and maybe they won't." She yanked her arm free and ran as fast as she could, dodging people on the sidewalk, ignoring their shocked glances. Once she was far enough that she felt safe, she glanced back over her shoulder. Rieker had disappeared.

Tiki slowed, her thoughts drawn back to his startling questions. The words he had uttered when he saw her birthmark echoed in her ears. *An fáinne sí.* The mark of the fey, he had said. What did he know of such things? And how could Rieker have known about the ring? Had he followed her all the way to the palace?

A sudden urgency filled her.

Tiki whirled around and raced back toward Charing Cross. She needed to change and go check on the ring. Now.

Chapter Five

W HERE'S the ring, Leo?" Arthur frowned at Leo from across the room. "Mother is positively apoplectic about the thing being gone."

"I don't *know* where the bloody ring is." Leo's voice echoed his frustration. "How many times do I have to tell you that? I had Harrison up half the night drawing up handbills. He went out this morning and posted them around town in places where thieves might congregate. Considering the reward I'm offering, *somebody* will know something about the disappearance."

"Could you possibly explain to me one more time why you felt compelled to get the blasted thing out of Mother's lockbox?" Arthur shook his head in disgust. "Honestly, Leo, you know better."

"I already told you. I wanted to see it. To confirm the ring was there." Leo's face hardened. "I don't need to ask for your permission."

"Surely you understand the seriousness of the situation." Arthur's expression was grim. "That's the ring of Ériu. The ring which is said to be the reservoir that holds the truce that bound the faeries to peace with us."

Leo snorted in disgust. "And have you confirmed this with the faeries, Arthur? Are they threatening war now?"

He shook his head and paced to the window, his back straight and taut. The wind raged and the rain beat against the pane with a staccato rhythm, tapping against the glass like someone trying to get in.

Arthur frowned. "No, but let's just say I'd rather not take any chances. You do remember the fire of 1809 that decimated the private apartments at St. James' Palace when the ring disappeared for a time? And you remember the floods on the east coast? Should the ring go missing, then forces beyond our ken can wreak havoc upon us." He strode closer to Leo. "It's not public knowledge, but there's talk among the family that the great fire of London in 1666 was a direct attack by the fey." He stood next to his brother, hands clasped behind his back. "It's not a legend to be trifled with."

"Maybe this is a test," Leo said. "Perhaps Mother found the ring and is testing us in some way. Measuring our devotion to the crown."

"A test?" Arthur repeated. His eyes narrowed as he contemplated the idea. "You think Mother hid the ring herself?"

"Your mother didn't hide the ring." A voice, shaky with age, interrupted them. "She's taken sick to her bed, she has."

"Mamie." Leo smiled at the diminutive woman. Macha Gallagher seemed as old as England herself. She'd been his mother's lady-in-waiting since Victoria had taken the throne at age eighteen. Now near eighty, she lived in her own little house nestled among the trees and birds at the far end of St. James's Park but still tended to Victoria upon her request. "Come for a visit, have you?"

"Your mother asked for me." She shook a gnarled finger at them. "She knew I would understand the significance of what's happened."

Leo's eyes shifted to his brother and back to the white-haired woman. "You can't be serious. It's a bloody ring, for God's sake. Don't tell me you two think the faerie curse is still real?"

"It wasn't a curse." Arthur raised his hands and let them fall back to his sides. "Can't you remember anything? It was a *truce*. Peace, for the right of their kind to walk among us undetected. If the ring is lost or destroyed, then the truce is void and the faeries are no longer bound to peace."

"And what does war gain them?" Leo asked. "Or walking among us undetected, for that matter." He didn't want to believe in faeries.

"Don't you remember anything I told you growing up? The fey will don a glamour, a skin that makes them look human, and cross over into this world." Mamie took a shuffling step closer to them. "There is a battle as old as time waging for control in the Otherworld. Those in the Seelie court believe joining with mortals will give them more power. But others, the UnSeelies, they like to take things, use nature to break things, create chaos. They like to steal mortals away." She lowered her voice. "Some even want to kill us."

"And you believe this, Mamie?"

"Leopold." Her bright blue eyes didn't blink. "Can't you feel them watching you? Haven't you seen their shadows move out of the corner of your eye?"

Leo tried to ignore the prickly feeling crawling along the back of his neck, unwilling to acknowledge the truth of her statement. He turned to his brother. "I mean really, Arthur, maybe when we were children, but you can't still believe these old wives' tales."

"Your mother's illness is not a coincidence," Mamie said. "Mark my words, young man, her health will continue to decline until the ring is back in her possession. This is just the beginning." The old woman's voice held a warning note. "Check your horses in the morning, if you don't believe me. See if any have gone lame." She held out a shaking hand and braced herself on the back of a chair. "The two of you must be very careful. And keep a close eye on Baby, your sister. The fey like young girls."

Arthur looked at Leo. "You can say the stories aren't true, and I can say they're not true, but who can really be sure? And more important, do you dare risk it?" He walked across the library and paused at the door. "Whether the truce is real or not, people *believe* it's real. History tells us it's real. We need to find the ring. And dear brother, since you lost the stone, it's your job to find the bloody thing. Find it *now*."

LEO rode hard across the field, working out the steed's muscles as well as his own frustration. Damn the ring! Why had he even taken the cursed thing out of its velvet-lined box?

It had been that chance encounter with Isabelle Cavendish upon her return from Paris. She was the one who had started him thinking about the ring. All of her questions, her curiosity, had piqued his own interest.

Black clouds of an approaching storm gathered in the distance, and the rumble of thunder mingled with the beat of his horse's hooves. Questions without answers ran round and round in his head, and no matter how hard or fast he rode, he couldn't escape them. If Isabelle hadn't looked so pretty, he would have ignored her queries. But Leo didn't remember her eyes being quite so vivid or her skin like a porcelain doll's when he'd seen her last summer. The Continent had agreed with her. It wasn't until after he had left her company that he'd felt a twinge of guilt at the information he'd revealed. It had been that same guilt that had made him take the ring from the hiding place to ensure its safekeeping.

When his mother had entered the Octagon Library so unexpectedly, he'd tossed the ring under the desk. But when he'd returned later to retrieve the stone, it was gone. For a moment Leo wondered if the faeries had reclaimed it, then cursed out loud for even letting the idea sneak into his head. There had to be some logical explanation.

Leo sat up straight in the saddle as an idea occurred to him. Arthur. His brother would think it a marvelous joke to get everyone stirred up at the thought of the ring gone missing. Arthur knew he'd dropped the ring under the desk. Could his brother have sneaked back into the library later and pocketed the stone?

Leo pulled Diablo to a stop as he contemplated the idea. The horse's sides heaved from exertion, steam rising from the beast in the crisp morning air, and Leo realized he had run the animal hard. An unusually strong blast of wind whipped his hair from his forehead, and Leo urged his mount forward at a slower pace, casting a wary eye at the black sky overhead. The storm was moving in quickly. He walked the horse along the lake within St. James's Park to cool him down and mulled over the idea of Arthur's involvement. The more he thought about it, the more he became certain that his brother was at the bottom of the mystery.

Damn him, anyway! Their annual trip to Balmoral was fast approaching, and he didn't want to be delayed by this foolishness of the ring's disappearance. At the same time, the sudden loss of the stone made him uneasy. What if there was something to the curse? Just as Mamie had predicted, one of their prized polo horses had gone lame this morning for no apparent reason. Perhaps it was a warning. Leo shook his head in exasperation. The ring needed to be found so he could leave without worry.

A sudden movement to the right caught his eye. It was a bit late for hare, but the moving shadow could have been a winter fox. He pulled Diablo up, peering into the brush. Something was amiss in the thicket at the bottom of an elm tree. With a start he saw a pair of eyes staring back at him.

"Come out of there at once," Leo commanded. He spoke more harshly than he intended, in an attempt to disguise how unsettled he felt at someone lurking among the trees.

For a moment, the eyes didn't move. Then, in a burst of energy, a small body came boiling out of the brush and ran in the opposite direction. Leo reacted by instinct. He kicked Diablo into a run, his eyes never leaving his prey.

The big horse broke into a gallop, and Leo leaned over in his saddle to grab the dirty vagrant by the scruff of the neck. After pulling his horse up, he slid ungracefully off the wrong side of the beast, still holding his struggling captive.

"Stop kicking and I'll set you down." Cautiously, he set his prisoner down, realizing as he did how small the boy was. "Now turn around and tell me what you're doing here."

The boy stood frozen for a moment, back stiff and straight; then, as if realizing there was no escape, the captive turned around.

"I do apologize, sir. I thought I was on the grounds of St. James' Park. Tell me, have I mistakenly traveled onto Queen's property here?" The boy spoke with surprisingly good diction.

"No, you're correct. You're in St. James' Park. But why were you hiding in the brush?" Leo's eyes narrowed as a flash of red caught his eye. "What've you got there?" He dropped Diablo's reins and took a cautious step closer.

The boy clapped his hands together and held his palms up, his scrawny wrists exposed from his oversize jacket as he wiggled his fingers. "Nothing, sir."

A strange black mark encircled the boy's wrist, reminding Leo of new leaves on a vine, just waiting to unfurl. "What is that mark on your arm?" He grabbed the boy's wrist and held it up to see better. "Are you a Gypsy?"

Quick as a wink, the boy jerked his slim arm free and stepped back, yanking his sleeve down. "Why do you ask?"

Leo eyed the dirty face shadowed by a battered cap. He tried to put his finger on what it was that bothered him beyond the tattered clothing and worn boots. A wild idea crossed his mind, and he gestured at the boy. "Empty out your pockets."

For a second the boy stood frozen, surprise etched on his face. Then, without warning, he sprang toward Diablo with a wild cry, waving his arms and yelling. Leo jumped, as surprised as his horse. He jerked around and watched as his frightened beast shied, then bolted.

Outraged, Leo spun back around, but the boy had disappeared.

Chapter Six

TIKI'S lungs burned as she neared Mr. Lloyd's shop, the ring heavy in her pocket. That had been a narrow escape. What would the prince have done if he'd found the ring in her possession? An image of a dank cell complete with the sound of rats scurrying underfoot clouded her vision, causing her to stumble.

Why had she felt compelled to check on the ring? She needed to focus on helping Clara get well. It was painful to listen to the little girl's hacking cough.

Tiki wiped her wet hair out of her face as she pushed her way into the shop, her boots loud on the wooden floor. Overhead, drying herbs hung in clumps from the wooden beams in the ceiling, casting a rich fragrance through the room. The combined scent of herbs and medicines that filled the air made her want to sneeze.

Mr. Lloyd, the apothecary, stood behind a wooden counter with glass panes that displayed a dizzying array of bottles. He was a thin, angular man with short, greasy black hair. His black mustache was just as thin as he was, little more than a black line painted above his lips. A pair of silver glasses perched on his hooked nose gave him the appearance of an emaciated owl.

At the sound of the door opening, he turned from where

he was arranging herbs on a rack and looked Tiki up and down. "What's your business?"

Tiki stepped up to the counter, pulling several coins from her pocket and jingling them in her hand. His eyes stopped on the coins long enough to see their color.

"I need something for a cough." Tiki's sides still heaved from her exertion. "For a child."

On the wall behind the druggist, shelf upon shelf held bottles of different colors. The blue green glass marked the poison, while the brown and clear glass bottles held liquids of different colors. Other items were lined up on the shelves: tins, jars, pitchers, bowls, and a multitude of canisters.

"A cough, you say?" Mr. Lloyd adjusted his glasses to peer over the counter at her. "How old is the child?"

"She's four." Tiki adjusted her cap. "And small for her age."

"Any red bumps or blisters?"

She shook her head, thankful Clara hadn't shown any signs of the pox.

"Hmmm. Sounds like croup." Mr. Lloyd rolled up his sleeves before plucking several bottles from the shelf. He slid them into the pockets of the great white apron he wore. "Does she have a fever?" he asked over his shoulder. He moved over to another counter, where he pulled the bottles from his apron and lined them up.

"No." Tiki watched as he mixed yellow leaves with a white powder and ground the mixture together in a small bowl. Then he poured in a red liquid that had a rich, pungent odor, reminding Tiki of fruit that had gone bad. After a moment, he poured the now orange concoction into a small brown jar and pushed a cork into the top.

"That'll be one shilling."

Tiki handed over a silver coin.

Mr. Lloyd leaned over the counter and adjusted his glasses as he handed her the bottle. "Give her a spoonful of this three times a day."

"What should I do if she gets a fever?"

The man unrolled his sleeves and then took the coin she offered. "St. Bart's will take emergency cases, but that's only if you can get in. Long lines up there." He jerked his thumb over his shoulder. "And there's the Great Ormond Street Hospital up in Bloomsbury. They only take care of children." He flipped the silver coin in the air. "But if I were you, I'd pray she don't get one." He grimaced and drew a finger across his neck in a slicing motion.

Tiki gripped the bottle as she left the apothecary's shop and slid it into the same pocket which held the ring. The worn fabric felt warm to her touch, almost as if the flames embedded in the stone had infused her pocket with an unusual heat. But she didn't dare keep the thing. Her brush with Prince Leo had almost been disaster. Better to return the ring to the elm tree for safekeeping until she could figure out a plan to sell it.

The park was sparsely populated when she arrived, the cold weather keeping most people indoors. She was pleased to find the area around the elm tree vacant and she scrambled into the tree unseen. When it came time to shove the ring back into the hole, she hesitated, toying once again with the idea of keeping it with her. The flames seemed to flicker, as if sending her a secret message, and she stared, mesmerized, into the heart of the stone for a long moment.

But in the end, common sense won out and she carefully covered the dirty scrap of cloth that held the beautiful stone with moss until the tiny package was impossible to detect. Still shaken by her close call with Prince Leo earlier, Tiki didn't linger. She shot a quick glance around the park, then jumped from the branch and ran for home.

The sun was on the wane as Tiki neared Charing Cross. Rather than walk through the middle of the station and possibly catch the eye of a bobby, she cut through the alley that ran alongside the station. There was a door there that led to the maintenance tunnels for the building. From the tunnels a sliding panel provided the back door to their small home.

Her nerves were so ragged from her encounter with both Rieker and the prince that she was jumping at shadows. All the way home she'd imagined that she was being followed. She saw shadowy faces, but when she looked again, they'd be gone. Tiki shook her head and shuddered. Maybe it was just guilt over stealing the ring.

"Are you cold, Tiki?"

"No, Fi, I'm just tired. I ended up walking a long way today and my feet hurt." Tiki shrugged her coat off as she moved toward Fiona, who sat on the floor near the stove at the back of the room.

Fiona adjusted the blanket that was wrapped around her shoulders. "Well, I'm cold. It's freezing in here today. Shamus went out to try and snitch some coal." She pulled her makeshift wrap tighter across her chest. "I hope he finds some."

Tiki spied Clara huddled in some blankets next to Fiona.

"Is she sleeping?" Clara's hoarse breathing was clearly audible.

Fiona nodded. She glanced down and smoothed the white blond curls from the little girl's face. "Her cough is gettin' worse again."

"She sounds like she can't breathe." Toots was perched in his usual spot, spying through a knothole onto one of the thoroughfares of the train station.

Fiona adjusted the blankets around Clara. "Did you get something for her?"

Tiki tried to push away the panic that threatened to engulf her. She dug into the pockets of her coat and pulled out a small bottle. "Mr. Lloyd gave me this. We're supposed to give her a spoonful three times a day."

"Do we have a spoon?"

Tiki cradled the small girl in her arms. "No, but she can just take a sip out of the bottle." She gave Clara a gentle shake. "Clara? Wake up."

Clara opened her eyes. "Teek, you're home." Her words ended in a gurgling cough. "I've been waitin' for you."

"No, you've been sleeping again," Toots said from his perch by the peephole.

"Have not." Clara pushed herself upright to glare across the room at Toots.

"Shhh." Tiki held a finger to her lips, motioning for Toots to be quiet. His orange mop of hair looked bright even in the shadows. "Stop it. Clara, I need you to take a sip of this. It should help your cough."

Clara eyed the brown bottle. "What is it?"

"It's medicine. Now be a good girl and take a drink."

The little girl took a sip and made a face. Her shoulders shook as she slipped into a spasm of coughing.

"Did you swallow it?"

Clara nodded.

"Good." Tiki tightened her grip on the frail little girl and held her close for a minute. She would give up the ring in a second if it would buy the four-year-old's well-being. But that was the whole problem—it took money to buy good health, to get the proper medicines to cure an ailment. And the ring was their only hope of getting enough money to afford a home of their own someday.

"Will you tell us another story, Tiki?" Clara gave Tiki a hopeful look. "One of those stories your mum used to tell you."

"Yeah, I'd like to hear a story, too." Toots moved away from the wall and came to sit closer to Tiki and the girls. "Tell us the one about the faerie who captured that soldier."

"Yes, please." Fiona looked up at her expectantly.

"All right," Tiki said. A story might be a good way to get her mind off the ring and Rieker. "He wasn't a soldier. He was the grandson of the Earl of Roxburgh, and it begins like this." Tiki affected a thick Scottish brogue.

"Oh, heed my warning, maidens all,
Who wear gold in yer hair.
Keep well away frae Cauterhaugh,
For young Tam Lin is there."

Clara giggled at her accent. "You sound funny, Tiki."

"Aye, it's because I'm Scottish, young lass." Tiki smiled at the little girl as she launched into the story. "Even though she had been warned, a young maiden named Janet went into Cauterhaugh Wood to pick the wild roses near a certain well. No sooner had she plucked the first stem when a young man named Tam Lin appeared. He asked her why she had taken something from Cauterhaugh without his command. Janet explained that her father owned the wood and had given it to her."

Tiki pulled a blanket closer around Clara's shoulders.

"Well, this young man was very handsome, and Janet spent the day with him, dallying in the sunshine. It was near twilight when her lover suddenly disappeared, and Janet feared that he was a faerie. But even so, when she left that day, she was sure she was in love."

"A faerie?" Clara squeaked.

Tiki nodded. "It wasn't long after she returned home that Janet's father noticed that she was going to have a baby. When he asked Janet about the father, she told him that he was a faerie and they were in love."

"Can faeries and humans fall in love?" Clara asked.

"Shhh," Fiona said. "Listen to the story."

"Well," Tiki continued, "Janet returned to Cauterhaugh Wood and went straight to the well, where she pulled an herb that grew there. Immediately Tam Lin appeared. Janet was desperate to find a way to stay with her love. So she said to him:

> *You must tell to me, Tam Lin,*
> *Ah, you must tell to me.*
> *Were you once a mortal knight*
> *Or mortal hall did see?"*

Tiki lowered her voice. "Tam Lin told Janet that he had been human once. When hunting in the wood one day, he had fallen from his horse. It was then that the Faerie Queen had stolen him away."

"Where did she take him?" Clara asked in a worried tone. "Did she keep him forever?"

Tiki shook her head, a solemn expression on her face. "No. You see, every seven years faeries have to make a payment. It's called a tithe."

"A payment?" Toots interrupted. "Who do they pay?"

"Shush, Toots." Fiona glared at him. "That's not important. Go on, Tiki."

Tiki started again. "The important part was that Tam Lin was afraid *he* was going to be the payment. He needed to escape before the Faerie Queen sacrificed him."

"How?" Clara asked. Then with a gasp she covered her mouth with her hand and looked at Fiona with wide eyes.

Tiki ignored the interruption. "Tam Lin had a plan. But it was dangerous. He needed Janet's help. Here's what he said:

Tomorrow night is Samhein
And the Faerie Folk do ride
Those that would their true love win
At Miles Cross must hide."

"What's Samhein?" Toots asked.

"Samhein is summer's end," Tiki said. "Right around the end of October when the harvests are over. It's said that the veil between our world and the Otherworld is at its thinnest then."

"Tell us what happened at Miles Cross," Clara said.

"So Janet went to the crossroads and hid behind a thornbush to wait. Close to midnight she heard the soft sweet sound of music. The magic strumming of a lute.

The eerie cry of a bagpipe, the haunting notes of a flute." Tiki's voice got softer. "A procession came into view led by the Faerie Queen herself, riding on her black horse. Janet could see the faces of the faerie lords and ladies, and there in the middle, astride a great white horse, was her own beloved, Tam Lin. She remembered what Tam Lin had told her:

First you let pass the black horse
Then you let pass the brown
But run up to the milk white steed
And pull the rider down.

"He had warned her that the faeries would change him into different shapes, making it difficult for her to hold on to him. But hold she must, for that was the only way he would be freed."

Tiki motioned with her hand. "As the horses drew near, Janet let the black horse pass, then the brown. When the white horse approached she sprang from her hiding place and ran over to pull Tam Lin down. Immediately he changed into a raging lion, but Janet buried her head in his chest and held on tight. Then he became a huge, coiled snake." Tiki's words became rushed. "Still, Janet wouldn't release him. From there he became a water serpent and finally a burning coal. Tam Lin had told her this would be the last transformation, so she threw the burning coal into the well, as Tam Lin had instructed her to do."

Tiki raised her hands above her head. "A great gust of steam rose from the well and a naked man stepped out. Janet quickly wrapped him in her green cloak and hid him from view, and Tam Lin became human again."

Tiki looked at each of them. "The Faerie Queen blazed with anger. She didn't think a mortal could ever outsmart her."

"What did she do?" Clara whispered.

"The Faerie Queen said:

If I'd have known of this, Tam Lin,
That some lady borrowed thee,
I'd have plucked out thine eyes of flesh
And put in eyes from a tree

If I'd have known of this, Tam Lin,
Before we came from home,
I'd have plucked out thine heart of flesh
And put in a heart of stone.

"And with that," Tiki said, "the Faerie Queen wheeled her horse around, and with her band of faeries following, she disappeared into the trees, leaving Tam Lin with Janet."

"And the Faerie Queen never stole him again?" Clara asked.

"No." Tiki shook her head. "He lived the rest of his days as a mortal."

"Do you think that story is true, Teek?" Fiona asked. "That Tam Lin really lived?"

Tiki smiled at her. "My mum said it was true."

"Do you think the faeries gave you the birthmark like your mum said, too?" Clara asked in a dreamy voice.

Tiki forced a laugh. "Well, if the faeries gave me my mark, they forgot to give me any of the powers that go along with it."

"But you see things," Clara insisted. "I know you do."

Startled at the little girl's comment, Tiki busied herself by poking at the coal in the stove. She did see things. She always had. Shadowed faces, there one minute, gone the next. Flashes of light where none should exist. The uncomfortable feeling that she was being watched. Perhaps it was time to pay more attention to things she had previously considered to be her imagination.

WHEN Tiki awoke the next morning, Rieker clouded her thoughts. She'd had a dream that his smoky eyes were floating in the sky above her, staring down, watching her. Then suddenly a million sets of eyes were watching her, every way she turned. Panicked, she'd run, but her feet moved in slow motion, causing her to stumble. Instead of landing on the ground, she'd fallen and kept falling into endless darkness. She'd jerked awake with a start, her heart pounding a frantic rhythm in her chest, the image of Rieker's eyes slowly fading.

"You awake, Teek?" Shamus asked. He was crouched in the back of the room, poking at the stove with the metal pole.

A deep hacking cough erupted from the blankets beside Tiki, and she sat up to pile another blanket on Clara's tiny form. "Did the stove go out?"

"Not all the way," Shamus replied. "We're almost out of coal, though. I just loaded the last in." His eyes locked on hers with a significant look. "We're going to have to round up some more coal, or find a way to buy some. It's a cold one out there today, and it feels like it's going to get colder."

"No luck yesterday?"

Shamus shook his head.

Tiki ran her cool fingers over Clara's warm forehead and smoothed the little girl's hair away from her face. She was asleep with her mouth partially open, her breath coming out in raspy gasps.

"It's too cold to go without. Use some of those coins I got from MacGregor the other night and buy some more coal." Tiki gave Clara's blanket a final adjustment, then moved closer to Shamus. "I'll see if I can pick some pockets. But we need to figure out a way to sell the ring." She paused to make sure she had his full attention. "I saw something yesterday. A handbill. The royals know it's gone and they're looking for it. Offering a reward, even."

Tiki reached for her tin mug that still had the remains of some tea leaves from yesterday and poured hot water into the cup.

"We've got to be very careful," Shamus said. "If they caught the likes of us with the queen's ring, we'd never see the light of day again."

"I know." Tiki's voice was grim. "I went and checked on the thing yesterday and saw Prince Leopold in St. James' Park. He practically caught me. I know he suspected something."

"What? Why did you go check on it?" Shamus sounded angry. "You run a risk every time you go near it."

"I couldn't help it." Tiki wasn't even sure why herself. "I just had to. Like the ring was pulling me somehow." She took a sip of the hot drink. "Then Rieker said something about it and I couldn't stop myself."

"Rieker? Where'd you see him?" Shamus frowned at her. "An' what's he got to do with the ring?"

"He was outside Charing Cross." Tiki took another

drink from her cup and tried to ignore the knot of worry that sat like a rock in her stomach. "I think he was waiting for me." Her voice dropped. "He knows I took the ring, Shamus. I swear I didn't tell him. But somehow he knows."

Shamus's lips pressed together in a thin line. His blond hair hung long around his face, shadowing the angles under his cheekbones. "This is getting dangerous, Tiki. First thing tomorrow we pick some pockets and get some coal. Then I'm going over to Cheapside myself and find out who can fence the ring so we can get rid of the thing."

Chapter Seven

TIKI heaved a sigh of relief as she sat on the bench in King's Cross Monday afternoon. Her feet ached with tiredness from the ground she'd covered, but she was pleased with her success. As the busiest railway station in London, King's Cross was always fertile ground for picking pockets. In one snatch she'd even slipped a small bag full of coins from a woman's satchel, no one the wiser. Tiki grinned. There were times when she even impressed herself.

Her grin faded, though, as she recalled one close call. It had only been because she'd become distracted by that girl again. Thinking of her, Tiki scanned the faces of the travelers hurrying between trains. More than once today, she'd glanced over her shoulder and seen her. Her beauty was striking, almost haunting. She had pale skin and blond hair, giving her an ethereal appearance. The graceful curve of her neck, the effortless way she moved, drew Tiki's eyes back to search for her time and again.

Tiki's eyes locked on a slim figure standing at a nearby bookstall.

There she was again.

She wore a flowing green cloak, and her blond hair hung in perfect ringlets down her back. As Tiki watched, the girl glanced over her shoulder and gazed directly at her. Tiki was startled by the challenging look in her eyes.

Was she another pickpocket? She wasn't dressed as though she scrabbled for a living. Tiki pushed off the bench and hurried toward her. She was going to find out why the girl was following her.

"S'cuse me," Tiki called to the girl. "Do I know you?" She was close enough now that she could see the blue green color of the girl's eyes, reminding her of the sea in summer. But there was something in the other girl's expression, in how her eyes were fixed so intently on Tiki, that was unsettling. Her mouth curved slightly, as if she were enjoying an entertainment.

"Not yet." The words were barely a whisper, but Tiki heard them as if she had shouted. Then the girl turned and stepped into a crowd of people and was gone.

"Nah, I don't think I knows you, boy," the bookseller said to Tiki. He scrunched his eyebrows down as he answered. "Who's you lookin' for?"

Tiki glanced at the bookseller in surprise, then darted after the girl, craning her neck this way and that, searching the crowd. But the girl with blond ringlets was nowhere to be seen. Uneasy, Tiki stepped back to the bookstall, where the vendor watched her with curious eyes.

"S'cuse me, did that blond girl buy anything?"

The bookseller crooked an eyebrow at her. "What blond girl are you talking about? I ain't seen no blond girl." His bemused expression turned into a frown. "Is this some trick so you can snitch something? Get out of here." He waved his hand at her. "Ye're not going to pull a fast one on ol' Dickie Betts."

Tired from her long day and suddenly wary, Tiki hurried from King's Cross and headed home. More than once she looked over her shoulder.

The lamplighter had already lit the streetlamps by the time Tiki returned to Charing Cross. As she drew closer to the station, hail started pounding down from the skies in a sheet of white, bouncing off the cobblestones as if thrown by some angry deity. She looked up in surprise at the unexpected onslaught and was immediately rewarded with the painful sting of the small ice chunks pelting her face. She yanked her jacket over her head and raced toward the entrance.

Several bobbies stood under a protective overhang, swinging their sticks and talking. Tiki decided not to chance catching their eye and veered over to the far side of the building to follow the alley to the entrance through the maintenance tunnels.

As suddenly as the hail started, the deluge stopped. Long shadows stretched between the tall buildings. Sometimes people slept in the darkness of the alleyway, when they had nowhere else to go or were too drunk to get there. Tiki could see an occasional silhouette of a body stretched along the cobblestones, sleeping or passed out. She counted her blessings again that Fiona and Shamus had taken her in and let her share the old clockmaker's shop two years ago. At least they didn't have to sleep outside in the elements, like these poor souls.

She was almost to the door that led into the maintenance tunnels when a hand clamped around her arm and yanked her backward. Only a sliver of light cut through the darkness of the alley, but it was enough for Tiki to see her assailant's face, twisted with emotions she didn't understand, staring down at her. He was beautiful in a dangerous way, with almond-shaped eyes, high cheek-bones, and black hair pulled back tight against his head.

She let out a scream, but her attacker clapped his free hand down hard over her mouth and pushed her against a brick wall with enough force to knock the breath from her body. He grabbed her hands and wrenched them over her head, pinning her thin wrists together with one hand.

"Aren't you a pretty pigeon. Larkin was right." His breath was hot on her face as he spoke, his lips too close to hers. His voice reminded her of the skin of a snake, dry and scaly. He chuckled under his breath, an evil, mirth-less sound. "What is it you know, little girl? What's your secret?"

Tiki squirmed and kicked, fighting to breathe, to break free. She was drowning in shadows, as if she were being pulled into an unfamiliar darkness.

"Let go of me!" Tiki thought she saw other faces in the dim shadows: frighteningly feral, vicious faces that laughed and jeered.

"Help!" She gasped. But then his lips descended on hers, cutting off her cries.

Tiki wrenched her face away and tried to kick him, but he lifted her off her feet. The toe of her boot caught her attacker's shin, and Tiki managed to free one hand. She clawed at his eyes but missed. Her grasping fingers grazed something folded along his shoulder blade.

She blinked.

Was that a *wing*?

"Marcus!" A deep voice cut through the shadows.

Before she could fully focus in the dim light, her at-tacker was yanked backward and after a moment seemed to dissolve before her eyes. Around her the air fluttered, the shadows still shifting where he had stood. Tiki gasped for breath, huddled against the rough brick wall, looking up at her rescuer.

"R-Rieker?"

"Tiki, are you all right?" His voice was low, urgent.

"Y-yes," Tiki stuttered, her teeth chattering with a delayed reaction. "Wh-who was that?" She grabbed Rieker's arm, her fingers clutching at his sleeve, and tried to catch her breath. "Where did he go?"

"His name is Marcus." Rieker moved close to her, as if to protect her. "Don't worry, he's gone now."

"Who is he?"

Rieker's lips twisted as though to hold his words in. "Someone who wanted to get my attention."

She peered at Rieker's face. His eyes were guarded, his emotions veiled. "Why?"

He reached forward and gently rubbed his thumb along the edge of her bruised lip. "You're bleeding," he said softly.

Tiki reached up to stop him, but her shaking fingers clung to the warmth of his skin instead. "You didn't answer my question," she whispered.

"They think I have something they want."

Tiki was uncomfortably aware of how close Rieker was standing to her, yet at the same time she felt pulled toward him, as though in the grip of a magnet. He leaned even closer and whispered in her ear.

"They think I have the ring, Tiki."

It took a moment for his words to sink in, and when they did, it was with a sickening tug.

"The ring?" Her words were faint.

"The ring you stole." He raised his eyebrows. "The royals aren't the only ones looking for it."

With him this close, she could see a long, narrow scar under one eyebrow and another along his jaw, giving him an air of danger. "What do you mean? Who else is looking?"

"The ring is old." Rieker's body was angled so she was shielded from any curious eyes in the alley. His voice was hushed as he spoke, and for a moment it was as though they were the only two people in the world. "But the secrets and alliances that it holds are ancient." His fingers tightened on hers. "The ring is a well, Tiki. A reservoir that holds things. *Important* things."

Tiki tried to back away, but the rough stones of the brick wall behind held her in place, trapping her.

"Did you notice how the heart of the stone burns with a fire?" Rieker's gaze didn't waver. "It's an eternal flame that binds the parties to an agreement that was reached and preserved there. If the flame extinguishes, then the agreement is void."

"How can a fire burn inside a ring?" But Tiki knew what he was talking about. She could still see the strange flames flickering in the depths of the bloodred stone.

Rieker's answer fell heavy on her ears.

"Magic." He leaned close, his breath warm on her cheek, and whispered, "Faerie magic."

Tiki's breath caught in her throat as a million thoughts crashed through her head at once. Her mother had believed in faeries. *They're around us, Tara Kathleen,* she had whispered to her when she was a child. *Watch closely and you'll see their shadows move.*

A cold hand clutched at her heart. Could Rieker be speaking the truth? Other memories flickered to the surface. Times when she'd seen strange faces one second that were gone the next.

"We'll both be safer if you just give it to me. If you do have the ring, they'll find you." Rieker's voice held a warning.

Tiki pressed her lips into a tight line. She would *not* give him the ring. That ring was her answer to saving Clara. To starting a new life for all of them.

"What if I don't have the ring?"

Rieker scowled at her. "For your sake, and the sake of those orphans you care for, you're going to listen to what I have to tell you." He tightened his fingers around her wrist until she winced. Seeing her pained expression, he let her go and his voice softened. "Tiki, come with me. I'll buy you a cup of tea inside the station. You *need* to listen."

Tiki followed without resisting, her nerves in a jumble at the idea that he might be speaking the truth.

Rieker led her inside Charing Cross and steered her to a tea shop that had small tables outside the storefront. He sat her down, then went inside to purchase a drink. Tiki pulled her coat tighter and shifted uncomfortably in her seat. She caught a few questioning glances from the other patrons, as though someone dressed in threadbare clothes didn't have the right to sit there. She was relieved when Rieker returned with tea and biscuits, dragging his own chair close to hers.

"I didn't believe it either, Tiki," he said, "at first." He shifted on his seat, his gaze never leaving her face. "What did you see when Marcus touched you?"

She froze, remembering the frightening shadows, the sense of another place, of darkness swallowing her.

"What did you *feel?*" Rieker's voice was a whisper.

Wings. She had felt a wing, springing from his back like that of an archangel, but without feathers. A wing as hard as stained glass, yet as fragile as a dragonfly's wing, reflecting the light in a thousand different directions. Even now she could remember how it fluttered, making the air vibrate around her, seeming to suck the breath from her chest. Her mother's voice echoed in her head. *Did you see that flash of light, Tiki? It was a faerie crossing over. Their wings reflect the light.*

Tiki lifted wide eyes to him. "He was a faerie?"

Rieker nodded. "Faeries exist, though their numbers are getting fewer and fewer. Their world is dying, which is why the ring is so important."

"*Faeries* are after the ring?" she whispered.

"The ring holds a truce between the British and faerie courts. As long as the flame burns inside the ring, then there will be peace between our worlds. Without the truce, it's war."

Rieker's eyes were locked on her, and Tiki found it hard to look away.

"But why do they want to fight us?"

"Because we're taking over their world. The fey fill a different space, in between where you and I can see," Rieker said. "But we share the same world. When our cities grow bigger, there is less space for them. Our mechanical inventions are replacing their magic." He gestured toward a steam engine waiting to pull out of the station, a gust of smoke bellowing from its sides like some mechanical fire-breathing beast. "As there are more of us who don't believe, their capacity for magic diminishes. Some in the Otherworld think that their only chance for survival is to eliminate us. To take back what was once theirs."

Rieker shifted in his chair, his voice low and hushed. "But to do that, they must destroy the ring first. To end the truce."

Could it be true? Was that why the royals wanted the ring back so desperately that they were willing to offer up a fortune?

"You're in danger, Tiki." Rieker's expression was deadly serious. "Some of them, Donegal and those of the Un-Seelie court, will stop at nothing to get the ring." He reached forward and took her hand, wrapping his long fingers around hers. "The fey have a weakness to iron. You should get a knife with a blade made of iron and carry it with you, no matter what." His voice dropped. "And you've got to be prepared to use it."

"Tiki!" A shout interrupted their conversation, and Tiki jerked around to see Toots running full speed toward them. She sat up in alarm.

"Teek," Toots gasped as he slid to a stop in front of her. His skin was pale under his orange freckles, and his green eyes were bright with panic. "Fiona sent me to find you. She needs you to come quick. Clara's taken a turn for the worse."

Chapter Eight

R IEKER stood as Tiki jumped to her feet. "Can I help?"
"No." Tiki answered more abruptly than she
meant. "I've got to go." Her eyes found Rieker's for just a
second. She was surprised by the compassion she glimpsed
there. Her breath caught in her throat.

"Hurry, Teek." Toots tugged at Tiki's arm.

She grabbed Toots's hand and they raced for home. She
glanced over her shoulder once to make sure Rieker wasn't
following them. She didn't trust him enough to let him
know where they lived.

"Please let her be okay, please let her get well," Tiki
whispered as they ran back to the abandoned clockmaker's
shop. She gasped for air as they slid into the little room.
It was as though a clamp had tightened on her heart.

Tiki hurried to Fiona's side where she sat cradling
Clara in her lap.

"She's hot, Teek. I think she's got a fever."

Tiki leaned down and put her hand on Clara's forehead. A deep foreboding filled her when she felt how dry
and hot the little girl's skin was. Mr. Lloyd's warning re-
verberated in her ears.

Toots hovered near Fiona, looking over her shoulder at
Clara, his face knotted up with worry. "Last year, before

my mum told me I was old enough to live on my own, one of my little brothers had the coughing sickness."

"And what did she do for him?" Fiona asked.

There was a long silence before Toots answered. "She buried him."

Clara's breath came out in a slow, raspy gasp and gurgled into a cough.

"Tiki?"

Her voice was so weak and low, Tiki could hardly hear her. The little girl opened her eyes just enough to make sure Tiki was there. A small smile flitted across her face, and she reached up. "Who's that pretty lady with long blond hair?" Tiki leaned down so Clara could wrap her scrawny arm around her neck. Even the skin on her arm felt hot.

"What blond lady, Clara?" Tiki asked.

Clara spoke slowly, every word an effort. "She's in the corner. Can't you see her?"

Fiona looked up at Tiki, fear in her eyes. "There's no one in the corner. Is she dreaming?"

Tiki shook her head. "She must be. It's from the fever."

"What do we do? Shamus has gone over to Cheapside. No telling when he'll be back."

Tiki's stomach churned. What could they do? An image of her mother and father flashed before her eyes, dying in their bed of consumption, wasting away to nothing. She hated doctors. They'd been no help when her parents were sick. Memories surfaced of the sharp features of Mrs. Thorndike, her strict governess, who had moved in with their family during her parents' illness. The woman had been cold and heartless, not allowing Tiki to see her mother and father even to say good-bye, telling her their bodies were contagious.

Tiki swallowed the lump in her throat. Her life before was like a distant dream now. Everything had been so easy when she'd lived with her parents. Hot food every day and clean clothes; servants to help with the cooking and cleaning. It was inconceivable that she would one day steal bread and pick pockets to survive. But lately her memories of her life before were beginning to fade. Images of those she cared about in the past were being replaced by Clara's face and the others. She didn't know if that was good or bad.

"There's a place up in Bloomsbury." Tiki smoothed Clara's hair back from her face. "A hospital for children. Mr. Lloyd told me. They'll help her." Clara's thin frame was racked with another coughing spasm. The blue veins in her eyelids that showed through her thin skin and the dark circles under her eyes made her look half-alive.

"How will we pay?" Toots asked. His eyes were wide and worried as he peered up at Tiki, his freckles stark against his pale skin.

"Don't you worry about that," Tiki said. Fear settled in the pit of her stomach like a snake coiled and waiting to strike. "We'll find a way." Even if they had to pawn the ring.

She began gathering the scraps of blankets they had collected and tucked them in around the little girl in Fiona's arms. "We'll have to wrap her up and try to keep her warm. It's bitter cold out there tonight. I'm going to put my dress on, too. Maybe that will help when we ask the hospital to take her."

Once she was changed, Tiki donned her cloak and took Clara from Fiona. The little girl stirred but didn't come fully awake as Tiki easily lifted her slight weight.

"Toots, why don't you wait here for Shamus to return so you can tell him what's happened?"

"You're not leaving me behind," Toots replied in a belligerent tone. "Clara might need me."

Tiki smiled at the young boy. "Of course, you're right, Toots. Grab your hat."

As they emerged into the alley, rain fell in a light mist. The wild weather from earlier in the day had dissipated, but now the night air was so cold that the drops froze when they hit the ground, making the cobblestones extremely slippery.

Tiki readjusted her grip and picked up the pace, Toots and Fiona close on her heels. Clara's frail body began to shiver in her arms, and Tiki tried to move faster. They cut across the front of the station and headed for the Strand, ducking their heads against the freezing rain. In her haste, Tiki slipped on the icy ground. She clutched Clara tighter in her arms, landing with a cracking thump on her hip. Her breath exploded from her chest in a sharp gasp.

"Teek," Fiona cried, reaching down to help her up, "are you okay?"

"Yes," Tiki muttered. She clenched her teeth against the burning pain as Fiona and Toots helped her up. She took a few limping steps, Clara unconscious in her arms. "Let's keep going." Already she could feel her arms beginning to shake with the cold and the strain.

A shout came from behind, but Tiki didn't slow.

"It's Shamus," Toots said.

"Teek . . ." Shamus's breath came out in small puffs of white air lit by the glow of the streetlamp. "What are you doing?"

"Oh, Shamus, thank goodness," she breathed.

"Rieker told me to get home." Shamus's worried eyes went from Tiki's face to the bundle she carried and back again. "Where are you going with Clara?"

"She's got a fever." Tiki's voice was rushed. "We're taking her up to Great Ormond Street. There's a hospital there for sick children."

"Is she that bad?"

"Yes, Shamus," Fiona said sharply. "An' she's getting worse."

Shamus glanced at Fiona but directed his comment to Tiki. "We run the risk of losing her if we take her there, you know. Hospitals won't give up orphans to other orphans." His voice was thick with warning. "They might even want to know about us—where we live, who cares for us."

Tiki shook her head and started walking again. She didn't want to hear what Shamus was saying. "We have to take the chance. She's burning up with fever."

Shamus reached forward and took Clara in his arms. "Let me carry her."

Tiki didn't want to relinquish her hold on the sick little girl, but it was a relief to let the weight of her body slip into Shamus's arms. He held the small, shivering child close to his chest as Fiona tucked extra blankets around her.

Shamus's long hair was soaked from the rain and plastered to his head. "We better hurry. There's bloody few cabs out tonight—it's too cold and icy." As if in response, a deep hacking cough that seemed to reverberate in the air around them rose from the pile of blankets that Shamus held.

"We'll go east and cut over at Aldwych," Tiki said. "Then head north on Kingsway. That's the fastest route. We should be able to get there in an hour."

The long walk to the hospital rattled Tiki's nerves. Coal dust hung thick in the air, making it difficult to draw a deep breath. Clara coughed often but never woke once to ask where they were going.

They turned on Southampton Place and stopped to ask directions from a milk-woman collecting her cans for the day.

"It's the white brick building down there, dearies." She adjusted the wooden yoke over her shoulders. Churns on each side swayed. "They only take very sick children, though."

Tiki thanked the woman, and they continued down the street at a faster pace. White columns framed the stone steps leading up to the entry of the three-story hospital. Tiki led Shamus and the others in through the front doors. They passed a room full of people; some of the men were sitting, others were leaning against the wall, many holding their hats. Women sat with children clutched in their arms, trying to ease their suffering as they waited to be seen. Muffled sobs could be heard, and the strident cries of a sick child rent the air. The despair that filled the room was palpable.

A stern-looking nurse in a black dress covered by a white apron and wearing a long white lace cap on her head eyed them from behind the entry desk.

"Excuse me, ma'am." Tiki took care to speak clearly. "My little sister is ill. Would it be possible for a physician to look at her?"

The woman frowned as she eyed Tiki. "Where are the child's parents?"

Before Tiki could reply, Clara began coughing. The nurse rose and walked to the bundle Shamus held. She peeled back the tattered blankets to look at Clara's face, her capable fingers resting on the little girl's forehead. Then she stepped away and disappeared into another room. It was only a moment before she returned, pushing a gurney.

"Put her on here."

Shamus stepped forward and gently lowered the bundle in his arms to the flat surface of the movable bed. He straightened the blankets around Clara's face, pulling them clear of her mouth.

The nurse pulled a device from around her neck, sticking two tubes in her ears while she placed a small hornlike instrument on Clara's chest. After listening for a moment, she pulled the tubes from her ears and moved toward the end of the gurney, forcing Shamus aside.

"The waiting room is down there." She pointed toward the room they'd passed.

Tiki threaded her fingers and clutched her hands together tightly. "Thank you for your help, ma'am."

The woman looked Tiki up and down. Her eyes skimmed over Toots, Fiona, and Shamus, then returned to Tiki. "Your parents will need to come in and discuss payment." She gestured toward the waiting room. "Now, go there and wait for me. I'll be needing information in a bit, but this one is too sickly to wait. What did you say her name was?"

"Clara," Tiki whispered. She bit her lip hard so she wouldn't cry. She was torn between fear of losing Clara and relief at knowing she would be getting the proper care.

"You better pray for Clara. She's going to need it." Then with quick, efficient movements, the nurse pushed the gurney down the hall and disappeared between two swinging doors.

Tiki moved toward the other room, her thoughts on Clara. Taking the little girl to the hospital was a risk, but if she didn't get the proper care, she might die.

"What do you think?" She cast a worried glance at Shamus.

"She doesn't sound good. I've heard coughs like that before." He shoved his hands in his pockets, and his shoulders sagged. "When my father used to force me to mudlark with him down on the Thames, he said some of the dead bodies we pulled from the river had died from coughing up blood. Consumption."

Tiki fought back a shudder. Her parents had died of consumption. She would never be able to erase the sound of their coughing from her memory. She tried not to allow herself to think of the possible outcomes. "We had to do it, Shamus."

"Where'd they take Clara?" Toots's voice wavered and he rubbed his eyes with a grubby hand, ducking his head as though he didn't want Tiki to see his tears.

Tiki slid her arm around his thin shoulders. "They're going to keep her here in the hospital and help her get well."

"For how long?"

"I don't know for sure. Maybe just a few days." Tiki

glanced in at the shifting crowd of people in the waiting area. A lone figure stood unmoving in the corner, staring at her. Tiki started in surprise. She recognized those blond curls. That exquisite face. It was the girl from King's Cross.

"Shamus," Tiki hissed. She tugged at his sleeve.

"What?"

She tilted her head toward the room, not wanting to give away her interest in the girl. "Do you see that blond girl in the corner staring at us?"

Shamus was silent for a moment as he peered at the crowd. "No, where?"

Tiki jerked her head up, intending to point out the girl, but she was nowhere to be seen. A chill crept down Tiki's arms. She scanned the entire room, but the girl wasn't there. Unnerved, Tiki grabbed Toots's sleeve and steered him out the door. They needed to get out of here. "Come along now."

As underage orphans and not relatives, none of them could stay and give information without risk of being taken themselves.

If they were sent to an orphanage, they would be separated and put to work in different places. They might not ever see each other again. Tiki had heard the tales of workhouse jobs that included oakum picking and stone breaking and not even being paid a wage for the backbreaking work but given day-old bread instead. She'd heard that the masters in the workhouses liked to beat the children. Her father had raged against the unjust conditions in the workhouses enough for her to know it wasn't any place she ever wanted to find herself or anyone she loved.

The image of a stone block cell shrouded in shadows formed in her mind. There was one alternative to the orphanage. That was prison. If she got caught for stealing the queen's ring, the workhouse might look like an inviting option considering what she'd be faced with. Conditions in Newgate Prison were said to be unspeakable, where rats feasted on your flesh and the cries of the insane kept you awake at night.

Tiki shivered, a fear filling her like she'd never known before. For the first time, she truly grasped what a dangerous game she was playing with the ring.

Once they were outside, Tiki took Toots's hands in her own. "Clara is going to be back home with us soon."

"D'you promise, Teek?" The hope in his voice put an ache in her chest.

Tiki whispered a silent prayer. "Yes, I promise."

"The hospital is going to make her well," Fiona said, sliding her arm around Toots's shoulders.

"Well, now what do we do?" Shamus asked.

"We might as well head back home," Tiki replied. "We've got more coal and we'll be able to build a bigger fire." She raised an eyebrow at Toots. "Maybe we can even get some warm pea soup on the way home."

Toots's face lit up. "Do you think so?"

"Yes. I think we've still got some bread and cheddar in the cupboard." Tiki forced a smile. "Clara will be home with us before we know it."

"Hey! You there!" A voice interrupted their conversation. Tiki glanced over her shoulder. The nurse in the black dress stood in the entrance to the hospital, staring at them. "I told you to wait. I want to know where that child has been living."

"Run!" Tiki cried.

Toots, Shamus, and Fiona all bolted in different directions. Everyone knew to split up. That way they were harder to catch. Tiki ran hard, ignoring the startled looks of strangers. It felt good to run, to run away from her sadness and fear.

Chapter Nine

TIKI was exhausted by the time she returned to Charing Cross. Her fear for Clara's health was now entwined with a sense of desperation. It would probably cost several pounds a day to keep Clara in the hospital. She would need to pay the hospital before they allowed her to take the little girl home once she was well. *If* they let her take Clara home. And the only way to come up with that much money was to sell the ring. But how to sell the ring without getting caught?

Tiki had spent the entire walk home trying to come up with a plan. All the while, her conversation with Rieker ticked in the back of her head like an annoying clock. *The ring is a well . . . A reservoir that holds things. If you do have the ring, they'll find you.* She shivered just thinking about it. If "they" were like Marcus, she didn't want anything to do with them.

The moon gleamed straight overhead as she pulled open the large doors of Charing Cross and trudged wearily down the main thoroughfare of the station. She checked the corridor for any bobbies, then eased into their home. Shamus's hunched form sat by the stove, whittling a small piece of wood while Toots's soft snores echoed from a dark corner.

Tears hovered close to the surface as Tiki collapsed

into one of the chairs. The day's events had finally caught up with her—the disturbing glimpse of the blond girl in King's Cross, the attack in the alley, her fearful belief that Rieker was telling the truth when he spoke of the fey's interest in the ring, and then Clara's admission to the hospital. It was almost more than she could bear.

"Where have you been?" Shamus whispered. "You scared the daylights out of me. I thought maybe they'd caught you."

Fiona sat up on the girls' side of the stove and rubbed her eyes. "Teek, is that you?" She wrapped herself in a blanket and tottered over to them, half-asleep. Yawning, she sat down across from Shamus, pulling the blanket tighter around her shoulders. "Can we go see Clara tomorrow?"

"I'd like to, but we might have to wait a day or two, Fi." Tiki sighed. "Clara's in good hands now. We've got to come up with some money. Fast. I've been trying to figure out how to sell the ring. It's the only way we'll be able to pay for Clara's care."

Shamus paused with his knife poised above the wood. "Selling the ring is our only hope, but if we're caught, they'll split us up and lock us away in prison."

"What did you learn over in Cheapside?"

"I talked to a couple of different gents, but I don't know, Teek." He shook his head. "Most of those men would sell their soul to the devil if they thought it would make them some money. I'm not sure we can trust them if someone comes asking about the ring. Who knows? The royals might give them money if they name us."

Tiki raised a shaking hand to brush a strand of hair from her forehead.

"Teek, are you okay?" Fiona asked.

"Something happened today." She told them about being attacked by Marcus. "There was something strange about him." Her voice faltered. She couldn't bring herself to tell them more. "We need to be extra careful right now."

"I still think we should ask Rieker." Shamus spoke with unusual stubbornness.

"Ask Rieker what?" Fiona asked.

"No," Tiki replied. "I don't want him involved." Faeries and truces. She pushed away the memory of Marcus's lips on hers, the strange feel of the . . . *wing* on his back. "He probably just wants the reward, like the rest of us."

Tiki closed her eyes and the backs of her eyelids were imprinted with the otherworldly faces she had seen, leering and snarling at her. Their images were suddenly replaced with the breathtaking beauty of the blond girl, silently watching her. Then Rieker's face . . .

Tiki bit back a gasp. Was Rieker trying to protect her or set her up to steal the ring?

Shamus shrugged. "I'm not so sure. I've heard things around. How he shares food with some of the street children and took care of some old bloke who was dying."

Tiki wasn't sure what to think of Shamus's comment. "I don't believe anyone would walk away from the fortune that this ring is worth. Rieker included."

"He knows the streets like the back of his hand," Shamus said. "And Rieker has connections."

"That's what I'm afraid of," Tiki retorted. "Connections that can make the ring disappear and we'll never see a farthing for the risk we took." She held her hands out to the warmth of the box stove. "I don't fancy going to prison either."

"The queen's ring?" Fiona asked.

"Yes." Tiki looked over at her. "We're talking about who will pay the most and how we can get the money without being caught."

"Oh." Fiona yawned again. "Why don't you just sell it back to the royals?" She gave them a sleepy smile. "They probably want it returned. Maybe they'll give you a reward."

Tiki's eyes locked on the young girl. Sell the ring back to the royals? An image of the handbill she'd found outside the station flashed before her. There was a reward being offered. It was clear that they were desperate for the ring's return. Why not pretend they'd found the ring and return it for the reward? Tiki's lips stretched in a big smile. "Fiona, you're brilliant."

AT first light, Tiki snuck out of the clockmaker's shop and hurried outside. There was a large section of wall on the front of Charing Cross that was designed to post information. It didn't take long to find another handbill tacked there. She ripped it free.

She skimmed over the words and came to a stop on the red letters scrawled across the middle of the page. Five hundred pounds! A fortune.

Her gaze riveted on one line: "If you have any information, contact Captain Davis-Smith of the Royal Horse Guards." Tiki hurried back inside and showed the handbill to Shamus, Toots, and Fiona.

"Five hundred pounds?" Fiona stared at Tiki with wide eyes. "We'd be bloody rich."

"We'd never run out of food again," Toots cried. He skipped around the room in excitement.

"But how can we tell the Guards we have the ring without getting arrested?" Shamus asked. "If we tell them we know where it is, they'll want to know how we know. It's not like a bunch of street rats are going to be able to hand them the ring and they'll hand us the reward." He shook his head. "Doesn't work that way."

"You're right." Tiki sighed. "Somehow, we've got to give them the ring without being seen."

Toots stopped and looked at her with wide eyes. "No way to do that unless you're invisible."

THEY spent hours discussing ways to collect the reward, but in the end there was always the possibility of getting caught. In the meantime, food needed to be either stolen or purchased with stolen coins.

Tiki nodded at Fiona, and they both edged closer to their mark. The woman's vivid red hair, with the blue hat pinned to the center of her head, reminded Tiki of an actress who used to shop at Mr. Potts's bookstore. But this woman was much larger, and her stout arms were so full of packages that she could barely see where she was going. Her bright blue handbag dangled on her arm like a sweet begging to be eaten.

"Flowers, mum?" Fiona called out to the woman, holding up a red rose she had snitched from a nearby shop.

"Oh, no, thank you, dear, not a hand to hold it with, I'm afraid," the woman replied. Tiki put her head down and moved forward, her shoulder bumping hard against the woman's arm as she reached for the coin purse within the handbag. Instead, the strap snapped and the whole thing fell into her arms.

"S'cuse me," the woman called in a singsong voice, unable to see Tiki below her bundles amid the thick Christmas holiday traffic. Tiki grunted in return as she shoved the heavy bag under the coat hanging over her arm and gave Fiona a slight nod.

"Hey, you there!"

Startled, Tiki glanced back over her shoulder. Her breath froze in her throat. A bobby was staring right at her.

"I want a word with you."

"Fi, run!" Tiki took off, tucking the coat and handbag under her arm as she raced around startled travelers. She skidded around a corner and headed down a hallway, zigzagging around people and trolleys filled with luggage. Daring a glance behind, Tiki saw the bobby's blue suit hurrying around the corner, his head swiveling back and forth as he looked for her. On impulse, she dove into Mr. Potts's bookstore, located along one of the walls within the station down from where the trains loaded. Her breath came in great gasps as she hurried into the store, looking for a place to stash the coat and handbag.

"Can I help you?" a wavery voice called.

Tiki raced to the end of the aisle, stopped in the darkest corner, and dropped to the floor. She pulled a number of books from the lowest shelf and shoved her dark coat with the bag wrapped inside onto the shelf in their place. With a grunt, she hefted the stack of books and dropped them on a nearby shelf.

Taking a deep breath, Tiki slid her hands in her pockets and whistled a soft tune as she tried to catch her breath. She sauntered toward the front of the shop, perusing the titles on the shelf as she walked.

"Wot you be about today, young miss?"

Tiki feigned surprise as she glanced up. "Oh, hello, Mr. Potts. Didn't see you when I wandered in." Large windows covered the front of the shop, providing a wide-open view to the railway station filled with passersby. Tiki eased toward the window.

"Didn't look like you were 'wandering' to me. Looked like you were flyin'." The stooped old man eyed her suspiciously. "Not runnin' from somebody, were you?"

"Who, me?" Tiki asked. "I don't know what you're talking about." She glanced at a stack of newspapers balanced on the corner of his old desk, the headline in bold print: QUEEN VICTORIA TO HOST A MASKED BALL FOR THE CHRISTMAS HOLIDAYS ON DECEMBER 16TH.

Four days away. She envisioned the piles of food she'd seen in the kitchens of Buckingham Palace, imagined the music of the orchestra playing in the distance. She wondered whether Prince Leo would be there.

Tiki scanned the area outside the store. "Have you got any new books for me to read?"

"As a matter of fact, I've got a new one right back here." The old man shuffled away, disappearing between the racks of books.

"Why did you leave the child?"

Tiki jumped and whirled around to stare in surprise at the familiar blond girl who stood behind her. Where had she come from?

"W-what?" Tiki stuttered.

The girl stepped closer, and for a second Tiki caught a whiff of something that reminded her of the succulent smell of honeysuckle on a hot summer day.

"I want to know why you took the child to that place and left her? She's *your* responsibility." The girl's striking beauty was diminished by the anger that blazed in her eyes. For a second, Tiki was afraid the girl was going to strike her.

Tiki took a step back. "Who are you? What do you want?"

A scream rang outside the bookstore, and Tiki jerked around. A bobby had Fiona by the arm and was marching her away.

Tiki rushed out the door and raced toward Fiona and the bobby. She slowed as she neared, sneaking up behind the two of them, keeping on her toes as she shadowed their steps. There had to be a way to get the bobby to release Fiona.

"Watch it!" a voice called on her left.

Tiki jumped out of the way as a porter pushed an overloaded trolley of suitcases toward her. As the cart veered to miss her, a small valise fell to the floor near her feet. Before the porter could slow the heavy cart enough to retrace his steps, Tiki wrapped her fingers around the soft sides of the bag. Her eyes shifted from the porter to the policeman. Clutching the valise in front of her, Tiki headed for the bobby.

When she was a step behind him, she yelled.

"Officer!"

The man's shoulders jerked in surprise, and he turned in response. Using both hands, Tiki shoved the valise as hard as she could straight into his stomach, forcing him to drop his hold on Fiona. As soon as he loosened his grip, Fiona ran.

"Found this, sir, someone must've dropped it," Tiki said. From behind, she could hear the porter shouting. She grabbed the bill of her cap and dipped her head, then turned and darted away through the crowds.

SEVERAL hours later, Fiona sat across from Tiki as they took turns pulling one item at a time from the stolen handbag they had retrieved from Mr. Potts's bookshop. Fiona pulled out a small silver box. She snapped open the lid.

"Look at this," she cried in delight. Inside, resting on a bed of red silk, lay a small silver filigreed brush and mirror. She pulled out the brush and ran it through her short, scruffy hair. "Aren't they beautiful?"

Tiki eyed the set. "I wonder how much they're worth?"

"Ooh, feel how heavy this is." Fiona pulled a small purse from the bag. She grinned as she shook it, the coins jingling inside.

"Open it, see how much there is," Tiki urged.

Fiona loosened the drawstrings and poured the coins into Tiki's hands in a tinkling waterfall. "Look at it all." Her face glowed with excitement.

Tiki nodded in satisfaction. "Hot-cross buns for Toots tonight, eh? Maybe we can sneak one into the hospital for Clara, too." She closed her fingers around the coins and noticed the dirt encrusted under her nails. Filthy, every single one of them. When was the last time she'd had a bath? When she was little her mother would bathe her two or three times a week with scented soap.

"What are you looking at, Teek?"

Tiki sighed. "Nothing. I was just thinking I need a bath."

Fiona laughed. "What for?"

"I'm tired of being dirty all the time."

"The way I see it, there's no point in getting all cleaned up unless you're planning on going to a ball. You'll just get dirty all over again the next day." Fiona leaned forward to peer into the depths of the bag, her short brown hair sticking up in all directions. "What else is in there?"

Tiki's eyes were riveted on Fiona. "What did you say?"

Fiona looked up in surprise. "I said, what else is in the bag?"

"No, before that."

Fiona gave her a confused look. "I said, unless you're going to a ball, what's the point of bathing?"

Tiki jumped to her feet. "Fi, that's it!"

The swinging plank of wood that marked the entrance to their home shifted to one side and Toots and Shamus came in, breathing hard. Toots collapsed on a pile of blankets next to Tiki, rolling on his back and gasping, his sides heaving in and out like a bellows. Shamus leaned against the wall, his hands on his knees.

Shamus gulped for air. "There's a lot of bobbies out there tonight."

"We had a little trouble earlier ourselves," Fiona said.

Tiki looked from one to the other. "What happened? Did you steal something?"

"Just this." Shamus grinned, opening his coat to reveal a large meat pasty. "And this." He pulled open the other side of his jacket, disclosing a loaf of fresh bread.

"And this," Toots added from the floor. He pulled a fresh chunk of cheddar from under his shirt and grinned with pride.

Tiki and Fiona laughed together. "A feast! We'll have food for a week!"

It was almost an hour later when Toots heaved a sigh as he passed a loud burst of gas.

"Ugghh, Toots, stop it," Fiona said. "Why do you always do that?" Next to her, Shamus plugged his nose.

Tiki groaned as she loosed her long braid. "Toots, does that only happen when you eat or if you just breathe the air?"

Toots giggled. "I heard a couple of the bobbies talking in the station today. They were saying that they've tripled the guards over at the palace. What with the queen's ring getting snatched and all. Guards on every door to make sure nothing else gets stolen."

"Yes." Tiki nodded. "But that's no problem for us." She paused, a smile playing at the corners of her mouth.

"Why's that?" Shamus asked.

"Because the royals aren't guarding against something being returned."

Three sets of eyes turned to look at her.

"What's that supposed to mean?" Toots asked.

"I've figured out how to collect the reward for the ring."

"You have?" Fiona gasped.

"Tell us," Toots cried.

Shamus gave her a questioning look, his response slow and measured, as usual. "Let's hear it, then."

"The queen is going to have a masked ball on the sixteenth." Tiki leaned forward, her eyes shining with excitement. "I'm planning on attending."

Fiona clapped her hands in delight. "A ball? Will you wear a beautiful gown?" She pushed herself off the floor and twirled in place, holding imaginary skirts out from her side.

Toots turned his nose up in disgust. "Why would you want to go to a ruddy ball?"

"What are you thinking, Teek?" Shamus asked.

"I'll sneak into the ball, hide the ring, and get out." She smiled, pleased with herself. "Then we'll collect the reward and tell the royals where the ring is after we have the money."

"That's brilliant, Teek." Toots jumped up excitedly. "How're you going to do that, exactly?"

"But will you dance first?" Fiona asked.

Shamus snorted out a disbelieving laugh. "I think you've gone daft."

Tiki smiled. "I have a plan. First, I'll have to find a dress," she said. "And then—"

"And what do you mean, you'll 'hide the ring'?" Shamus interrupted.

Tiki shifted her gaze to him. "It's obvious we can't just walk up to the Guards and hand someone the ring. We've gone round and round trying to figure out a way to trade the ring for the reward, but in the end it's just too risky."

"But where are you going to hide it at, Teek?" Fiona asked. Her face was alight at the idea of Tiki attending a royal ball.

"I'm going to hide the ring in bloody Buckingham Palace. Right back where I found it." Tiki beamed at them. This was the solution they'd been looking for. Not only would she not have to worry anymore about being arrested for stealing the ring, but she would be able to claim the reward and also be rid of Rieker and the faeries at the same time. It was perfect.

"You've lost your bloody mind." Shamus paced back and forth, his hands behind his back.

Fiona twirled and hummed a snippet of a tune. "I'd like to go to a ball."

"But how will they know where to look?" Toots asked.

"Shh, the lot of you need to be quiet and just listen for a minute." Tiki leaned forward again, her voice low. "I'm going to sneak into the ball and hide the ring. Someplace where no one will think to look. Then I'm going to sneak back out. They won't even know I was there. I'll be invisible, just like Toots said." She smiled over at the young boy.

"I said that?"

"Then," Tiki continued, "we'll contact the Guards and tell them we have the ring."

"But how . . . ," Shamus started. Tiki held up her hand.

"We'll strike a bargain with the royals," Tiki said. "If they give us the reward, we'll tell them where the ring is." She sat back. "It will be so simple."

Chapter Ten

I N theory, the idea was simple, but with only four days to put the plan into action, it was the details that presented the challenge.

"What will you wear to a royal ball?" Fiona asked in a dreamy voice the next morning. "Oh, I wish Clara was here. She'd love to see you all dressed up."

"I know," Tiki said. "I've been thinking about her so much. Let's go up and see her tomorrow."

"Do we dare?"

Tiki nodded. "I've been thinking of a way. If we pretend to be from a church and stop by as a charity visit to see the children, I think they'll let us in without asking questions about our parents." She eyed Fiona's soiled trousers and shirt. "We'll need to go over to Petticoat Lane and find you a dress to wear, though."

"A dress?" Fiona's voice rose in surprise.

"We're going to pretend to be girls."

"But you *are* girls, aren't you?" Toots asked from across the room.

Tiki laughed. "I'm not sure half the time anymore."

P ETTICOAT Lane was over in Aldgate, next to Spitalfields Market in the East End. They were lucky to catch a boot there, as it was almost half a day's walk from Charing Cross.

The streets of Petticoat Lane were jammed with shoppers when they arrived. The Lane was one of two main exchanges where secondhand clothes were sold.

"Fruiiiiiit. Get yer fruiiiiiitt. Apples and oranges, fresh all day." The cries of the costermongers were like birdcalls, sharp and piercing.

Tiki had brought the coin purse they'd picked off the woman in Charing Cross yesterday—it was stuffed into the depths of her trousers pocket, deep enough where no one could pick *her* pocket. They were going to need every one of those coins today.

She stopped at the cart of a costermonger selling an assortment of metal items. The glint of a small knife had caught her eye, and Rieker's words came back to her: *The fey have a weakness to iron. You should get a knife with a blade made of iron and carry it with you, no matter what. And you've got to be prepared to use it.* She slipped her fingers around the hilt and turned the knife back and forth, letting the blade glint in the soupy light of the day. The memory of Marcus grabbing her in the alley was never far from her mind. She would not be caught unarmed again. Shamus could show her how best to defend herself with a knife.

"Ah, that's a beauty, my fine fellow." The man moved close to her, his squinty eyes measuring Tiki to determine her ability to pay. "Pure iron blade on that one. Slice through the thickest meat."

"How much?" Tiki's attention was drawn to a young man standing behind the vendor. There was something about the intensity with which he watched their transaction that disturbed her. His hair was long and dark, like the feathers of a crow, pulled back behind his head. His features were striking, almost foreign, with large black eyes that seemed bottomless. She shuddered and turned back to the vendor.

"A special price for you today, young sport," the vendor replied. "Only one shilling, fourpence."

"Done." Tiki was digging the coins out of her pocket when a sickening realization of who the young man reminded her of twisted her stomach. He looked like her attacker in the alley. The one Rieker had called Marcus. She looked up, but he was gone. With a sense of desperation, Tiki stood on tiptoes and twisted her head, trying to locate him.

She dropped the coins into the vendor's grimy hands, anxious to get away. With a shaking hand, she took the knife and slipped it into a small pocket on the back of her trousers, where it could easily be reached.

Fiona raised her eyebrows. "What's that for?"

"Protection."

"From who?" Fiona grinned, a dimple appearing on one cheek. "Rieker gettin' a bit cheeky?"

Tiki forced a laugh as she fingered the cool, wooden handle. "Something like that." She wouldn't tell Fiona the truth. There was enough to worry about without scaring her as well.

"Friiiied fish! Oysters, three for a penny!" The cries of a nearby fishmonger cut through the air. An omnibus filled with passengers blocked the middle of road, its two horses jerking their heads, causing the reins to jingle, as they waited impatiently to move forward.

Tiki and Fiona cut around the carriage, always careful to avoid the steaming piles left behind by the horses. A brewer's dray and a hay wain waited as well, along with private carriages and pedestrians. To add to the cacophony and chaos, street children darted in and out of the masses of people, shouting and laughing. Along the front of every shop hung rack upon rack of secondhand clothes for sale.

Several times Tiki thought she'd spotted faces that didn't seem to belong in the crowd, their skin too perfect, their features almost flawless; but when she'd look again, they'd be gone. An unsettled feeling wormed its way through her chest, a fear that she was starting to imagine things that weren't there. Damn Rieker anyway.

As they drew near to the racks of clothes on display, Tiki crinkled up her nose. "What is that smell?"

"It's the clothes. Most have never been washed," Fiona said. "Come on." She grabbed Tiki by the hand and pulled her along, weaving through the crowd. Her head turned this way and that as she examined the goods hanging in front of each store. "We need fine ladies' clothes, not these rags that any woman on the street would wear."

Tiki looked at Fiona in surprise. "How do you know what fine ladies wear?"

Fiona tossed her head. "I'm not blind. I know how a lady dresses. Besides," she sniffed, "you know perfectly well that my mum was a seamstress before she passed." She lowered her voice. "Remember, she used to work for MacGregor."

Though it had been almost two years since Tiki had escaped from the drunken attacks of her own uncle, she would never forget the abject fear she'd felt whenever he was near. Fiona had told her that MacGregor had the same mean streak, that he liked to beat women and children.

"Wait." Fiona came to a stop, her head swiveled to the left as she spotted another rack of clothes. "Let's go look over here." She pulled Tiki toward a shop with an entire rack of dresses on display.

"What are you looking for?" Tiki asked.

"You need something fancy, but that won't draw too much attention. A full skirt, but without a crinoline. How anyone can even walk in those things, I'll never know." Fiona was muttering to herself. "Something that gathers in back a little that might pass for a bit of a bustle." Her eyes scanned the rows. Suddenly she stopped. Her dirty hand reached forward and pulled out the skirt of an ivory-and-gold-colored dress, twisting it this way and that in the light. "This might do."

Tiki considered the gown Fiona had found. "The neck looks a little low," Tiki said. "And big."

"It's meant to be worn off the shoulder," Fiona replied. "Simple lines, the gold overskirt could really be quite spec-tacular in the right light, and we all know gold is a color the royals like." She turned and looked Tiki up and down before turning back to the gown. "Might be a bit big, but we can take in the waist."

Tiki pulled up one edge of the skirt to survey the ex-panse of material. "That's a lot of fabric, Fi."

"This dress has a lot smaller skirt than most of these, especially the dresses meant to go over a crinoline."

"Will I look odd if I don't wear one?"

"No." Fiona snorted. "You don't need one of those big old hoops anyway." She hugged Tiki's arm. "You're going to be the most beautiful girl at the ball when I'm done with you."

Tiki smiled but didn't reply. It was difficult to re-member what it felt like to be a girl and impossible to even imagine being beautiful.

Fiona shoved the gown back between the other gowns so it could barely be seen. "Come on. Let's make sure we haven't missed anything else."

Tiki followed through the rows of stands and hanging garments, feeling slightly lost and disoriented. She'd never had much interest in clothes when she'd lived with her parents. Now, she knew how much more freedom there was in a pair of trousers.

"How much've we got in the coin purse?" Fiona asked.

Tiki recited the amount in a low whisper close to Fiona's ear so no one else could hear. "But we have to use some of it for a top hat for Shamus. And some slippers to wear with my gown. And we still need a dress for you to visit Clara."

Fiona stopped dead in her tracks. "A what for Shamus?"

Tiki giggled. "Shamus is going to be my driver, of course. He needs a hat."

Fiona laughed out loud. "Shamus is going to be a ruddy gentleman. This I have to see."

THEY'D searched through most of Petticoat Lane before Fiona led her back to the first dress. As they passed a shop window, Tiki stopped.

"Fi," she called. Fiona retraced her steps to stand next to Tiki in front of the bay window. Inside was a display of masks. Sequins sparkled from around the cutouts for the eyes, and feathers arched from the brow. Tiki motioned to the contents of the window. "I need a mask."

"Oh, good Lord, you're right," Fiona said.

"Something simple," Tiki warned. "I don't want to draw attention to myself."

"Look at that gold one in the back." Fiona pointed. "That will go with your dress."

Tiki gazed doubtfully at the frilly feathers attached to the center of the mask. "I can't imagine wearing half a bird on my face."

"You'll be glad for it when you're there and everybody else is wearing one," Fiona replied. "Especially if you're sneaking around." She nudged Tiki with her elbow and smiled.

They returned to the shop where Fiona had spotted the gold-and-ivory dress.

The shopkeeper eyed them with a frown. "What do you two lads want with a dress?"

"It's a gift," Fiona snapped. "I'll give you three shillings for it."

The man's eyes narrowed. "The price is six shillings."

"I'll give you three shillings, sixpence, but you'll throw in some slippers," Fiona replied.

Tiki glanced over her shoulder as Fiona negotiated, trying to ignore the uneasy sense that she was being watched. They were paying for the dress. She had nothing to feel uncomfortable about. Still, there was something that pricked at her senses.

Fiona haggled back and forth with the shopkeeper until they finally agreed on a price and she managed to have him throw in a plain brown dress as well.

They left with Fiona gaily swinging their bag of purchases. "If only that old codger could see you when you're all fixed up," she said. "He'd probably lose his teeth. When I get done with you, he wouldn't recognize his own dress." She grinned over at Tiki. "I bet he'd think you were bloody royalty yourself, he would."

Tiki giggled. It was hard to imagine looking much different from the way she did every day, masquerading as a boy in her dark trousers and oversize jacket. "He'd probably only wish that he'd struck a harder bargain for the dress."

Fiona barked out a laugh. "That's true, too."

THE next afternoon, Tiki entered the hospital wearing her one blue dress. She'd scrubbed her face and hands with the water from the fountain in Trafalgar Square, and her hair hung down her back in soft, dark waves.

Beside her, Fiona was wearing the simple brown dress they'd bartered for in Petticoat Lane. Being dressed like a girl brought back bittersweet memories of Tiki's life before. Having tea with her mother, dressing for dinner. It was when an image of her uncle surfaced that she pushed the memories away. His dark, brooding stare and the memory of his volatile temper still gave her shivers, even now.

They entered the hospital and approached the woman at the front desk.

"Excuse me, miss." Tiki was pleased that the attendant was not the nurse they had met the night they'd brought Clara in. "We're here from St. Timothy's Chapel to visit the ailing children today."

"Oh, that's so sweet of you girls," the young nurse replied, looking Tiki and Fiona up and down with a smile. "What nice, upstanding young women." She got up from her chair. "Let me show you the way."

Tiki and Fiona followed her down a long hallway and paused outside a door.

The nurse lowered her voice. "Some of the children have no family visiting, so they'll be extra glad to see you. Bless you, girls." She smiled again and disappeared back down the hall.

Tiki drew a deep breath as she entered the hall, trying to suppress the anxiety that filled her. Clara was going to be better, she repeated to herself. Most of the sick children were sleeping, but those who weren't just stared at them with hopeless eyes. By the time they reached the sixth bed and still hadn't found Clara, Tiki could feel a fluttering in her chest, making it hard to breathe.

They circled the room again.

Clara wasn't there.

Tiki looked in Fiona's eyes, now brimming with tears, and saw the question there. She wouldn't allow herself to believe it. Not Clara, too. She turned and looked over the beds in the room again, making sure that she hadn't somehow missed the little girl.

A deep hacking cough came from a nearby room, and Tiki jerked around with a start. She hadn't noticed the closed door before. She hurried over to peek in through the glass window embedded in the door. There was another, smaller ward behind the door. Only four beds there, each of them filled.

Tiki read the word on the door, QUARANTINE, before she yanked it open. She could see a small tousled blond head lying on one of the pillows and rushed over, Fiona on her heels.

Clara was lying on her side with her thumb in her mouth, eyes closed. She was pale and drawn.

Tiki reached out and put a gentle hand on the little girl's head, unable to hold back the tear that ran down her face. The drop landed on Clara's cheek, and she opened her eyes to look up at Tiki. Her eyes sprang to life and she lifted her arms to hug the older girl as sobs shook her frail little shoulders.

"I thought you'd left me," she sobbed. "I thought you didn't love me anymore."

"Shhh," Tiki said. "Shh, little Clara, everything's all right. We will always love you and will never leave you, I promise."

"Clara, we brought you a hot-cross bun," Fiona said in a bright voice. She pulled the squashed bun from the pocket of her dress and showed it to the little girl.

Clara gave a hiccuping sigh. She pulled Tiki's hand to her cheek, then reached out to take the bun from Fiona.

"Are you working hard at feeling better?" Tiki leaned down close to Clara's face as the little girl laid her head back down on the pillow.

"I will now." She rested her cheek on Tiki's hand. "Now that I know you'll come for me."

"Clara, we'll never leave you. We're your family," Tiki said. "We only brought you here because you were too sick to stay with us. We needed the hospital's help to get you well. That's why you're here. And when you're feeling much better and stop coughing, then you'll come home with us."

Fiona leaned down, slightly breathless. "And we're going to live someplace new with food in the cupboards and Tiki's going to go to a ball at the— Ouch!" Fiona narrowed her eyes at Tiki. "Why'd you kick me?"

"We'll tell Clara about all that later." Tiki gave Fiona a look before she turned back to Clara. "But for now, all you need to concentrate on is getting well enough to come home. And we'll all be together again and I'll tell you a story every night before bed."

"Okay." Clara sighed, her eyes beginning to droop again. "Will you tell me more faerie stories, like your mum told you?"

"Yes, of course. For now you need to sleep, but listen to me, Clara. Even if you don't see us for a few days, we are thinking of you always and love you very much. We will be back for you. Never, never forget."

"And we'll bring you another bun," Fiona added.

Clara nodded, watching Tiki's face with adoring eyes. "You look pretty, Teek."

"It's going to be different when you come home. We're going to be warm all the time and we're always going to have enough food to eat." Tiki felt Fiona giving her a questioning look, but she ignored her.

"Truly?" Clara whispered, her eyes brightening again.

"Yes, truly." Tiki smoothed the blond curls from her forehead. "Now the very most important thing is for you to sleep and eat everything the nurses give you so you can get stronger and come home. Okay?"

"Okay." Clara nodded as another deep cough shook her body.

Tiki pulled a piece of lavender lace from inside her coat. It was a shred she'd kept from one of her mother's dresses. "Here, let me tie this around your wrist. If you ever doubt me, you look at this piece of lace and know this is my promise to you that I'll be back."

"It's preetiful," Clara said in an awestruck voice. She ran a little finger over the delicate lace, her lips curving in a tired smile. "Thank you, Tiki."

"You're welcome. Now close your eyes and we'll stay here for just a minute and hold your hand while you fall asleep, just like always."

Tiki clutched the small hand in hers and leaned down to gently kiss her cheek. "I love you, little Clara," she whispered. "Get well soon."

It took only a few moments before Clara fell asleep, a smile on her thin face.

"Come on, Teek, we better go." Fiona tugged at Tiki's sleeve.

Tiki laid Clara's hand on the pillow, the little strip of lavender lace around her wrist a spot of color against her pale skin. She straightened up and followed Fiona from the quarantine room. They went down a long hall. Several carts filled with items for the hospital rooms were parked in between doors that led to other wards.

Tiki gazed up and down the hallways as they wound their way back to the entrance, trying to explain the unsettled feeling that rode her shoulders like a witch's cat. Flickers of faces, brief images of people standing near her, came and went so fast that she tried to tell herself she was imagining things. Rieker's warning was never far from her mind. The sooner she could get rid of the ring and return the stone to the royals, the better.

As they passed the waiting room on their way toward the exit, Tiki glanced in at the throng of people waiting to be seen by the doctors. Her eyes stopped on a blond head, and her heart skipped a beat. A familiar face stared at her. It was the girl she'd seen at King's Cross. The same girl from Mr. Potts's bookstore, the one who had asked about Clara. She was sure of it. Then the crowd shifted and she was gone.

Chapter Eleven

THE day of the masked ball at the palace dawned cool and clear.

Tiki was a bundle of nerves from the minute she woke up. The idea of pretending to belong to a crowd who hobnobbed with the royals was almost beyond her imagination. Pure desperation was the only excuse she could think of for how she came up with such a crazy idea.

She pushed her way out their room and wandered down the bustling hallways of the railway station, trying to calm the fear bubbling in her stomach. Saturdays were always the busiest day of the week at Charing Cross, and today was no exception. The crowds were thick and the people seemed harried, rushing this way and that, trying to avoid the overloaded trolleys that weaved through the throng.

Tiki sank onto a bench outside Mr. Potts's bookstore, mentally reviewing her plan one more time.

"What's the scowl for? Not enough people to pickpocket for you?"

Rieker slid onto the bench next to Tiki, his long legs stretched out, his shoulder brushing against hers. She flushed at the unexpected contact, and a wave of nervousness washed over her. Damn Rieker anyway. Why did he always make her feel like this?

"Hello, Rieker." She made sure her voice stayed even.

He rested his elbows on his knees and crooked his neck to look back at her. "How's your little girl?"

Not for the first time, she noticed how straight his nose was, somehow fitting the contours of his face perfectly. A light stubble was evident along his jaw, and when his hair fell back Tiki could see another scar just behind his ear. The mark was a jagged shape, bleached white with time, and looked as though it had been quite painful once. She fought the urge to reach out and trace the scar, as though to wipe away the hurt the wound must have caused.

Instead, she threaded her fingers together in her lap. "She's in hospital," Tiki said quietly. "I couldn't help her."

To her surprise, Rieker reached over and slid his big hand over hers. "You did the right thing, Tiki. They have the means to care for her there."

The purple shadows that had colored the skin under his eyes previously were gone today. He looked well rested and healthy, his smoky eyes calm and reassuring. She wanted to believe him.

"But what if I can't bring her home again?" Tiki bit hard on her bottom lip, hoping Rieker hadn't heard the telltale waver in her voice.

"If I know you, Tiki, you'll find a way." Rieker gave her a half-smile. The timbre of his voice was mesmerizing and seemed to pull her toward him. His brow dipped in a quizzical frown. "I may not have mentioned this before, but you have the most beautiful green eyes I've ever seen. They're like—"

"Just like the green hills of Ireland," a voice interrupted them. "Yeah, yeah. It's what ol' Potts says all the time."

Toots came to a stop in front of them. "What are you do-ing out here, Teek? Fiona's been looking for you."

Tiki pushed off the bench and got to her feet before Rieker could see the blush that warmed her cheeks. She wondered if he was silently laughing at her. No doubt his compliments were simply a ploy to try to talk her out of the ring. Well, after tonight there was no chance of that.

Rieker stood, too, towering over the two of them.

"Have you thought any more about our conversation, Tiki?" Rieker moved closer, his hand brushing the back of her arm. His words were soft. "I need your help."

Tiki jerked her arm back and stepped away. "I'm sorry." She was surprised to find that she meant it. "But I can't help you, Rieker. I don't have what you're looking for." She felt a twinge at the lie, but she reminded herself that it would be the truth soon enough.

DID you get it?" Toots asked in a hushed voice. The sun had just set as they gathered in their little room in Char-ing Cross. Everyone's eyes were locked on Tiki.

"Yes." She dug into the deep pockets of her trousers and pulled out the wad of dirty fabric. "I've got it right here." She balanced the bundle on the palm of her out-stretched hand and peeled the folds back. Gasps of awe filled the room as the queen's ring was revealed.

Tiki held up the ring so the others could see the bloodred stone wrapped in gold. The flames flickered deep within the gem as brightly as ever, infusing her hand with a strange kind of warmth.

"Oh, it's so beautiful," Fiona cried. "Can I hold it?"

"Don't drop it," Toots said.

"Are you daft? I'm not going to drop it, you—"

"Shh . . . we can all take turns," Tiki said. "Then I'm going to put it away until I leave." They didn't know about the truce, so she didn't tell them that she was afraid the faeries might know it was in her possession and come after her. Damn Rieker anyway. Sometimes she wished she didn't know the truth.

After they had all had time to gaze into the depths of the stone, Tiki took the ring back and wrapped it within the folds of the dirty cloth. She shoved it back in her pocket with a sense of relief.

"I still don't know where you came up with this mad idea, Teek," Toots said. A wide grin split his face. "But I think it's bloody brilliant to sneak into the ball. Are you planning on picking a few gems off those fancy ladies?" His eyes were round with wonder. "It'd be like being in a shop full of sweets."

"I still think it sounds too risky," Shamus said in a low voice. He sat before the stove, whittling again, a worried expression on his face.

"Well, she's going," Fiona interrupted. "And she can't go looking like a crossing sweep. So you two better hustle down to the fountain and fill those buckets we nicked from Mr. Binder with some water for her to wash." Fiona put her hands on her hips and scowled at Shamus and Toots.

The boys scrambled out the back door to do Fiona's bidding, and Tiki laughed in a giddy sort of way. Strange bubbles filled her stomach, making her feel light and heavy and tipsy all at the same time. It *was* madness to think she could attend a royal ball. What would they do to her if she was caught? But she pushed the thought away. She had to do it. Returning the ring was the only way to get the reward. And she needed the reward to pay for Clara's care.

It wasn't long before Shamus and Toots returned with full buckets. The only way to heat the water was to put the bucket on top of the stove. Since that quantity of water would take too long to heat, she and Fiona arranged the two buckets of cold water behind the tattered blanket that worked as their privacy screen.

Tiki poked her head around the edge. "Why don't you two go visit Mr. Potts for a bit? And maybe you can round us up something to eat."

Shamus's face colored. "Oh. C'mon, Toots." He nudged the younger boy, and they slipped out into the station.

"Do you want to wash, too?" Tiki looked over at Fiona and motioned to the water.

"Nah." Fiona grinned at her. She had smudges of dirt along her jaw and over one eye from wiping her brow with the back of her hand. "What's the point?" She dug into the pocket of her trousers. "But look what I nicked from the hospital when we were there." Balanced on her dirty fingers was a chunk of white soap.

"Where did you get that?"

"There was a box of them sitting on a cart we walked by." Fiona shrugged. "It looked like they had plenty to me. Let's wash your hair first so it has time to dry."

Tiki couldn't hold back a gasp of shock as Fiona slopped the cool water on her head. The other girl scrubbed vigorously, trying to spread the soap through Tiki's thick, dark hair.

"Easy, Fi. I don't want my head to start bleeding."

"Sit on the floor and lean back and I'll dip your head in the bucket," Fiona instructed. "That's the only way we're going to get all the soap off." By the time they were done, there was more water on the floor than left in the buckets. Tiki was shaking uncontrollably, but her skin was clean and even her hair smelled fresh.

She shivered as she rubbed herself dry with the cleanest edge of one of their tattered blankets, anxious to move closer to the heat of the box stove. She slipped on a long shirt that doubled as her nightgown and pulled a crate over near the warmth. Fiona came and stood behind her, finger-combing the long strands.

A moment later, Tiki squirmed as Fiona tugged at her hair with the small filigreed brush. "Careful, Fi," Tiki warned her. "I want to leave some hair on my head."

"It's just so tangled. You should brush it more often," Fiona said, unconcerned. "Especially now that we have a brush. Sit still, I'm almost done."

An hour later, Tiki's hair was almost dry and she was warm and comfortable next to the fire. The boys still hadn't returned.

"Okay, let's get this dress on," Fiona said, "and see where I have to take it in."

Tiki's heart was beating like a stick on a tin can, and her fingers were fumbly, which was a rare state for her.

"How will you do that?" she asked.

"I've got a bit of thread and a needle. It's all you need." Fiona picked up the dress. "Lift your arms up."

"Don't poke me." Tiki's voice was muffled as yards and yards of fabric seemed to swallow her. She wiggled to maneuver the dress over her head, and then the gown settled like a cloud over her shoulders and down her hips.

"Pull the sleeves down, they're meant to be worn off

your shoulder," Fiona said. "Now stand still and let me get all these buttons." She pulled at the back of the dress, bringing the pieces of fabric together. After she finished securing the buttons, Fiona turned Tiki around and gave her an appraising glance. She reached forward and pinched the loose fabric at Tiki's waist. "I think just a little bit here on each side. . . ."

After an hour of measuring and stitching, trying on, and more measuring and stitching, Fiona pronounced her ready to go.

"Now for the finishing touches on your hair." Fiona pulled Tiki's long, dark tresses away from her face, then secured them at the top of her head. "I know just the style for a ball." Tiki debated asking Fiona how she knew such a thing but decided to let her have her fun.

Fiona hummed as she worked, something that sounded like a waltz. She twisted and braided Tiki's hair to gather at the back of her head, then let the thick strands cascade down her back in soft ringlets. Tiki wondered if the whole mess wouldn't collapse from the weight of the pins.

"Okay, turn around, Teek." Fiona stood back with her hands on her hips.

Tiki turned, and the dress swung out with a graceful *whoosh,* then settled down around her ankles.

Fiona's jaw went slack and she stood speechless for a moment. "Cor, Tiki, you look like a bloody princess," she whispered, then clapped her hands together in delight. "Wait till the boys see you."

Just then the panel for the back door swung to the side.

"Can we come in?" Shamus called.

"Yes, come see," Fiona replied. She yanked the blanket across the rope in front of Tiki to hide her while Shamus and Toots entered the room. "Ta da da dumm," Fiona sang, sounding as though she were announcing the arrival of royalty.

"Oh, stop it, Fi." Tiki brushed the blanket aside. "This is business tonight."

A stunned silence fell over the room.

Unsure at their reaction, Tiki looked down, nervous at the amount of creamy skin that was revealed. Her sleeves, worn off her shoulder, were slim to just above her wrists, where they fanned out in a spill of lace. The neckline dipped down in a V, revealing the tops of her breasts. Fiona had taken in the sides of the gown until it fit snugly around her small waist. From there, the skirt dropped away in shimmering golden folds to puddle on the ground around her bare feet.

Tiki put her hands on her hips and looked from Shamus to Toots. "What's wrong with you two?"

"God bless the queen," Shamus uttered. "Fiona, what have you done to Tiki?"

"You look like a princess," Toots whispered.

"That's what I said." Fiona laughed. "Ain't she grand and beautiful?"

"Stop it right now. I'm nervous enough as it is," Tiki said. But she was secretly pleased that they liked the way she looked. She couldn't help but wonder what Rieker would think if he could see her dressed like this.

NIGHT had fallen as they finished the last of the hard bread. Tiki was almost afraid to move for fear she would damage the dress or knock her hair askew. She clutched her fingers together tightly in her lap to still the rumbling in her stomach.

"Have you got Binder's wagon, Shamus?" Tiki asked.

"Yes. Toots and I went by earlier to get things ready."

"And he doesn't mind that you're going to use it tonight?" Fiona looked from one to the other in surprise.

"Ol' man Binder doesn't mind what he doesn't know." Shamus smiled and raised his eyebrows at her. "Some generous bloke left him a pint of gin this afternoon, and last time I saw him, he was dozing off."

"What if he wakes up and finds the wagon gone?" Fiona asked.

"He won't be waking up anytime soon." Shamus pushed himself to his feet. "I'll go get it. You lot go out the back way and wait for me in the alley."

"Wait, Shamus." Tiki motioned to Fiona.

"Oh, right." Fiona hurried to the far corner of the room and moved aside a pile of blankets. She turned and held up a black stovepipe hat. "This is for you, Shamus. From Tiki." She gave a sly glance at Tiki, then looked back at Shamus. "So you look respectable." Then she burst into laughter.

Shamus looked over at Tiki. "You got that for me?"

"Of course. I think you're a gentleman, Shamus." She smiled. "You'll look handsome in it."

Shamus took the hat out of Fiona's hands and positioned it at a cocky angle on his head and struck a pose, a broad grin across his face.

"Shamus McFerguson, at your service."

Toots looked from Tiki to Shamus and slapped his hand to his forehead in perfect imitation of Mr. Potts. "Oh, fer the love of Pete."

* * *

WHILE Shamus ran to get the "carriage," Fiona and Toots helped Tiki navigate her way out the back door and through the maintenance tunnels to the alley.

"Hold her skirt up," Fiona snapped at Toots.

"I am, but there's a lot of cloth. It keeps slippin'."

They worked their way to the edge of the alley. It wasn't long before Shamus returned, driving a black wagon, pulled by a single horse. The words BINDER'S BAKERY were written in black on a white sign above the doors. The horse jerked his head against the reins, and the jingle of bells echoed in the night air.

Tiki turned to Fiona and Toots.

"Okay, back inside, you two, and don't budge until we get back. Shamus will have to stay and wait for me, but we won't be gone too long. I just need to get in, take care of business, and get out."

Fiona threw her arms around Tiki, careful not to crumple her dress or dislodge the elegant hairdo. "Oh, Teek, I wish I could go with you," she cried. "You look so ladylike and fancy. Be careful."

Toots hung back, looking awkward. "Yeah." He couldn't seem to pull his eyes away from Tiki. She turned to climb in the carriage when Toots stopped her. "Uh . . . Teek, what about your mask?"

"Oh, good Lord, the mask." Tiki gasped, putting her fingers up to her face. She turned to Fiona. "Can you run inside and grab it, Fi?"

Fiona was back in just a few minutes, holding the elegant gold eye mask festooned with white feathers. With great care she positioned it over Tiki's face, tying the lace ribbons in back to hold it in place.

"There." Fiona stepped back to examine her. "Even I wouldn't recognize you," she breathed. "It's a shame Clara's not here to see this. She'd be so excited."

Tiki smiled at the mention of the little girl, and her nerves relaxed. Clara and the three standing before her were the reason she was doing this. Her family. It was worth the risk to try to find them a better life.

Chapter Twelve

TIKI sat on the hard wooden seat and stared out the small window as they passed the Queen's Park. Mr. Binder's wagon was a delivery truck, so the inside had only one bench, which faced multiple wooden shelves where he stored his baked goods. But it was a way to get to the ball, and that was all she cared about.

Her plan was to sneak in the same way she had before— through the door that led to the kitchens. If anyone stopped her, she would say she'd become lost. She hoped no one would ask to see her invitation.

The gas lamps were blazing on the front of Buckingham Palace as they drew near. A line of black, elegant hansom cabs formed a queue to drop their occupants off at the front of the palace. Shamus steered the old horse along the road between St. James's Park and the palace, headed toward the Royal Mews. No one paid any attention to the bakery wagon.

He pulled the carriage to a stop, hidden in the shadows under several low-hanging trees in an area of the side yard.

Shamus climbed down and opened the door. "This is as close as I can get."

"Is there anyone about?" Tiki asked.

"It sounds like everybody's out front. There's a door propped open on the side of the building here."

"That's it." Tiki gathered her skirt and lifted it so she could climb out the door. She hopped to the ground and shook out the folds of her gown, taking a deep breath to slow the wild beating of her heart.

"Teek . . ." Shamus's voice was soft. "Remember, you're more of a lady than anyone else in there tonight."

Tiki leaned forward and kissed his cheek. "Thank you, Shamus. Wish me luck." She adjusted her mask, making sure it would stay firmly in place. "I'll try to hurry."

Holding her head high, Tiki swept into the dim hallway that led to the immense kitchens, praying that no one would question her. She had never attempted a deceit this daring before. Once again, pots were banging amid a babble of conversation. Over it all Tiki could hear the voice of the cook, barking instructions.

Tiki slowed as she neared the door, afraid of being seen. Then, with a deep breath, she drew herself up and walked by the door as if she owned the place. If anyone from the kitchens saw her, they didn't try to stop her, which gave her renewed confidence.

She hurried along, following the swell of conversation that echoed in the distance. She took several wrong turns in the maze of hallways before she spotted a footman up ahead.

"Excuse me," she said, her voice wavering with nerves. "I seem to have gotten turned around."

The footman didn't make eye contact with her, which gave her an odd sensation of feeling invisible. Instead, he stared at the opposite wall as he swung his arm out. "This way to the ballroom, miss."

"Thank you." Tiki inclined her head as she glided by,

wishing she could remain invisible for the rest of the night.

After checking her mask one last time, Tiki moved into a larger room and followed a swell of beautifully dressed people toward the stairs. The sound of violins, cellos, and flutes wafted toward them from the ballroom upstairs. Women wore gowns of every color, from vibrant rich satins to ethereal silks. The matching masks were adorned with gaudy feathers and sparkling sequins, making their owners look like exotic birds. Men were elegant in their black tails, wearing crisp white shirts with white cravats tied neatly under black vests.

Tiki's fingers shook as she slid her hand along the shiny black handrail of the Grand Staircase, trying not to stare in awe at the glittering gold design of the railing. Above her on the walls, life-size pictures of the royal family were displayed, and she could feel the weight of their painted eyes as she passed underneath.

Lessons she had learned as a young girl, of how to stand straight and carry her head just so, came back to her. Tiki straightened her shoulders as she tried hard not to stare at the glittering jewels on the ladies around her, knowing how easy it would be to lighten their burden without their knowledge.

Not yet. She couldn't give in to the temptation until she had taken care of the real reason she was here.

As she entered the ballroom, Tiki's jaw went slack. Her first impression was of a room created from gold. The walls and ceiling appeared to be carved from the stuff, such was the quantity of elaborately sculptured gilded trim. High on the walls, huge oil paintings framed in gilt were interspersed between gold-trimmed windows. Gold moldings circled the room at multiple levels on the walls.

Near the ceiling, luxurious painted images of cherubs danced among otherworldly beings with wings. The ceiling itself was divided into precise squares of gold, each painted and stair-stepped to a center containing an enormous sparking chandelier ablaze with lights.

Beyond the din of people talking, the notes of an orchestra swelled from one corner as dancers swirled on the floor in the intricate movements of a quadrille. The sound of a piano blended with violins and horns and enveloped her with a wash of music. The rustle of silk and velvet, the sparkle of gold and jewelry, all glittered together like an exquisite painting come to life.

Tiki patted her bodice, making sure that the small package she had hidden down the front of her dress remained in place. Her eyes scanned the exits as she worked her way around the perimeter of the room. Where could she hide the ring?

It was with a measured pace that Tiki made her way through a door and down a hallway. Her eyes roamed over the huge paintings that lined the walls as well as the tall, ornate vases and elegant furniture that filled the corridor. She was in a different part of the palace tonight.

A small alcove set off to one side caught her eye, and with a quick glance over her shoulder to make sure no one was watching, she slid behind the partially closed drapes. The small room looked out to a view of a beautiful garden lit by hanging lanterns. Two carved chairs were positioned adjacent to each other beneath a painting hung on the wall.

Tiki caught her breath. In the painting, a man held his hand out to a woman. Her beauty was riveting, reminding Tiki of the blond girl. But what truly caught her eye were the ethereal wings that adorned the woman's back, as thin and delicate as the wings of a dragonfly. Faerie wings?

I didn't believe it either, Tiki. Rieker's hushed words came back to her. *What did you see when Marcus touched you? What did you feel?* Tiki's stomach lifted with a sickening motion. The wing she had seen in the alley that night, the wing that had been on Marcus's back, had had a similar stained-glass appearance as those in the painting before her.

With a trembling hand, she ran her fingers along the gilt frame of the picture. The wood had been carved in elaborate swirls of loops and curls. Tiki reached around the back corner of the frame. Behind the picture she could feel a small nail used to hold the canvas in place.

Tiki cast a cautious eye up and down the hallway, but there was no one to notice her hidden in the shadows behind the curtain. With a trembling hand, she reached down the front of her dress and retrieved the small package she had hidden there.

Oh, pardon me." Tiki smiled at the woman she had just purposely bumped. "I'm so sorry."

"Quite all right, dear," the older woman replied. The faded eyes behind her green velvet mask were a bit glassy as she raised her goblet and drank deeply. "It's not a ball if we don't rub elbows a bit." She swayed slightly on her feet as her eyes narrowed at Tiki.

"Enjoy your evening," Tiki murmured as she patted her hair, letting the emerald earring slide down her sleeve.

As she moved away, she heard the woman gasp, and for a second Tiki thought she had already missed her jewels.

"Have you forgotten your crinoline, my dear?"

Tiki dodged behind a stout old man who reminded her of a penguin in his black-and-white dress clothes. She found herself trapped by people on all sides in the crowded room.

"May I offer you a drink?"

Tiki turned with a start. A servant inclined his head over a silver tray.

"Oh, yes, thank you." Tiki reached for the glass, filled with dark red liquid. She took a sip and coughed, trying to catch her breath from the pungent flavor of the wine.

"Are you all right?" a new voice inquired.

"Y-yes." Tiki coughed again, her eyes watering at the corners.

"I often have the same reaction to fine wine," the young man said. One corner of his mouth lifted as he gazed down at her.

Tiki's stomach dropped like a rock into a pond. His chiseled face was partially hidden beneath a black mask. Though the mask was of a simple cut, the quality of the embellishments suggested that this was a young man of means. The outside corners of the eye cutouts were shaded with glittering gold, and an intricate design of gold embroidery embellished the area above the eyes and down the center portion over his nose. A single black gem sparkled from the center amid the embroidery at the top of the mask.

"Would you like me to fetch you something different to drink?"

He stood straight and tall, immaculately dressed in black trousers with a shirt, waistcoat, and cravat of the purest white silk, covered by an overcoat of black tails. His gray eyes watched her with amusement through the slits in his mask.

"I don't . . . ," Tiki started.

"Perhaps a sweeter negus?" he said. "Or, if not that, could I offer you some tea?"

"Wills, you're not hiding this scrumptious tidbit from the rest of us, are you?" a voice interrupted.

The dark-haired young man turned. "Oh, hello, Leo."

The newcomer moved into view, and Tiki was surprised to recognize Prince Leopold, the youngest son of Queen Victoria. Though he wore a mask, his short brown hair and receding hairline were unmistakable. He was without a doubt the young man who had stopped her in the park. She dipped into a low curtsy, relieved the package was gone from the depths of her bodice.

Leo reached for Tiki's hand and assisted her in straightening up. He inclined his head.

"You are breathtaking tonight, miss," he said. "And so cleverly disguised that I cannot discern your identity, but something tells me we've not met before." He paused, as though hoping Tiki would offer her name, but she remained silent. "Therefore, I will be forced to call you the Unknown Beauty until I learn your true name."

"Another to your list of Unknown Beauties, Leo?" Wills chuckled. "How do you possibly keep them all straight?"

The prince turned to face the young man. "Perhaps you could save me from this awkward moment, then, Wills, and introduce me to your friend."

"So you can sweep her away? What do you take me for? A complete fool?"

Leo laughed out loud. "A contest for the hand of the Unknown Beauty, then?" He nudged Wills in the ribs. At that moment, the orchestra struck up a waltz. Before Wills could respond, Leo turned to Tiki.

"Shall we dance?"

Chapter Thirteen

O H, well . . . I'm . . . not a, er . . . very good dancer,"
Tiki stuttered.

"Nonsense, I'm sure you're an excellent dancer." Leo
leaned close. "And I am an excellent dance *partner,* so
between the two of us, I daresay we shall be fine." He took
Tiki's glass and handed both drinks to his friend. "Wills,
old chap, would you be so kind?"

Without waiting for a reply, Leo held out his hand and
led Tiki into the swirl of dancers.

Hours of dance lessons she'd been forced to endure
came back to her as she followed the prince's lead. One,
two, three, one, two, three. Tiki stared at her feet as she
concentrated on counting the waltz steps in her head, the
familiar tune reminding her of practicing the dance with
her father.

Her dance instructor, Madame Broussard, had been
most insistent that a waltz, or a valse, as she liked to call
it, was an essential bit of knowledge for any properly
brought up lady. A valse was the easiest dance to learn if
you knew the simple steps, she had insisted. Tiki stumbled over Leo's foot and immediately felt a blush stain her
cheeks. Why had she not thought to practice before coming to a dance? How could she be so daft?

"You're doing beautifully," Leo whispered in her ear.

He whirled her around until her gown flared out with every turn and Tiki began to enjoy the rhythm of the music. "I've danced with many"—he rolled his eyes in a charming way—"*far* too many of the ladies here, and I can say with confidence that you are one of the better dancers in the group. And certainly one of the prettiest."

"How very kind of you," Tiki replied. She was starting to enjoy the game she played. A prince of England was flirting with her. She couldn't wait to tell Fiona. What a laugh they'd have over this. "Please forgive my ignorance, but do I call you sire, sir, Your Highness . . . ?" Her voice trailed off.

"Just call me Leo. I don't need any fancy titles among friends." He gave her a warm smile.

"Then, tell me, Leo," she said, "do you pay such outrageous compliments to all of your guests? Or just those who need dance instruction?"

"No, of course not." Leo pretended to look aghast. "I only fawn over those who can provide some political advantage to the crown, those who might be related to the crown, and those who live on or near lands held by the crown. Let me see"—he pretended to think—"have I left anyone out?"

Tiki giggled and shook her head. "No, I don't think so."

"Good." Leo smiled at her. "Then perhaps I've earned my keep here for another day." He twirled her again and then drew her close. "And how do I categorize you? Are we related?"

"No," Tiki said. "But, if we are to share confidences, tell me where your favorite places are in London."

Leo frowned and regarded her for a moment. "Now that's a question I'm rarely asked." He paused to consider his answer as he swept her along in the dance. "There's the Birdkeeper's Cottage in St. James' Park. A woman who has tended my mother most of her life lives there. Her husband was the birdkeeper for many years. It's surrounded by gardens and overlooks the lake. I like to ride out there when it's warm. The gardens are very picturesque and you feel like you've escaped into another world."

"That sounds wonderful," Tiki murmured. "And where else do you like to ride?"

"Well, if you follow Rotten Row, over in Hyde Park, you'll pass by the Upside Down tree—have you seen it?"

"I don't believe I have."

"Fascinating tree and quite old. Some type of cypress, I believe. The branches grow toward the ground rather than the sky, creating an umbrella effect. You can walk right underneath and be hidden from the world."

"Surely your guards don't let you ride alone?"

Leo grinned at her, his youth suddenly evident. "What they don't know won't hurt them. It's finding the time to escape my responsibilities and obligations that is the difficult part." He winked and lifted his arm to twirl her again. "But one can't live life being followed and coddled *all* of the time."

The violins and piano swelled to a grand finale as the waltz concluded. Tiki dropped into a deep curtsy. "Thank you for the dance and the lovely conversation." She turned and made her way to the edge of the dance floor. She hadn't planned on dancing tonight, as if she'd actually been invited to the ball. Now that she'd placed the ring, she needed to get out, just as she'd told Shamus she would do. And somehow manage not to be caught.

"But wait." Leo took a few hurried steps to catch up

with her. "You've not told me anything about yourself. How am I to discover who hides behind the mask if you don't give me any clues? What is your name?"

Tiki laughed. "I'm quite sure there's nothing about me that you'd find interesting," she replied. She took a few more steps, then realized that this was her golden opportunity. With a coy look she said, "However, there is something about you that I find fascinating."

"Only one thing?" Leo asked in mock disappointment.

"I've wondered why the palace has offered such a high reward for the queen's ring that has recently gone missing."

"Oh." The prince's expression hardened. "You've heard of the ring?"

"I just overheard some ladies talking about it," Tiki lied.

"Yes, well, it holds great sentimental value for my mother, and she wishes to have it returned."

"And it was stolen?"

"Unfortunately, yes. We know where the ring was last seen, but we can't locate it now and have to assume it's been taken. My mother is quite insistent upon having the ring returned. And believe me"—Leo lowered his voice— "you don't argue with my mother."

Tiki walked along beside the prince, her hands clasped in front of her. "Have you any clue what happened to it?"

"No," Leo replied. His expression sobered. "The disappearance is quite worrisome, actually." He came to a stop at the edge of the dance floor and turned to face her. "May I offer you something to drink?"

"But you've offered a reward because you think it was stolen?"

A small frown flitted across his brow. "Impossible though it seems, there's really no other explanation. We've questioned the staff and posted handbills, but it seems to have vanished." He eyed her with curiosity. "Tell me again how you know of it?"

"I heard several ladies discussing it over there." Tiki pointed to the far corner of the crowded ballroom.

Leo's gaze followed the direction she pointed, his eyes scanning the crowd. "Hmmm, that's curious." He took two goblets from the tray proffered by a footman. "Wine?"

Tiki nodded. She was treading on thin ice, and would feel more confident holding something in her hand.

"It sounds like a great mystery." She gave Leo her best smile. "But if the thief wanted to claim the reward, how would they return the ring without being arrested?"

"Yes, well, that is a very good question indeed." Leo surveyed the crowded room again before he lowered his voice. "I suspect the thief would somehow convey a message to one of the palace guards, then we would negotiate the proper exchange of ring for reward." He took a drink from his glass, letting out a contented sigh. "Now, where were we? Ah yes, your name . . ."

"Elizabeth." Tiki said the first name that popped into her head.

"Elizabeth." Leo sighed. "A lovely name for a lovely girl. Elizabeth suits you." He peered closer at her mask. "Did you know your eyes are a most unusual shade of green? They remind me of emeralds."

Tiki smiled at him, thinking of the emerald earring tucked in the folds of her dress. "Thank you, Leo. But, tell me," she persisted, "how would a thief contact a guard without being caught? I'm sure if you truly want the ring back, then you must have a system of exchange planned out."

Leo sighed. "I'm sure we can find more interesting topics of conversation other than thievery and blackmail, but being the gentleman I am, I will strive to satisfy your curiosity. There have been occasions in the past when we've exchanged goods in certain, shall we say, *extreme* situations, where a person sends a sealed note or letter that contains some identifying information that would suggest they are indeed in the company of an actual missing item." He leaned forward and put his lips near her ear. "For instance, the missing ring has an inscription inside the band that has never been publicly revealed." His eyes dropped to the low-cut neckline of her dress and lingered there.

At his words, Tiki was transported back in time. It was as if she stood in the library again, peering at the inscription inside the ring. *Na síochána, aontaímid: For the sake of peace, we agree.* She could see the flowing script inside the gold band reflected in the flickering light of the gas lamp perfectly.

Leo took another sip of wine. "Only someone who has handled the ring would have that information," he continued. "So should a person provide a letter claiming possession of the ring with the words from the inscription, along with instructions of where to leave a large sum of money, we would be inclined to believe what they said and most likely do as they ask."

"I see." Tiki nodded, trying to hide her elation. Without thinking, she took a sip of her drink and immediately started coughing again. The stuff was awful!

"Too much wine?" A familiar voice spoke.

"Ah, Wills, there you are." Leo turned with a broad

smile. "And Isabelle Cavendish." He nodded at the tall young girl in the striking blue dress. Her brown hair was uplifted in an elegant pile of curls, and a few stray strands of hair dangled around the creamy skin of her narrow face. Her mask was adorned with peacock feathers, and their iridescent colors seemed reflected in her blue green eyes.

"Leo," she said in a low, seductive voice, "I've been wondering why you didn't invite Wills to your parties anymore." Her lips curved in a mischievous smile. "I thought perhaps he'd left town."

"He's always invited." Leo chuckled. "Getting him to show up is the challenge. I saw that the two of you took a turn on the dance floor." Leo's gaze traced the exotic feathers that adorned Isabelle's mask, then dropped briefly to the brilliant blue sapphires that glittered from her chest. "You make a fetching pair, you know."

Tiki caught the wink that Leo threw to the dark-haired young man, and she turned in curiosity to see his reaction.

"Actually, I'm anxious to make the acquaintance of this young lady as well." He inclined his head toward Tiki. Isabelle shifted her gaze toward her, and Tiki was stunned by the malice in her eyes. "Allow me to introduce myself. I'm William Becker Richmond."

"Oh, allow me, Wills," Leo interjected. "So sorry, I thought you two knew each other. This is Miss Elizabeth, uh . . ." He turned to Tiki, expecting her to fill in her last name. Instead Tiki dipped into a deep curtsy.

"So pleased to meet you, Mr. Richmond." She fought the panic that was fluttering in her chest. She needed to find a way out of this room. Too many questions, too much attention. There was something about the intensity of this dark-haired stranger that worried her. Not to mention Isabelle Cavendish trying to burn her with her eyes.

To her amazement, instead of returning her bow as she expected, the tall young man reached for her hand and took a firm grip. He lifted her fingers to his lips, his eyes never leaving hers. "The pleasure is all mine," he said. Beside him, Isabelle's lips pinched together in anger.

As if in slow motion, Tiki watched his hand lift hers. The thick lace at the end of her sleeve fell back, revealing the dark swirls of her birthmark. For one long second, William Richmond's gaze shifted to her wrist before his eyes returned to hers with startled surprise.

The sound of a wineglass shattering on the marble floor disrupted the low hum of conversation. As one, heads turned to find the source of the noise.

With a gasp, Tiki jerked her arm away, allowing the sleeve to cover her wrist again. Her eyes flicked over to Leo. He stood with his mouth ajar, his now empty hand still frozen in place.

Leo's eyes were transfixed on her arm.

"What is that mark on your wrist?" Leo's voice was faint as he raised questioning eyes to her.

Panic stopped Tiki's breath in her throat. He recognized her.

This was the only opportunity she was going to get to escape.

"My gown!" she half shrieked, staring down in horror at the red wine splattered all over the skirt of her gold dress.

"M-my apologies," Leo stuttered. His focus shifted to the reddish purple stains on the front of her dress. "I don't know how that glass slipped out of my hand." Several footmen converged from different directions to clean up the mess. "I will certainly pay for the repair of your gown, Miss . . . Miss . . . Elizabeth . . ."

"Excuse me, please," Tiki cried. She lifted the skirt of her gown and hurried through the stunned crowd, praying the prince wouldn't follow her. Several of the women turned as if they might try to help, so she sped up.

"Pardon me . . ." Tiki shouldered her way through the crowd. "So sorry. Excuse me."

Tiki raced out into the long hallway. She took a sharp turn to the right, then turned hard again and hurried down the Grand Staircase, making a dash for the hidden servants' passageway that would lead to the exit by the kitchens. She dared one glance over her shoulder. No one had followed her yet.

She raced past the kitchens, and with a gasp she exploded into the coolness of the night. It was all she could do not to scream Shamus's name at the top of her lungs. Tiki scanned the shadows beneath the trees, but a fog had moved in, making it difficult to see. She had to escape before the prince came and found her. Or worse, his dark-haired friend.

She hurried down the steps, her long gown floating behind her, and ran into the misty night.

"Miss, wait!" a woman's voice called from behind. "Are you lost?"

Tiki raced on, pretending she hadn't heard. The queue of carriages that had delivered their passengers to the front of the palace now stretched along the side road that led to the Royal Mews. Where was Shamus?

She hurried toward the line of hansom cabs, her eyes searching the night for any sign of Binder's wagon. The pebbles in the courtyard hurt her feet through the thin soles of her slippers, but she welcomed the pain to help keep her alert. She was on dangerous ground right now in more ways than one.

There. She saw Binder's wagon across the street, ready to depart at a moment's notice. "God bless Shamus," Tiki whispered as she ran.

Shamus spotted her and slapped the reins, urging the horse to move in her direction. The dark silhouette of their borrowed wagon, with the signs propped above the doors, was a welcome sight. Shamus pulled up on the reins, intending to dismount to help her into the carriage, but before he could move, Tiki waved him off. She reached up and yanked the door open.

"Go, Shamus, go as fast as you can." She got one foot on the step and dove ungracefully into the wagon, falling to her knees on the floor. She didn't bother to get up. Tiki turned and gathered the trailing mounds of her gown, pulling the door closed. Outside, Shamus slapped the reins again and the wagon jerked forward.

As they clattered their way down the tree-lined lane and Buckingham Palace disappeared from view, Tiki leaned her head back against the edge of the seat and let out a sigh.

She'd done it.

A wave of relief washed over her, leaving her feeling giddy. She'd danced with a prince, mingled with the aristocracy, and best of all—she'd hidden the queen's ring in the palace without getting caught. They were safe once again. Safe from the royals, from faeries, maybe even from Rieker. They couldn't take from her what she didn't have. A ripple of laughter erupted from her lips, and she had to cover her mouth for fear she would laugh hysterically until she cried.

Tiki gathered her skirts and climbed onto the seat as Shamus drove them through the night toward Charing Cross. She closed her eyes, imagining the magnificent ballroom and beautiful gowns. All of it was like a glorious dream. She hummed along with the music in her head.

Another shaky laugh escaped her lips as she thought of Leo. The look of shock on the prince's face when he saw her birthmark was almost laughable. The word *thunderstruck* suddenly took on a whole new meaning. And little did he know that he had provided her with the exact bit of information she'd needed to claim the reward for the ring.

Suddenly she sobered, her happiness tainted with a sliver of fear. Leo had recognized her birthmark, she was sure of it. The expression on his face as he had stared at her arm made her stomach turn. But even if he did put together the fact that "Elizabeth" and the street urchin he'd met in the park were one and the same, it didn't matter, she tried to reassure herself, for the prince would never see her again.

Tiki freed the emerald earring she had nicked from the small pouch she had created in the voluminous fabric of her dress. She examined the gem with a critical eye. Her work tonight had paid off handsomely. This would give them a good start toward being able to pay for Clara's care. Once she negotiated the reward for the return of the queen's ring, they would never be hungry again.

Chapter Fourteen

T HANK you, Leo, for that timely diversion." Arthur spoke in a dry voice as he entered the library. "Lord Howard was a little too far into his cups to exit under his own locomotion. Your clumsiness gave us the perfect opportunity to help him out the door and ah . . . pour him into his carriage, as it were."

Collapsing into one of the leather chairs, Arthur crossed his legs and let out a loud sigh. "The last of the guests have finally departed, thank God, and I have survived yet another masked ball." He turned to face Leo. "By the way, who was the dark-haired enchantress that so captivated your attention?"

Leo stood by the fire, one arm leaning against the carved mantel. "I don't know her name," he replied, "but I'm determined to find it out."

"You don't know her name?" Arthur said. "Aren't you acquainted with her?"

"No."

"Whom did she arrive with? Did you just strike up a conversation with her?"

"She was talking with Wills, and I joined them," Leo said. "For the sole purpose of finding out who she was, without success. She was quite striking in that gold gown, wasn't she?" He chuckled. "Imagine the nerve of not wearing a crinoline *or* a bustle."

"Yes, she was quite unusual. Thanks to you, I'm sure tongues were wagging about her long after she left."

"She did tell me her first name."

"And . . . what was it?"

"Elizabeth." Leo stared down into the flames of the fire. "She told me her name was Elizabeth."

"Well, that's common enough. Did she share who her family is?" Arthur chuckled. "Or was she taking the masked ball as a literal event?"

Leo sighed. He didn't know what to think. Elizabeth had been beautiful in an unusual sort of way. She wasn't like the others who attended ball after ball during the Season. There was something fresh, unspoiled, about her.

The lines of her dress accentuated her thin build, and beneath the mask he could see how delicate her features were. But what he had found most entrancing about the girl was the fact that she was not afraid to have a conversation. It was clear that she had not been impressed or intimidated by him. There had even been a subtle hint of sarcasm in some of her comments, which reminded him of another recent encounter. Had he not seen the mark on her arm, he would never have put the two incidents together. But now it was all he could think about.

"Leo?" Arthur tried again.

"What?" He barely turned to acknowledge the question.

"Leopold!" Arthur spoke in a harsh tone.

Leo stared in surprise at his brother. "Is there a problem?"

"Yes, *you,* dear brother. It's like you're in another world. What is wrong with you?" Arthur shook his head with irritation. "I'll ask you yet again: Do you know Elizabeth's family?"

Leo turned from the fire and slouched into a chair, thrusting a long leg out to dangle over the arm. "No. I have no idea." He closed his eyes and for what seemed the millionth time pictured the dirty little urchin he'd spoken to under the tree in the park. He focused on the strange marking he'd seen on the boy's wrist. Swirls of black. Almost a Celtic design. Whatever the pattern, he'd seen the exact same marking tonight, when Wills had taken Elizabeth's hand.

"Did you feel that earthquake this afternoon?" Arthur asked, changing the subject.

Leo scowled at him. "Are you sure that's what it was? It only lasted a few seconds."

"Enough to cause the chandeliers to sway in the Blue Drawing Room." Arthur raised his eyebrows. "I saw it for myself, and believe me, it wasn't a comfortable feeling watching those behemoths swaying above my head. I'd hate to have one of those crystal lights fall." He pushed himself up in the chair and crossed his legs. "And then there was the freak storm down in Portsmouth last week. The sea rose without warning and flooded part of the city. Significant damage to the dockyards. The block mills suffered damage, too." He looked over at Leo. "Some of our most important industrial areas."

"Yes, I heard about it."

"And, as Mamie predicted, Mother has taken a turn for the worse. She stayed at the ball for less than thirty minutes before retiring to her bed, yet again." He stood up and walked toward Leo. He lowered his voice. "Do you think it has anything to do with the ring gone missing?"

Leo scowled at him. "Don't start with me, Arthur. I'm not in the mood for your dire predictions tonight."

Arthur shrugged. "I'm not making predictions. Simply sharing the day's news. Record snowfall up in the Cotswolds, too. If it melts off too fast, it can cause the Thames to rise and parts of London are at risk for flooding." He stared at Leo. "What has your man found out? Is there *any* news of the ring?"

"No!" Leo shouted. "We've questioned all the servants who might even remotely have access to the library, Harrison's posted the handbills, but there's been no word. No hint of anyone having knowledge of the ring's whereabouts. He's sent men out to talk to the pawnshop owners and some of the street thieves, but nobody claims to have seen it."

He turned back and faced the fire, grinding his teeth in frustration. Did his mother's illness and these strange twists of nature have something to do with the ring being unguarded?

"I saw Isabelle Cavendish dancing with Wills," Arthur continued. "Any chance they might have an interest in one another?" His tone was lighter now, as if he were making an effort to find a noncontroversial topic. "It would do Wills good to find someone."

At the mention of Wills, Leo jerked his head up. "That's it! Wills was talking to Elizabeth. He might know who she is or how to find her." He pushed himself out of the chair in excitement. "I can't believe I didn't think of that before. Arthur, do you know, is he staying in town for a few days or do you think he's heading back to his estate immediately?"

"*Find* Elizabeth?" Arthur gave him a surprised frown. "Why does it really matter? Though I do admit it's a bit odd that she seemed to be unescorted and no one seems to know her name. But, you know how Wills is, very close to the vest about everything. One never knows what his plans might be until you see the whites of his eyes." Arthur didn't even attempt to stifle his yawn. "I am so tired."

Leo debated whether to tell his brother his suspicion about the mark he had seen on Elizabeth's wrist. But even as he considered the idea, he realized how idiotic it sounded. How could that dirty boy in the park and the beautiful girl at the ball possibly be the same person? And if by some leap of the fantastic they were, what did it mean?

He remembered Elizabeth's curiosity about the ring. Could she somehow be involved with its disappearance?

Like a balloon that had lost its air, he sat down with a thump. It simply wasn't possible. He massaged his forehead as though trying to erase any further deliberation of the mysterious Elizabeth from his mind.

"No," he agreed, "it doesn't matter. None of it matters. I suspect we will never see the girl again."

Chapter Fifteen

S EVERAL days later, Tiki stood in Mr. Potts's bookstore, browsing for a new book to borrow. "Gone to
Balmoral?" she repeated in disbelief. "Scotland?"

"That's where the royals go in the winter, missy, when
they want to hunt for great stags." Mr. Potts coughed a
phlegmy gurgle as he reached up to scratch the top of his
balding head. His thin, hunched shoulders were covered
by an old olive sweater, the sleeves flopping over his ar-
thritic hands as he rearranged and tidied his stacks of
newspapers near his counter. "Did you bring the book
back wot you borrowed t'other day?"

Tiki's eyes darted to Mr. Potts's face. She swung a leg
over and perched on a stool behind the counter, trying to
hide her guilty expression. "I'll go get it in a bit." She fingered the edge of the book in her hand. "Besides, I just
finished it. How long will they be in Balmoral, do you s'pose?"

Potts shrugged, settling down on his old wooden stool
next to her. Behind him stretched several aisles of shelves,
filled with books top to bottom. "A coupla weeks, most
likely. Might spend Christmas up there."

"A couple of weeks," Tiki wailed, her shoulders sagging.
That sounded like forever. Already her nighttime trip to
the palace seemed like a far-fetched dream.

Mr. Potts gave her a sharp look. "Oh, fer the love of

Pete, wot difference does it make t'you when the royals come an' go?"

Tiki forced a laugh. "Oh, I was just hoping to catch sight of the queen in one of her grand carriages, you know," she said. "See the pretty trimmings and all." She fidgeted on her stool and stared out the paned windows that faced the station. How could she collect the reward if the royals weren't even in residence?

Tiki heaved a sigh. For some reason, she was having a hard time just being Tiki again. Dirty clothes and light-fingering food wasn't enough anymore. She had allowed herself to dream of something beyond pickpocketing the rich folks going through Charing Cross. She wanted something more for herself as well as for Clara, Shamus, and the others.

Restless, she hopped down from her stool.

"Go git my book," Mr. Potts said in a gruff voice. "An' remember the rules. Return one before you take another."

"I won't forget, Mr. Potts," Tiki said. "I'll bring it by later." She exited the store and walked down the thoroughfare of the railway station, not in a hurry to go anywhere. With the royals gone, it would take that much longer to collect the reward and bring Clara home. Home to someplace other than an abandoned shop alongside a railway station.

Tiki glanced up at the big clock in the center of the station. One thirty. With a pang, she thought of Clara. She and Fiona had gone up to the hospital yesterday and visited. The little girl had looked so much better. She had color in her cheeks and had hardly coughed at all while they were there. Tiki smiled. Clara was going to get well. She was sure of it.

Spotting an empty bench, Tiki ambled over and sat down. She pulled a coin from her pocket and shuffled her fingers, letting the silver dance across her clean knuckles. Since the ball, she had started washing her hands and face every day. She'd even eyed some soap at the market and was thinking about washing her clothes. Yesterday, Mr. Potts had glanced at her, then looked again really quick, as if he'd caught some stranger dressed in her clothes. "Umphf," was all he'd said. But at least he'd noticed, Tiki thought.

With a flick of her wrist, she made the coin disappear, hardly conscious of what she was doing. She needed to figure out her plan to claim the reward for the ring. What rotten luck that Leo and the royal family had left for Scotland. For just a moment, she let herself wonder what she would think of Leo if *she* came from money and moved in his circles. He would still be spoiled and royal, she decided.

"Better be careful who you show that trick to or people will think you're a thief."

Tiki jumped at the smooth voice in her ear and turned to find Rieker leaning over the back of the bench. His long, dark hair flopped over his forehead, shadowing his eyes. His lips curved in a mocking grin.

"Rieker," Tiki said with dismay. "What are you doing here?"

"Tiki." One corner of his mouth lifted. "You don't sound happy to see me. You're not still mad about that little chat we had, are you?" His eyes traced her face with a new sort of intensity, and Tiki was sure that he'd noticed she'd bathed, too. But instead of feeling pleased, she was embarrassed.

"What do you want?" She wished he would go away. "We can't keep having the same conversation over and over."

"Where've you been?" he asked. "I haven't seen you for a few days. I thought maybe you'd started picking pockets in another part of town."

"What does it matter to you?" She crossed her arms tightly over her chest. "I thought King's Cross was your turf. Why are you always down here?"

"Because I think you have the answer I seek, my little Tiki," Rieker said. "That's why."

She turned her head away, trying to ignore the tugging inside at the way he spoke to her. His words had unexpectedly brought back memories of her father calling her "my little Tiki," the nickname he had bestowed on her as a child. She felt weak with longing for something that couldn't be.

"I don't have the ring," Tiki snapped. Might as well get right to it. For a second, she wondered what it would be like when Rieker wasn't hunting her down anymore, trying to get information about the ring. Would she be happy when he was gone?

"Maybe not, but I've a feeling that you know where it is." Rieker didn't move. "I'm afraid for you, Tiki." His voice was low and serious. Tiki's eyes dropped to a dark stain coloring the sleeve of his jacket.

"What's that?" Tiki pointed. Rieker followed her gaze and stepped back abruptly. Tiki grabbed his wrist. "You're bleeding!"

The blood on her fingers felt warm and sticky. She pulled at his sleeve. He resisted, but she refused to release him.

She worked his sleeve up far enough to see a long gash stretched across his forearm. The wound was raw, and blood dripped freely from the cut. She looked at Rieker, aghast. "What happened? Who did this to you?" She twisted his wrist to examine the cut. "That needs to be cleaned and bandaged. You stay here. I'll be right back."

Tiki raced through the station back to the clockmaker's shop. She slipped in through the sliding piece of wood and wiped her hands on an old cloth before she rummaged through their blankets, looking for anything from which she could tear several strips of relatively clean cloth.

Tiki went to the back wall and opened a cupboard. It wasn't often that one of them got injured, but every once in a while a nail would catch somebody or a piece of glass would slice a finger. She grabbed the small bag of chamomile she'd nicked from a stall over in Covent Garden. She'd read a book from Mr. Potts's shop once that had said a poultice made from chamomile wrapped in a damp cloth would take the red out of a cut.

She shoved the cloth and the herbs in her pocket and hurried back out into the station. As she approached the bench, Tiki slowed to a walk. Rieker was no longer there. She stopped and swiveled her head from side to side, looking for his tall silhouette and wild dark hair. But he was gone. *How stupid can I be? Running off to help him, as if we were friends or something.* Tiki shook her head. *What a laugh he must be having right now.*

"Looking for someone?" A soft voice came from behind her.

Tiki whipped around. "Rieker! Stop doing that. Why can't you just walk up like a regular bloke, instead of scaring the daylights out of me all the time?"

"Who wants to be regular?" He laughed.

"Where did you go?" Tiki was suddenly uncomfortable. Was this a trick to find out where she lived?

Rieker shrugged. "Just for a walk. I don't like to stay in one place for long."

"Well, come over here and sit down so I can put something on that cut." She pulled him over to the bench. "Pull your sleeve up." She winced as she looked at the raw wound on his arm.

From inside her pocket Tiki pulled out several strips of cloth. "Don't move." She gave him a warning look before hurrying to a nearby water fountain. She dipped the cloth into the water and returned to the bench.

"Now tell me what happened." She leaned down to examine the raw edges of the wound, grimacing at the depth of the cut. It looked as if a claw had ripped through his skin.

"They want the ring, Tiki. They think I know where it is." He shrugged, but his eyes were serious. "It was more of a warning than anything, I think."

Tiki dabbed the wet cloth on the cut, trying to clean the pus and dried blood away. "What do you mean, a warning?"

"The fey, Tiki." Rieker's voice was low. "They know the ring has been moved. They know the royals don't know where it is. This is their golden opportunity to destroy the truce."

"But why would they hurt you?"

"The UnSeelies think I know something. I tried to walk away from one of them, and she stopped me."

"She?" Tiki asked, horrified. "What's she got, claws?"

"They can have or be whatever they want. They're

shape-shifters. They wear glamours to look human. When they're angry, faeries are vicious. They can rip you to shreds with their hands or their teeth."

Teeth? Tiki shuddered. They didn't sound like faeries, they sounded like monsters.

"She thinks I know where it is." Rieker flinched as Tiki pressed down too hard on the cut. "She's frustrated that I won't tell her anything, so she sent me a message." He hesitated and Tiki looked up. "It would seem that my life lies in your hands." He said the words lightly, but the intensity of his gaze was like a weight on her shoulders. "If you know where the ring is," Rieker said softly, "you need to tell me."

Tiki balanced the poultice on his arm, then pulled another long strip of cloth from her pocket and wrapped it around Rieker's arm. Once the cut was covered, she tied the ends in a neat knot.

"Try to keep that on for a few days, just to give it enough time to heal a bit before it scabs over." She rubbed her hands on her trousers.

Rieker twisted his wrist and moved his arm up and down. "Feels better already. Thank you, Tiki."

Embarrassed, Tiki looked away. Rieker was making her feel guilty, if that was possible. Her eyes scanned the crowd in the large open area of the station. Was Rieker really in danger because of her? Her eyes stopped and backtracked. There, standing in a doorway not far from where she sat, was a face she recognized.

Marcus.

He didn't try to hide from her. Instead he nodded at her in acknowledgment, his lips twisted in a grin that was somehow threatening. Tiki jerked her head away, her heart beating a rapid tattoo in her chest. How long had he been watching them? She thought of what Rieker had told her. Was Marcus interested in her because of the ring?

Tiki glanced over her shoulder, an eerie sense of being hunted making the hair on the back of her neck stand up. But Marcus was gone.

Chapter Sixteen

THAT night, Tiki woke to what sounded like a cat-fight out in the alley. Hissing, yowling, and screeches split the night. She rolled over, closing her eyes again. Strange noises in the alley were common around the full moon. She'd learned to sleep through them.

It was the shout of either rage or pain that made her bolt upright from her pile of blankets. She was wide-awake now, her nerves tingling as she listened for other sounds.

"What was that?" Fiona whispered through the darkness.

"I don't know," Tiki replied in a quiet voice. She got to her feet and tiptoed toward the back entrance. Silently, Shamus fell in step behind her.

"Did you hear it?" she whispered over her shoulder.

"Yes. Sounded like somebody getting stabbed," Shamus said.

Stabbed? She hadn't thought of that. Goose bumps popped up on her arms as she carefully opened the back door. They wound their way through the short tunnel to the entrance that opened out to the alleyway.

"Let me go first." Shamus put his hand on the door above Tiki's head before she could open it.

"Suit yourself." Tiki shrugged, taking a step back so Shamus could move in front of her.

Shamus pulled the door open just enough to put his eye up to the crack and survey the area outside. "There's somebody backed up against the wall," he whispered. "He's got a knife."

"Who is it?"

"It might be Rieker."

"Rieker!" Tiki's voice came out much louder than she intended, and Shamus turned back to glare at her.

"Quiet. Do you want him to hear you?" He put his eye back to the crack. "God's love, I think he *did* hear you. He's looking this way."

Her heart crashed in her chest in an unsteady rhythm, making her breath catch in her throat. Who was out there? Tiki balanced on her tiptoes to see around Shamus's shoulders. She squinted through the dim shadows. With a start, she realized there were other figures—really more like shadows—in the alleyway.

"There are three others, can you see them?" Tiki whispered.

"Where?"

"Right there." Tiki pointed.

One of the shadows moved, and for a second Tiki thought the person was looking at her. She gasped as she was able to discern his features and clutched at Shamus's arm.

It was Marcus. And he *was* looking their way.

His mouth curved up in an evil grin as he took a step toward her. Suddenly, the person against the wall moved and Tiki recognized Rieker's tall form. What was he doing in this alley in the middle of the night? He raised his arm, and in a blink everything happened at once.

One of the shadows lunged at Rieker. Another moved

toward them so fast, he was just a blur. Shamus sprang through the door with a knife drawn, but somehow Rieker got there first. With an animal-like growl, he sank his fist deep into the dark shadow's stomach. Tiki heard a strange keening sound, like the wind high up in the trees in St. James's Park. Then, as she watched, the shadow folded and disappeared.

Tiki's mouth dropped open in horror. Who were these people? *What* were they?

She looked to Rieker for his reaction, but he and Shamus had moved to face the others still hovering in the alleyway. The moon emerged from behind a cloud, and a shaft of light pierced the dimness. At the far end of the alley, watching from a distance, Tiki recognized another shadow.

Staggered, she reached for the brick wall to brace herself. The girl from King's Cross. From the hospital. Clara's hospital. What was *she* doing here? Tiki wanted to cry at the thought that she knew where they lived. Was there any place they were safe?

As if sensing they had lost the advantage, Marcus and the other shadow shimmered and were swallowed up by the night. Tiki tried to track which direction they'd run, but they were gone as if they'd simply disappeared on the wind. She glanced back toward the end of the alley where she'd seen the girl, but the spot was now vacant.

"Rieker." Tiki hurried through the door.

Still in a defensive crouch, Rieker glanced at her over his shoulder. "Go back inside, Tiki," he said. "It's not safe out here."

"He's wounded, Teek, help me get him inside." Shamus stepped up to slide his arm under one of Rieker's.

"Wounded?" Tiki ran forward to see for herself. Three long claw marks had ripped a bloody path down the front of his left thigh, and blood had soaked through the leg of his trousers. Aghast, she looked at his face and saw another cut running along the line of his chiseled jaw.

"Who were they?" she whispered. "What are you doing here?"

"Just trying to protect you, Teek." He grinned, his teeth gleaming in the darkness. Tiki wondered if he enjoyed the danger.

"Stop talking and get him inside." Shamus slung Rieker's arm over his shoulder to bear the weight of his wounded side. Scrambling around him, Tiki grabbed his other arm and a sticky warmth squished between her fingers that felt suspiciously like blood.

As they came through the tunnels, Tiki could see Toots and Fiona watching wide-eyed by the door. They had lit several candles and the room held a soft, welcoming glow.

"Did you capture someone?" Toots asked. The young boy was barely able to conceal his excitement. "Who's that with you?"

"It's Rieker," Shamus said in a calm voice.

"R-Rieker?" Toots's mouth formed an O of amazement. Fiona scampered away like a little field mouse and burrowed into some blankets in a far corner, her gaze transfixed on their visitor.

"Put him over here." Tiki pointed to one of the rickety chairs.

"I'm fine," Rieker said, but he seemed grateful to sit. His eyes circled the long room, taking in the blankets on the floor, the stove in the corner, and the upturned crate and piece of wood that served as their table. Without commenting, he glanced down at his leg and scowled. "They'll pay for that, I promise you."

"Who are 'they'?" Tiki asked. She wasn't even sure where to begin with all of the questions rolling around in her head. Instead, she focused on his injury. Should she try to clean the wounds on his leg? But he would have to remove his trousers. . . . "Is your arm cut or is that blood from the first wound?" she asked instead.

"My arm?" Rieker looked down in surprise at the blood dripping down his sleeve. Fiona let out a squeak from the corner at the sight of the blood. Tiki ran to grab a cloth to stanch the flow as Shamus helped Rieker peel his coat off.

The makeshift bandage that Tiki had wrapped around Rieker's arm earlier had been torn away during the fight, causing the wound to bleed freely again. She grasped his wrist and pulled his arm forward to get a better view of the injury. Her fingers tingled with an unusual warmth when they brushed his skin. Surprised, she glanced at his face to see if he had felt the same thing. Expecting his usual aloof expression, she saw instead that his smoky eyes were locked on her face and the walls that he usually hid behind were gone. There was something that looked almost like longing in his expression.

"What do you mean, you were protecting Tiki?" Shamus asked in a low voice. Thankful for Shamus's interruption, Tiki tightened her grip on Rieker's wrist and dropped her eyes. She focused instead on pressing a corner of the cloth against the cut to stanch the flow of blood.

Shamus pulled up a chunk of wood they used as a stool and sat down across from Rieker. "I didn't know you two knew each other that well."

Tiki ducked her head to hide the guilty expression she was sure was on her face. Had Toots and Fiona wondered why she'd been talking to Rieker so much the past few weeks? Especially after she had protested against asking him to help pawn the ring. Shamus was probably wondering why she was willing to help him now.

A surprised frown etched across Rieker's brow, and his eyes shifted over to Tiki. "You haven't told them?"

Shamus's eyes went from one to the other and back again. "Maybe you'd like to tell us now."

"Tiki wouldn't hide nothin' from us," Toots said. Then he turned to her and whispered in a loud voice, "Teek, are you hidin' something?"

Tiki glared at Rieker, but he returned her look with a steady gaze, one eyebrow slightly crooked, almost as though daring her.

She would not be the first to flinch.

The seconds ticked by.

"Do you want me to tell them?" Rieker finally asked. "It's your choice, Tiki. But you have to understand that tonight was more than a warning. The fey are looking for something and they think you or I know where it is. To get to me—they'll attack you. To get to you . . ." His words died off as he looked from Shamus to Toots to Fiona and then dropped down to his bloody leg. His eyes returned to Tiki. "I think you get my meaning."

A chill filled Tiki. "That was Marcus . . . ," she said hesitantly.

"Yes." Rieker nodded, a grim look on his face.

"What are the fey?" Shamus frowned, looking from Tiki to Rieker.

"Do you know the girl?" Tiki's gaze was fixed on Rieker.

"The blond one? Her name is Larkin," Rieker replied. "Though I didn't see her tonight." A shadow crossed his face. "She's worse than Marcus. Much worse."

"Blast it," Shamus said heatedly. "Who are you two talking about?"

If Rieker was surprised at Shamus's outburst, he didn't show it. "The fey are ancient creatures of old that occupied this world before humans," he said. His tone was as casual as though he were talking about the weather. "They're still here, of course. We share the same air with them, but we can't see them unless they choose to let us. We are slowly taking their world from them, and they want it back."

"Ancient creatures?" Shamus asked, his frown deepening.

"Most mortals know them by the name faerie," Rieker said.

"Faeries!" Toots repeated in a breathless shriek.

"Like the Faerie Queen in 'Tam Lin'?" Fiona whispered.

"Oh, stop it, Rieker," Tiki interrupted. "You're going to scare everyone for no reason."

"There is a reason, Tiki. And you know what it is." Now he sounded angry. "I'll protect you as long as I can, but everyone's at risk. . . ."

"I saw the girl tonight," Tiki said in a low voice. "She was at the end of the alley."

"What girl are you talking about?" Shamus interrupted again. "I didn't see a girl."

Tiki jerked her head in his direction. It was unlike Shamus to interrupt. "You didn't see her either? It was the same girl I pointed out to you in the waiting room when we took Clara to the hospital." A thrill of fear went through her, causing her voice to waver. "I've seen her other places, too."

"What do you mean, you saw her at the hospital?" Rieker asked abruptly. "And what other places?"

"I think she's following me," Tiki admitted softly.

"She's dangerous, Tiki." Rieker's words were low and urgent. "You've got to stay away from her. Don't talk to her. Don't even *look* at her."

"But what does she want?"

"Why do you need to protect Tiki?" Shamus raised his voice above theirs, his irritation obvious. "Just what in bloody hell is going on?"

Rieker's gaze was heavy on Tiki, and she fought not to squirm under the accusation in his eyes. "The fey are after something I think Tiki has," Rieker replied. He didn't take his eyes from her face, as though by staring at her he could force her to confess.

Tiki dropped the cloth on Rieker's arm and sat back with her arms crossed over her chest.

"And what do you think Tiki has?" Shamus's eyes narrowed.

Tiki and Rieker answered at the same time. "The queen's ring."

There was a moment of total silence.

"Rieker thinks the queen's ring holds a truce between faeries and the royals." Tiki spoke quickly. "If the ring is unguarded, faeries can attack and destroy the truce."

Shamus's eyes drifted for a moment, then came back to Rieker. "A truce?"

Rieker nodded. "If the truce is broken, then faeries will overcome London. Already there's been bodies being pulled from the Thames that have strange marks on them. Savage wounds that are out of the ordinary. And the weather has been unpredictable. Floods, storms. I heard there was an earthquake up round Liverpool yesterday."

Toots inched closer, his eyes shining with excitement and a hint of fear. "Faeries?"

From the corner, Fiona held a corner of a blanket up to her chin, ready to cover her eyes if need be.

"And they've done that"—Shamus nodded at Rieker's leg—"to you because they want the ring?"

Rieker nodded again.

Tiki looked from face to face, then finally settled on Rieker's. She had to admit that Fiona was right. Rieker was handsome. The wild waves of dark hair that framed his face created shadows under the angles of his cheekbones. His straight nose somehow gave him an aristocratic appearance, and his firm jaw was shadowed with a hint of dark whiskers, making him look dangerous somehow. But it was his smoky eyes framed by those long black lashes that Tiki found most captivating. What secrets did those eyes hold?

"Can't we just tell the faeries I don't have it anymore?" she finally said.

"Where is it?" Rieker wasn't smiling, but he didn't look as angry.

"I put it back." Tiki braced herself, somehow knowing her answer would make him mad.

"You put the ring *back*?" He enunciated every word, as though he couldn't believe what he'd heard. "Put it back *where*?"

"I put it back in the palace." Tiki raised her chin and braced herself.

"When?"

"Three nights ago. At the masked ball."

Rieker's face twisted into a strange expression.

"What's wrong?" Tiki asked.

"*You* were at the masked ball?" Rieker asked.

"Yes." Tiki's lips were pressed together.

Rieker chuckled and he stared at the ceiling for a moment. Then his eyes raked Tiki up and down. "Excuse my ignorance, but what do you own that could possibly be suitable to wear to the queen's masked ball?"

"I bought a dress." Her voice could have turned water to ice.

"An' she looked like a bloody princess, she did," Toots added in a rush. "All gold and shimmery, with her long dark hair done up fancy-like." He smiled at Tiki with dreamy eyes. "You were beautiful, Teek."

Rieker nodded, a disbelieving smile playing about his lips. "Did you talk to anyone there?"

"As a matter of fact, I did. I talked to a young man named William Richmond, and I danced with Leo."

"William Richmond," Rieker repeated. "And you danced with *Leo*." He paused. "Prince Leopold?"

"Of course." Tiki knew she sounded snobbish and full of herself, but Rieker deserved it.

Rieker nodded for a long time, his eyes far away.

"So can't you just tell the faeries that the ring is back where it belongs and they've missed their chance?" Tiki asked.

"You really put it back?"

"Well, not in the same spot." Tiki's lips curved into a smile despite her attempt to stay irritated at Rieker. "That's the best part of the plan. The ring's back in the palace, but it's in a place where it will never be found unless I tell them where it is." The white of her teeth flashed in the candlelight. "Of course, I intend to collect the reward before I do that."

Pleased with herself, Tiki sat back. "There's no way they can accuse me of stealing it, because the ring's already back in the palace. So, nothing has really been stolen at all." As far as she could see, it was a foolproof plan. She just needed the royals to return from Balmoral. She leaned forward to press the cloth against Rieker's arm where the blood was starting to drip again.

"We're gonna be rich!" Toots's voice was loud with excitement.

"Toots, quiet. Remember it's still the middle of the night." Shamus reached out a hand to calm the younger boy.

"So, do you feel better now, Rieker?" Tiki asked. "I don't have the ring. Now we just have to let the fey know that the truce is intact and they have to continue to live by the agreement."

Rieker leaned back and ran his hands through his hair. "No, it just means that we have to steal the ring again."

Chapter Seventeen

STEAL the ring again?" Tiki jumped out of the chair and clenched her fists at her side. "Why in bloody hell would we do that?"

"Fight, fight." Toots giggled, scooting back in the corner closer to where Fiona sat.

"Wait a minute." Shamus stood up, holding his hands out for calm. "What's this about a truce?"

Rieker shifted his gaze to Shamus. "The truce is an agreement for both sides to live in peace. But not all of the fey want to abide by the truce. There are courts within the world of Faerie, just like the Liberals and Conservatives in the House of Commons; factions who band together and believe one thing or the other. In the Otherworld, there are those in the UnSeelie court, faeries who have fallen from the grace of the Seelie court, who do not want to live by the truce. The UnSeelies are the most malicious, malevolent, and evil faeries. They take great pleasure in harming humans."

"So they attacked you tonight believing you had the ring?"

"Yes." Rieker nodded.

Shamus glanced over at Tiki. "Did you know about this truce?"

Tiki shrugged. "Rieker mentioned something about it the other day."

"Why didn't you tell us?"

Tiki tried to ignore the guilt that crept through her. "Shamus, I wasn't sure if I believed it myself. I thought Rieker was trying to get the ring so he could claim the reward."

"I see." Shamus nodded.

Tiki looked over at Rieker. "Why do you want to steal the thing again?"

"The only people the fey can't steal the ring from are the bloodline of those that bound their oath to the truce, which is the English royal family, or the faerie lineage of Eridanus."

"How come I've never seen a faerie?" Toots interrupted.

Rieker smiled at the young boy. "You probably have. You just don't realize what you're looking at. Sometimes a faerie will use magic to create a glamour, a humanlike skin, that they wear so they look like you and me." He shifted in his seat, readjusting his leg. "Other times they cross over and don't reveal themselves. Have you seen shadows move out of the corners of your eyes, or sparks of light? Then, when you turn, there's nothing there?"

Toots's eyes got wide. "I do see shadows move. I always thought I was just seeing things."

"You won't see them unless you've been given the sight."

"The sight?" Fiona asked. She had crept out of the corner and now sat beside Shamus, staring transfixed at Rieker. "Tiki has told us lots of faerie stories. Is that when you can see into the faerie world?"

"Not quite." Rieker shook his head. "No one can see into the Otherworld unless a faerie carries you over. But there are those that gain the ability to see the fey who have crossed over to our world." He straightened his leg with a grimace. "It's starting to stiffen up," he said apologetically.

"I'll get something to clean it with," Tiki said. Glad for an excuse to get up, she hurried over to the cupboard. "Did talk of the faeries scare you, Toots?" she asked.

"No." He curled his lip with scorn, but he remained silent beyond that and cast a cautious glance toward the dark corners of the room.

"Beatrice Wilson claimed to see faeries," Shamus said. "Said they stole her baby." His eyes narrowed as he gave Rieker a calculating look. "So how do you know so much?"

"I've learned things over the years," Rieker said. "I met someone who taught me about the fey. I recognize the signs when I see them now."

Returning to the table, Tiki pulled her dagger out of the little pocket in the back of her trousers and reached for Rieker. It was a subtle movement, but Tiki saw him flinch. "I have to cut away the fabric to clean those cuts on your leg." She pulled her chair close to Rieker's. "If we're going to trust each other, we better start right now."

"I agree," Shamus said.

Tiki couldn't stop herself from glancing up to see Rieker's reaction.

Rieker's shoulders relaxed and a rare smile transformed his features. He looked so much younger when he smiled. "Then we share each other's trust from this day forward."

"Could you tell us why you need to steal the ring again?

It sounds like returning it to the palace is the safest place for it," Shamus said.

"I am not stealing that ring again until I get paid for stealing it the first time," Tiki muttered.

"First of all, if the royals don't know where the ring is, then it's considered unguarded and can be stolen," Rieker replied. "Even if it is in the palace."

"And second?" Shamus asked.

"I think the fey have found a way into the palace. Even if the royals knew where the ring was hidden, I'm not sure it's safe there anymore."

Tiki contemplated his words as she slipped the flat side of the knife inside Rieker's torn trousers. A faerie spy within Buckingham? With a quick jerk, she brought the edge of the knife through the shredded fabric and made a neat slice through his trouser leg.

"You seem to handle that blade with ease," Rieker commented. He grimaced as the back of the blade skimmed the top of his leg.

Tiki nodded. "Shamus has been teaching me. You can be sure I won't be caught in an alley alone and unarmed again." She gave Rieker a significant look. "One more cut." She folded the cloth over the edge of the knife and sliced it neatly through the fabric. "There we go." Tiki held up the square piece of material for a moment before dropping it on the floor. "Now let's take a look at what we've got here."

She leaned forward to inspect the three gashes down Rieker's thigh. "These look deep. But these marks look different than your arm. Was this the same faerie who scratched your arm?" she asked.

"Marcus did this to my leg, tonight." Rieker pulled the

edge of the fabric back to peer at his exposed leg. "But Larkin was the one who scratched my arm. She can be vicious, though I think this was more a warning." His lips curled down in a scowl. "She is particularly motivated. She's even sought by her own kind."

Tiki listened without commenting. The blond girl's name was Larkin. A faerie. That would explain how she could disappear so quickly. But why would Larkin be following her?

"She?" Shamus said. "A girl did that to your arm?"

"Girl, woman." Rieker shrugged. "Faeries don't age like humans. Though she may look like a girl when she's in her glamour, she is actually quite old."

"And why is she after you?" Shamus asked in a quiet voice.

Rieker grimaced as Tiki dug into the wound to clean it. "It's complicated. Larkin has shadowed me since"—he paused, a frown crossing his brow—"for a number of years now. At first I thought it was curiosity. But now I realize it's something more." His voice drifted off as he contemplated his words.

"Something besides the ring?" Tiki raised her head from tending to Rieker's wound and looked him straight in the face. She sensed he wasn't telling them the whole story.

"I'm not sure." He brushed his hair out of his eyes. "Did you say that you had seen her at the hospital?"

"Yes, I thought I did," Tiki admitted. "I've seen her other places, too. I saw her in Potts' bookstore once, and she asked me why I'd left Clara at the hospital."

Rieker jerked forward in the chair. "She talked to you?"

Tiki gave Rieker a guilty look. "Just that once."

"And what did you do?"

"I ran away."

Rieker sat back in the rickety chair with a thump, causing the whole chair to shake unsteadily. "Don't talk to her, Tiki. Don't even let her know you can see her."

"What does she want the ring for?" Shamus asked. "To end the truce so she can destroy you?"

Rieker's lips tightened in a thin line, and his eyes were dark as he returned Shamus's stare. "Perhaps."

"So"—Shamus began again—"she's after you because she believes *you* have information about the ring. You're following Tiki because you think *she* has information about the ring. If Larkin is following you, have you led her straight to Tiki?"

"Of course not." Rieker sounded defensive, and his eyes flicked uncertainly from Shamus to Tiki. "I'm protecting Tiki."

Surprised, Tiki watched Rieker's face for a moment. "But why? Why would you protect me?"

Rieker turned his dark eyes on her. A strange fluttery feeling filled her chest, and Tiki found it hard to draw a deep breath. For a moment everyone else melted away, and it was as though only the two of them were in the room. She stared back, the slow thud of her heart suddenly noticeable in her chest.

"Because"—Rieker's voice softened—"you need protection. You don't seem to understand what you're part of."

Tiki busied herself with tending to Rieker's leg. "It doesn't matter now, Shamus," she said. "What is done is done. The truth is, I did have the ring and maybe somehow Larkin knew that. What we have to figure out now is how we get paid for returning the thing and to stop the fey from stealing it."

She pushed her chair back and stood up. "Now, take your trousers off." The shocked looks on both Shamus's and Rieker's faces made her laugh out loud. "I have to wrap these wounds, but I can't do it with your trousers on," she said in a matter-of-fact voice. "You're going to have to take them off and tie a blanket around your waist until I've got those cuts wrapped, then you can put your trousers on again."

Rieker complied, and Tiki finished wrapping his leg.

"Do I need to be looking over my shoulder for this Larkin creature?" Tiki tried to sound nonchalant.

"You've got to be on your guard. Larkin is vicious and volatile. Until the ring is either in the fey's possession or the flame in the heart of the ring is extinguished, they are bound by the truce, so I don't think she can kill you. But she can make your life miserable. And Larkin has a temper."

Tiki glanced at Rieker out of the corner of her eye. Larkin couldn't kill her? Was that supposed to be reassuring? Tiki turned away and busied herself by stoking the fire in the small box stove. Could this all be a ploy to collect the ring and claim the reward for himself?

She eyed the bandage wrapped around his leg and decided Rieker wouldn't stoop to the level of injuring himself to make her believe him. Besides, she had seen Marcus and Larkin for herself tonight. She shivered at the thought of their eerie shadows in the alley, almost like wisps of air, yet deadly real at the same time.

Tiki's thoughts drifted to Clara. She was anxious to visit her again. If Clara continued to improve, the little girl would be ready to come home in the next few weeks.

That meant Tiki needed to collect the reward soon so she would have a decent home for her return.

"All right, Tiki?" Rieker interrupted her thoughts. "Are we in agreement that we need to secure the ring again? To protect the truce?"

"But how would we do that?" she asked.

"There are ways," Rieker said confidently. "Is there any chance that the ring will be found by someone in Buckingham first?"

"No." Tiki shook her head.

"Then we need to find a way back in so you can recover the ring from wherever you've hidden it."

"Are you daft?" The words exploded from Tiki's mouth. "How in bloody hell would we get back into the palace? I don't think the royals are planning on having another masked ball anytime soon."

Rieker stood to face her, towering over Tiki. Toots and Fiona both scooted back toward the corner. Shamus pushed his chair back with a low screech and stood, too, almost as tall as Rieker.

"You're clever, Tiki. I'm sure you can find a way to sneak in again and grab the thing and get out," Rieker said. "Or if you tell me where the ring is, maybe I can find a way."

Tiki took a step back, uncertainty bubbling inside her. Was this his plan? To get her to reveal the location of the ring?

"I'll help you, Tiki," Rieker said softly. He held his hands out to her. Tiki wavered. She wanted to believe him. She wanted to do the right thing. But what about Clara? She had to find a better place for the little girl to live. Someplace warm and clean, with food in the cupboards.

And the only way to get that was with money. She couldn't just walk away from the reward, could she?

"Teek?" Shamus asked softly.

"All right," Tiki agreed. She would go along with Rieker for now, just so she wouldn't have to keep arguing with him. But if the opportunity presented itself, she was going to claim the reward, whether Rieker liked it or not.

Chapter Eighteen

R IEKER was gone the next morning, almost as if he'd never been there at all. The only sign of his presence was the bloodstained coat he'd left behind. The shredded sleeve flopped over Tiki's arm as she picked it up and smoothed the fabric. For a second she held the lapel close and inhaled Rieker's scent, imagining him standing before her again.

After folding the garment neatly, she stacked it in a pile with the blankets. She could wash the jacket and Fiona could stitch the sleeve and the coat would be good as new. If Rieker didn't want it anymore, maybe Shamus or Toots could use it.

SEVERAL days later, Tiki walked over to Mr. Potts's bookstore.

"The royals are back," Mr. Potts said as she walked in the door.

She looked up in surprise. "I thought you said they'd be gone for a couple of weeks."

Mr. Potts reached out and smoothed a stack of newspapers. "Bad storm up in Scotland." He coughed as he shuffled down the row of papers, straightening the already straight piles. "Guess they's afraid the river's goin'ta flood."

Finished with the row, he sat down on his stool. "Plus, I 'eard Queen Vic's been ill."

"How do you know all that? Is it in the daily?" Tiki asked, scooting over to scan the headlines.

"Dickey's brother-in-law works up at Bucking'am, and I 'eard a bit from 'im."

"Oh," Tiki said, trying to hide her elation at the news that the royals had returned. "I brought your book back." She smiled brightly, holding up the thin tome for him to see.

"Eh? Which one was that?"

"*Emma* by Jane Austen." Tiki moved around the counter into the shop and shoved the book back in the proper slot on the shelf.

"Oh, right. That one." Mr. Potts gave a half-laugh. "That story'll teach yer to not meddle in other folks' affairs, eh?"

"Yes, that's for certain." Tiki grinned at him. "I won't be trying to find a match for you, Mr. Potts, if that's what you're worried about."

The old man was suddenly seized with a fit of coughing. "God bless the Queen, I should 'ope not," he finally choked out as he wiped tears from the corners of his eyes. "You can borrow another one, then." He pointed a crooked finger toward a lower shelf. "What with Christmas around the corner, you might want to try one of those. You'd probably like *The Cricket on the Hearth*."

"Oh, my father read that one to me a few years ago." She squatted down to look at the lower shelf. "It was one of our favorite Christmas faerie tales." Spotting the title, she slid the book off the shelf and flopped the pages open in her hands. "My father was a barrister, you know. A practical man, but he loved to read faerie tales. He and my mum both."

Tiki sat back on her heels and gazed up at the old man. "Sometimes I think they really believed in faeries. Almost like they knew something more than just the stories they were telling me."

Mr. Potts raised a shaking hand and smoothed the few hairs that were left on his bald pate. "There's an awful lot of faerie tales out there. It's hard t'believe they're all spun outa whole cloth." He shuffled away as if he didn't want to continue the conversation.

Tiki snapped the book closed and pushed up to her feet, wondering at his strange comment. "I'll take this one," she said, sliding the book inside her jacket. She smiled at the old man. "The Cricket should bring back good memories. Thanks, Mr. Potts."

Anxious to find Rieker and Shamus and tell them the news about the return of the royal family, she hurried from the shop.

"Stay outa trouble," Potts called after her in a gruff voice.

Tiki waved as she exited the door and skip-walked back toward the abandoned clockmaker's shop. No sense attracting attention by running.

A large group of travelers moved in front of her, blocking the way. Tiki stepped aside to avoid colliding with them, and someone bumped into her. A burning sensation ripped down Tiki's arm. She jerked back in pain and was shocked to recognize Larkin. Pure hate emanated from the girl's beautiful face.

"Give me the ring."

The words were barely audible, yet they seemed to permeate Tiki's mind as clearly as if they'd been shouted at her. Then the group swept by and Tiki was left staring in disbelief at the back of her blond head of ringlets.

"What in bloody hell?" Tiki whispered, pushing up the ripped sleeve of her jacket to look at her arm. Several long scratches had left a trail of red, raised skin. The sharp angle of the marks immediately reminded her of the jagged wound she'd tended on Rieker's arm.

Tiki shivered as Rieker's warning came back to her: *Don't talk to her. Don't even let her know you can see her.* Tiki glanced back in the direction Larkin had gone, but her group had been swallowed up by the crowd. *She's dangerous.*

Larkin was after the ring. Tiki hesitated, fear suddenly thick in her throat, making it hard to draw a deep breath. Was Marcus nearby as well? She scanned the crowd, but if the black-haired faerie was watching her, he was hidden well. Tiki pulled her sleeve down over her stinging arm as an uneasy dread stirred in the pit of her stomach like a cauldron of bubbling stew. They didn't know she had put the ring back in the palace. Would they attack her in search of it?

Oh, fer the love of Pete, wot'cha goin' to do? Write the queen a letter?" Mr. Potts cackled at his own joke when Tiki asked to borrow his pen and ink. She smiled and laughed along, enjoying his unwittingly accurate guess in a perverse way. He squinted and peered close at her. "D'you know 'ow to write?"

After assuring him that she did indeed know how to form her letters, Tiki took the long, fine-pointed pen with the silver tip and the black inkwell and went to a corner in the back of the shop. After setting her tools carefully on the hard floor, she knelt and pulled out several blank pages she had torn from the back of a Grimm Brothers faerie tale book they had stashed at their home. Shamus had snitched it for her and Fiona as a Christmas gift last year. Once she'd smoothed the fold out of the paper, she laid it on the floor and picked up the pen.

She'd hardly slept the last few nights, worrying about Rieker's insistence that they had to get the ring out of Buckingham again. Even though she hadn't seen him for a few days, she was sure he would soon be back around, pestering her about the ring again. Now Larkin was threatening her. Attacking her, really.

The only logical thing to do was to claim the reward for the ring and return the thing to the royals, putting the truce safely back in their hands. The sooner the better. Then she and Clara and the others could move out of Charing Cross to a place where the faeries could never find them again.

Tiki got down on her knees and leaned over the page.

Now what to say?

Dear Sirs? Dear Madam? Dear Queen Victoria? Tiki's hands were clammy as she clutched the pen. Nothing sounded right.

Making up her mind, Tiki dipped the tip into the black ink. She pulled the pen out and realized she needed to blot the tip. She spied an old newspaper and reached for it, trying not to drip. Mr. Potts would have a conniption if she got ink on his floor. She slid the paper over and firmly planted the tip on the page, causing a large dot of black ink to spread in a circle from the end of the pen. Satisfied, Tiki lifted the silver point and started scratching letters across the page.

To Captain Davis-Smith:

*I am in possession of the missing item. I would like
to collect the reward which has been posted but I do not
seek attention and would like to keep my identity a
secret. For that reason, please leave the reward in a large
black bag,*

Tiki paused and chewed on the wooden end of the pen handle. Where was a safe place to leave the reward? She knew from watching the hordes of people constantly moving through the railway station that everybody carried black bags. That would be the easiest way to hide and move the reward. But where to leave it so the police wouldn't catch her picking it up?

An idea struck her, and she leaned forward to finish the note. Satisfied, Tiki blew gently on the page to dry the ink. She could hear Potts's slow footsteps shuffling her way.

"All done," she said brightly, jumping up with the pen and inkwell in her hand. "Where do you want me to put these?"

"Eh? Oh, well, put 'em back 'ere on the front desk." Potts stopped and peered down the hallway at her. "Got yer letter written, then?"

"Yes, thanks." Tiki smiled at the old man as she hurried by him to put the pen and ink on the desk. When she turned back, she was horrified to see him bending down to read her letter, which lay drying on the floor.

Tiki ran down the narrow passageway and turned sideways to scoot past Mr. Potts, bumping him with her sore arm as she did. "S'cuse me," she squeaked as she swept the page from the floor.

"Who'd you write to?" His eyes followed the page in Tiki's hand.

"Oh, just a note to an aunt who lives up in Liverpool," Tiki said. "I lost her address but thought I'd try anyway."

"What aunt in Liverpool?" another voice asked.

Startled, Tiki turned toward the dark shadow near the door.

"What are you doing here?" Tiki slid the paper inside her jacket and prayed that the ink was dry and wouldn't smudge.

"Looking for you." Rieker backed up so Mr. Potts and Tiki could move into the main part of the little shop.

"Lookin' for a book, you say?" Mr. Potts eyed Rieker up and down with a frown. "Or you want a daily today?"

Rieker's hair was brushed back from his face, and a dimple peeked from one side of his cheek as he smiled at the old man. "I am looking for a book. What do you recommend?"

Tiki's stomach fluttered with an unfamiliar feeling. It surprised her that Rieker could be so charming at times.

"Oh, well, hmmm . . ." The old man cleared his throat. "'Ow's about this one?" He pulled a copy of *Oliver Twist* from the shelf. "Seems like it might be a story you'd enjoy."

Tiki pressed her lips together to hide a smile as she read the title. She knew the story of Oliver, an orphan boy who got caught up with a band of pickpockets. Her eyes darted to Rieker's face to watch his reaction. Did he have any idea of Potts's insult?

Rieker reached for the book and eyed the title. "Yes, this looks good. I've heard of this chap Dickens. What's it about?" He looked to the old man for an explanation.

Potts cleared his throat and cast rheumy eyes on

Rieker's tall form. "'Bout a boy, grew up 'ere in London. Falls in with a bunch of ruffians. Bad news."

"Sounds interesting." Rieker grinned at Potts. "How much?"

"One shilling, sixpence, and no IOUs," Potts mumbled. He appeared surprised at Rieker's willingness and ability to purchase.

Rieker reached into his pocket and Tiki could hear a jingle of coins as he pulled out a handful. He picked out a silver shilling and six copper pennies and handed them over to Potts. "Maybe I can get Tiki to read it to me."

"She's a reader, that girl," Potts said over his shoulder as he shuffled to the counter to lock his money away.

Rieker smiled over at Tiki. "Yes, but does she know the story of Oliver Twist?" His eyes twinkled, and Tiki had the sudden suspicion that Rieker had already read the book he had just purchased. "It has a happy ending, you know," he whispered, too low for Potts to hear.

So Rieker could read, too, she thought. Not a surprise, really, given his posh diction. Still, it made her wonder what other secrets he might have.

"Ready?" Rieker asked. He escorted Tiki to the door of the small shop, and Tiki could feel Mr. Potts's eyes watching the two of them as they left.

"Thanks, Mr. Potts." Tiki waved over her shoulder. "See you tomorrow."

The old man waved a gnarled hand and turned back to straighten his stacks of newspapers.

"How did you know I was in there?" Tiki asked, suddenly suspicious.

Rieker shrugged, putting the book inside his jacket

and sliding his hands into the pockets of his trousers. "Just a lucky guess. What were you doing in the back?"

Tiki hesitated. Somehow she needed to convince Rieker that it would be better to give the ring back to the royals so they could protect it again.

"I wrote out the note to the royals," Tiki said quickly. "You know, the one for the reward." She held her breath as she waited for Rieker's reaction.

Rieker didn't reply. He was silent as they walked, his eyes staring off into the distance. Tiki wondered if he was angry. The farther they walked, the more uncomfortable she got. Finally she stopped and tugged at his arm, forcing him to turn and face her.

"What's wrong?"

"Tiki . . ." He sounded as if he were forcing himself to stay calm. "We can't collect the reward if we're not going to return the ring. Like I said before, I think the fey have infiltrated the royal circle. Right now, we don't know who we can trust and who we can't. If we tell the royal family where the ring is, its location could be revealed to the fey. We can't take that chance." Rieker gave her a pleading look. "Can't you see, we just have to go back in and get the thing and let the reward go?"

"I am *not* letting the reward go." Tiki was horrified at his suggestion. "Can't you see that is the only way I can bring Clara home?" She could hear the hysterical note in her voice, but she couldn't stop. "I have to be able to *have* a home. Someplace clean and warm where she won't keep getting sick."

"Why is she your responsibility?"

"Because she doesn't have anybody else," Tiki snapped.

"She was lying in a pile of trash on the street when I found her. She was almost dead. She would have died if I hadn't fed her and cared for her." Tiki gritted her teeth to fight back the tears that suddenly pressed against her eyes.

"What if Shamus and Fiona had said the same thing about me when I was forced to run away? Even though I didn't know how to survive on my own, I couldn't stay with my uncle one day longer. He would drink and then he'd want to touch me—" She stopped abruptly. She didn't want to think about him. Her voice got louder. "If Fiona hadn't shown me how to pick a pocket, I probably would have starved to death that first month. Or been forced into being a beggar or a prostitute to feed myself."

"Tiki, calm down."

She took a deep breath and lowered her voice, but the urgency remained. "Even then, I barely survived. If they hadn't let me live with them in Charing Cross, I might be the one lying in a pile of garbage today, half-dead." Her anger fueled her nerve. "Look around you, Rieker. Can't you see all the children who need help?" She flung out an arm. "They're everywhere. Toots' own mother threw him out when he was only nine years old because she couldn't afford to feed him anymore. She had too many other children to care for. If their parents can't or won't do it, then who cares for the street children? Somebody's got to care."

Incensed at his lack of understanding, Tiki jerked around and started to walk away, but Rieker's hand shot out lightning fast and grabbed her arm to stop her.

"Tiki, wait . . ." As his fingers pressed against the cut on her arm, Tiki gasped with pain.

"What's wrong?" Rieker looked down at her sleeve as if he already knew what he'd find. His grip tightened around her wrist, below the cuts, and his eyes locked on hers with a knowing look. Tiki wanted to pull away but doubted she could with Rieker holding her wrist so tight.

"You're making a scene," she said through clenched teeth. She looked around self-consciously and tugged on his arm to try to get him moving again. He didn't budge.

"Where was she?" Rieker asked.

"Here in Charing Cross," Tiki finally admitted. "I was walking from Mr. Potts' shop." Tiki shrugged as if the encounter had been nothing, even though her stomach was grinding uncomfortably.

"This was no accident, Tiki." Rieker sounded furious. "Larkin must know you're involved. Did she say anything?"

Tiki's eyes met his. "She said she wants the ring."

"No," he whispered.

For a second, the emotionless expression that Rieker so often wore cracked and Tiki caught a glimpse of something that looked like desperation.

"That's the other reason why I think we need to send the ransom note to the royals," Tiki said hurriedly. "That way the fey will stop following me."

Rieker's hand slid from her wrist to her hand, and his fingers entwined in hers. Before she could move, he wrapped his arms around her shoulders and pulled her close. Instead of being afraid, Tiki felt an odd sense of safety.

"Tiki, I understand why you want to protect Clara and the others. I really do," he said softly, his lips against her hair. "It's the same reason I want to protect you."

Her head rested against his chest and she could hear the slow beat of his heart. She inhaled his scent and closed her eyes, a strange yearning pulling deep inside. If only she could trust him.

"But you don't understand what's been done." His words were firmer now. "It's not so simple as just giving the ring back. It needs to be protected." He grasped her by the shoulders and held her away from him. "We can't take the chance that there is a faerie spy within the royal circle." He gave her a little shake. His eyes were dark, intense. "Don't you see? If the truce is destroyed, there's no going back. Ever."

A surge of anger shot through her, and she jerked free from his grasp. "And don't *you* see? I'll never have another opportunity like this to get us out of Charing Cross. I have to pay the hospital, I have to find someplace clean to live. I have to find food for my family. I *have* to get that reward."

Before Rieker could answer, Tiki turned and ran.

Chapter Nineteen

L EO rode low over Diablo's neck, enjoying the wild rush of wind against his face. With weather like this, it was easy to believe the reports that a tornado had destroyed a barn and torn up several fields in Devonshire yesterday. His horse shied as the wind whipped the branches of a nearby tree from side to side in a feverish dance. Leo worked the reins with a firm hand, the bite of the cold air somehow sharpening his ability to think.

Tucked inside his jacket was a page where he had sketched the flowing lines and swirls he had seen on Elizabeth's skin as he remembered them. There was one person who might know something about the strange mark.

Leo had known Mamie all of his life. His mother's old lady-in-waiting was a fascinating woman, if a bit eccentric. She favored using herbs and flowers to tend to cuts and ills, and said the birds and plants spoke to her. As boys, he and Arthur had whispered that she was a witch, but a good witch. She had told them many interesting stories of faeries and legends of old as they were growing up, always as though the stories were true. There were a few, even now, that he couldn't say were fact or fiction. If anyone would know if this mark meant something or not, it would be Mamie.

She lived at the far end of St. James's Park in a cottage

known fondly as the Birdkeeper's Cottage, as her husband had for many years tended the black swans, pelicans, and other birds that lived in the park. Leo was pleased to see a feathery plume of smoke drifting from the brick of her chimney as he approached.

He pulled up to the small cottage and dismounted, tying the reins to the gnarled branch of a nearby apple tree. His knock sounded loud on the small wooden door, echoing in the still afternoon air. He shuffled his feet as he waited, nervous for no reason.

The old woman opened the door and blinked in surprise when she saw him standing there. "Prince Leopold?"

"Hello, Mamie." Leo leaned down to kiss the remarkably soft skin of her cheeks. "How are you?"

"I'm well, dear boy, and you?" the old lady replied in a soft, melodic voice. She peered out the door and raised an eyebrow at him when she spotted the black horse grazing nearby. "Here on your own, are you?"

"Yes, ma'am. I didn't think I needed an escort to ride in the park," Leo said.

A corner of her wrinkled face lifted in a smile. "You always were one to do as you pleased, weren't you?" She waved her hand at him. "Come in, come in. Did you see the hailstorm earlier?" She shuffled back inside. "Hail the size of chestnuts. It's a message, sure as sure."

Leo followed, ducking through the small frame of the door, debating whether to ask who would send a message of hail.

"Can I get you some tea, dear?" Mamie asked. "The kettle's on. I've chamomile today."

"Thank you, but no," Leo said. "I can't stay long."

Mamie sank into an old wooden rocker with a worn

floral cushion on the seat. The windows of the cozy room overlooked a long stretch of lake, with Buckingham Palace visible in the distance. Mamie reached for a delicate china teacup and took a sip, holding the cup and saucer cradled in her hands. "How is your mother?"

"She continues to decline. The doctors aren't quite sure what to make of it."

Mamie eyed the young prince. "Have you any word on the ring yet?"

A frown crossed Leo's face. "Well, that's getting to it straightaway. No, Mamie, there's been no word on the ring. But there is something." He reached inside his jacket and pulled out the paper, the page crackling as he unfolded it. He moved closer to the old woman, resting one knee on the floor to be at eye level with her.

"Have you ever seen a mark that looks something like this?" He held the drawing out for her to see.

The old woman set the teacup back on the little table and reached for the paper. She stared at the drawing in fascination and after a moment ran a crooked finger over the swirls. Without lifting her eyes, she asked, "Where did you get this?"

"I drew it." Leo's eyes moved from his drawing to Mamie's face and back again, trying to decipher her reaction.

Her blue eyes searched his face. "You've always been an exceptional artist, Leo. Did you see this somewhere?"

"Well, yes, as a matter of fact I did." His eyes flitted uneasily around the room. "It was a mark on someone's arm. Very unusual, you see, and for some reason it caught my fancy, so I thought to draw it." He gave Mamie what he hoped was a charming smile. "With your knowledge of nature and cures, you were the only one I could think of who might be able to explain it to me. Have you seen this mark before? Is it caused by some sort of ailment?"

"Beautiful, isn't it?" Mamie's voice had a hushed quality to it, as though the mark represented something sacred.

A surge of excitement blazed through Leo's chest. "Yes. In a strange sort of way. But what is it?"

"An fáinne sí," Mamie said softly. "The faerie ring."

"A *faerie* ring?" Leo repeated. The sudden brightness he'd felt quickly turned to black despair. His suspicion that Elizabeth and the urchin had something to do with the disappearance of the ring flared again.

Mamie looked over at him. "It is a mark of the fey."

His stomach spiraled downward in a circle of dread as his worst fears were confirmed. Faeries. Arthur had been right. He stared down at the swirls and arcs that etched across the page. He could still see the same black lines dancing around Elizabeth's thin wrist. He frowned at Mamie. "I thought a faerie ring was a circle of mushrooms growing in a field."

Mamie smiled. "The fey do love to play jokes on mortals. The mushroom circle is one of their favorites." She ran her fingers over the drawing again, a thoughtful expression on her face. "But a true faerie ring is not found on the ground. This particular mark is quite rare. It comes from a line of fey who were said to have died out centuries ago." She raised her head to eye him curiously. "Who is it that bears the mark?"

Leo hesitated. "A girl at the masked ball. She was asking questions about Mother's ring."

Mamie frowned. "Someone at the party was marked?" Her hands tightened on the page. "Is anyone missing?"

"Missing?" Leo looked at her in surprise. "No. At least, not that I know of."

Mamie didn't release her grip. "You need to assign a guard to watch your mother at all times. And keep an eye on your sister. Baby is too young to protect herself." She shook her head. "We've feared it for years, you know."

"Feared what?"

"That the battle in the Otherworld would spill over into London again." She was silent for a moment as her eyes traced the contours of his face. "You're eighteen. Old enough now to know the truth." She leaned forward and spoke in a soft voice. "There's a spy in our midst, Leopold."

Leo narrowed his eyes at the old woman. "A spy? What kind of spy?"

"Fey." Mamie's chin quivered. "We've never been able to figure out who it might be, exactly." She sat back, a worried expression creasing her wrinkled face. "Until now, we thought we had stymied their attempts, but I'm afraid the ring gone missing changes everything. The stakes have been raised." She lowered her voice to a whisper. "There are some fey who will do *anything* to get the ring. Even murder."

Leo tried not to let his shock show on his face as his thoughts raced in circles, crashing into one another. Murder? "Does Mother know?"

"Of course she knows."

"How long have you suspected?"

"Many years, my boy. Many, many years." Mamie put her hand on his arm. "We were close once. Thought we had him."

"But I've never even seen Elizabeth before. How could she be a spy?" Leo sputtered.

"There's the trouble," Mamie said. "They can change the way they look, assume a glamour, or simply cross back over to the Otherworld and we have to start all over again."

"But what do they want?"

"They want England, Leopold." She whispered the words. "They want to reclaim the world that once belonged only to them."

Leo swallowed a gasp. "Do you really think the girl who had this mark could be a spy?"

"It's possible," Mamie replied. "But there's a bigger problem now. With the ring unguarded many have crossed over." She clutched at his sleeve, her grip surprisingly tight. "I've seen them, Leo, hiding in the shadows at the palace, lurking among the trees on the grounds. The fey are throughout London. Their numbers are growing and they're becoming bolder." Her eyes burned into his. "As long as the ring is missing, they'll push the boundaries and encroach on our world. Your mother is particularly at risk. You *must* find the ring."

Leo took a deep breath, trying to quell the sense of panic that tightened his chest. Was she telling him the truth, or had she gone completely mad in her old age? "Mamie . . ." His voice sounded ragged. "You speak about this as though it were fact. Do you truly believe faeries are real?"

Mamie reached up and caressed his cheek with her old hand, just as she used to do when she would soothe him as a child after his frequent nightmares. "Dear Leo, I don't *believe* faeries are real. I *know* they are."

Chapter Twenty

THE day was dark and cold, like an echo of the emotions that warred inside her. Fog had settled in early and trapped the coal smoke that constantly clouded the air above London. It was one of those dreary winter days where night never really seemed to lift and daylight never really arrived. Tiki fought back a cough as she inhaled the gritty air.

Overhead, a round black bristly broom emerged from a small brick flue, followed by a small boy, who scrambled out of a chimney covered head to toe in black soot. Tiki shuddered at the idea of climbing down into that unlit, cramped space. Before, when she'd lived with her parents, before she'd been forced to survive on her own, she'd never considered who tended the chimneys. The idea had never occurred to her that *children* would be forced to clean the innumerable smokestacks that stretched across London's skyline. She'd heard that some employers even lit straw beneath a cleaner's feet to make him move faster.

She glanced at the small boy again, a black smudge against the sky. He could be Toots. Or, God forbid, Clara. It made her heart break to think of the thousands who had no one to care for them. It strengthened her resolve to do everything she could for Toots and Clara. And Fiona, for that matter.

Tiki hurried across Whitehall Street toward the Mall, ducking between the clacking wheels of the carriages, trying not to breathe through her nose. The steaming deposits left behind by the horses seemed especially pungent today. She eyed the back of a particularly large carriage going by and wondered for a moment if she dared try to jump in her dress. But the carriage moved past and Tiki missed her opportunity.

She hugged her thin arms tight to her chest, trying to stay warm. She thought again of her argument with Rieker yesterday about retrieving the ring. She didn't know how he planned to do that now that the royals were back in residence at Buckingham, but she didn't really care. She had made up her mind she was going to claim the reward first.

Tiki cut toward the entrance to St. James's Park across the street from Buckingham Palace. She stood in the shadows under the trees and surveyed the crowd.

There.

A scruffy young boy, probably only seven or eight years old, loitered on the sidewalk with his broken broom, waiting for the opportunity to sweep the street. He would be perfect for what she needed. She walked toward him.

"Hey there, boy, come over here," she called. The boy put his thumb to his chest with a questioning look. At Tiki's nod, he jogged over. She leaned down to look him in the eyes. "I've got a small job for you. Want to make a decent wage for your work today?"

"Yes, miss." The boy bobbed his head, holding his cap in his hand. He was thin and dirty, just as she was most of the time. Just like so many other children living on the streets of London. But he had a brightness to his eyes and what looked to be quick feet.

Tiki dug into the pocket of her overcoat and pulled out a halfpenny. She held it up. Then she pulled out the folded ransom note. "I'll give you this coin for taking this note over to the guard there. Tell him it's for Captain Davis-Smith." She smiled at him. "But you have to run away before he asks you any questions. Do you think you can do that?"

"Yes, miss." The boy smiled, already reaching for the coin.

Tiki pulled another coin from her pocket, this time a copper penny. "And how about if you don't go anywhere near the guards for a really long time? So they'll forget what you looked like?"

He nodded with even more enthusiasm.

"Okay, off you go, then." Tiki handed him the other coin and the ransom note. She stepped back into the shadow of the tree and braced a hand against the rough bark as she watched. The boy tucked his broom under one arm and scurried away. He ran straight up to a guard and tugged at his sleeve. The guard ignored him until the boy waved the paper in front of his face. With a frown, the guard reached for the page. Good as his word, the boy turned and ran. In a blink, he had disappeared into the crowd.

As Tiki watched, the guard unfolded the page and read the words written there. For just a moment he stood frozen, then he disappeared into the guardhouse.

A glimmer of excitement ignited inside her. It was started. Satisfied that her task had been accomplished, Tiki stepped from behind the tree and walked back the way she'd come, her steps quickening as she headed toward the Great Ormond Street Hospital.

Close to two hours later, Tiki hesitated as she entered the hospital. The harsh woman who had admitted Clara sat behind the desk.

"Good afternoon, ma'am." She bobbed her head. "I'm from St. Timothy's Chapel, here to see the children." She rushed her words as she pointed down the hallway. "I've been here before. Should I just go down?"

The woman looked up from the page on which she was writing notes. She gave Tiki a quick glance, nodded, then turned back to her paperwork without a word.

Tiki hurried down the hallway. She was anxious to see Clara. They had moved her out of quarantine almost a week ago and in with the rest of the children. Fiona had been up to see her the day before yesterday and said she'd made even more improvement. To celebrate, Tiki had brought her a small bite of chocolate. Tiki's eyes darted around the room, looking for the little girl's curly blond head.

The metal frame beds in the ward were crammed together, using every available inch of space. Every bed was occupied. A thin aisle threaded its way down the middle of the room between the footboards with just the smallest space for a person to stand between the beds. Small windows lined two of the walls, though the gray light of the day did little to dispel the aura of sickness in the room. Tiki tried to ignore the muffled cries and moans of the sick children. At the far end of the room, a single nurse bent over a bed.

Tiki's heart beat a little faster as she searched the beds, unable to find Clara. Where was she? She bit her lower lip in fear as her head swiveled from one bed to the next. Had they moved her? Tiki's worst fear bubbled up and threatened to choke her. Had she gotten worse again?

Tiki rushed over to the door of the quarantine room and peered inside. Had Clara had a relapse? But only three beds were occupied, and Tiki could tell by the color of the children's hair that Clara was not among them. Dread settled across her shoulders like a heavy cloak as she hurried from the room and headed back to the woman at the front desk.

"Begging your pardon, ma'am. There was a little blond girl in here, named Clara." Tiki clutched her hands together under her cloak. "I told her I'd show her something special today and I can't seem to find her. Has she been moved?"

"Clara?" the lady repeated in a tired voice. She glanced at a chart with a list of names. "Oh, right, that one. Her relatives came to pick her up yesterday." She shook her head. "Can you believe it? The little thing's been in here for nigh on two weeks and they just now come to see her. Then they up and take her." She shuffled her papers some more. "One hopes they'll take better care of her this time round."

"Her relatives?" Tiki couldn't keep the shock from her voice. "What did they look like?"

"A man and a woman. Well-dressed, average-lookin' folk." The nurse peered at her. "What difference does it make?"

"What color hair did the woman have?" Tiki asked.

The woman shrugged. "Blond hair—just like the little girl. In the prettiest ringlets. Didn't look old enough to be her mother, but you never know, these days."

Tiki dug her fingernails into the palms of her hands

and swallowed. She couldn't seem to draw a steady breath. "Do you . . . know . . . where"—she took a shaky breath—"they took her?"

"No, we don't ask where they're taking them. Especially if they're relatives. They just have to sign for them and off they go."

Tiki swallowed hard. "Could I see their names? I'd love to stay in contact with that little girl." She bowed her head as if overcome with sadness and whispered, "We became friends. She reminded me of my little sister that I lost to the fever."

"Oh, I know just what you mean." The woman sighed. "So many dead."

She reached for a clipboard and ran her finger down a list. "Here it is. Clarence and Emma Houghton."

The names echoed in Tiki's head. "Did they leave an address or anything?"

"Actually, she came in as a charity case. Strangest thing. I was on duty that night and a bunch of the dirtiest children you ever laid eyes on brought her in. One of them said she was her sister. But I doubt any of them had parents. Looked like a bunch of street urchins to me." She ran her finger along the name and stopped. "They left an address for the bill. Up in Soho. Forty-six Oxford Street."

"Oxford, you say? Thank you." Tiki backed away and hurried for the front door.

"Good luck," the nurse called after her. "I know it's hard to say good-bye to those sweet little dears when they go home, but it's for the best."

Tiki waved a hand in response. As soon as she was through the doors and out on the street, she ran. She ran as fast as she could, arms pumping, skirts flying around her legs. She ignored the shocked stares of the people as she flew by.

She darted into the street and bit back a scream as she narrowly avoided a collision with an oncoming hansom cab, causing the horse to rear in alarm. Tiki sprinted on, choking down the bile that rose in her throat. Fear like she'd never known boiled in her stomach, fueling her legs.

Clara was gone.

Chapter Twenty-one

A RTHUR, you've returned," Leo cried as he hurried into the library. "I've got to talk to you. I've learned something."

His brother fixed him with a steely gaze from where he stood next to the fire burning in the hearth. "We've received what amounts to a ransom note."

Arthur's words had the same effect as being dashed with a bucket of ice water. Leo stopped and gasped for breath, staring at his brother in stunned silence.

"You may shut your mouth now." Arthur paced toward the glass doors that overlooked the gardens at the other end of the room. "It was delivered to your man in the Horse Guards this afternoon by a street urchin. He ran away before the guard could question him."

"A ransom note?" Leo finally choked out. "For the ring?"

"Are we missing anything else for which we have offered a reward?" Arthur said. "Of course it's for the ring."

"And did it mention the inscription?"

"Very clearly. They've asked for the reward to be delivered in three days' time. No bobbies. No guard." Arthur gave Leo an appraising look. "They want you to deliver it, on Diablo, at midnight, in the woods alone." He turned away and pulled a piece of paper from inside his vest and snapped it open in front of his face. "Allow me to read the note to you.

"'I am in possession of the missing item. I would like to collect the reward which has been posted but I do not seek attention and would like to keep my identity a secret. For that reason, please leave the reward in a large black bag. On Tuesday night have Sir Leopold come ALONE . . .'" Arthur looked over at Leo. "They wrote 'alone' in capital letters." One corner of his mouth lifted in a wry grin before he continued, "'. . . at midnight on his black horse with the reward to the large elm near the blue bridge in St. James' Park. There will be a message in the crook of the tree telling him where to go next.'" Arthur raised his eyebrows at Leo and cleared his throat. "Second paragraph.

"'We will be watching. Do not try to follow Prince Leo. We will not harm him.'" Arthur looked up. "That's certainly a relief, wouldn't you agree? Let me continue: 'I know others seek the ring. So please follow these directions precisely and do not try to identify us. We hope the following is true: *Na síochána, aontaímid*—For the sake of peace, we agree.'"

Arthur folded the letter and held it up for Leo to see. "Apparently they know of the truce."

"Oh, my God," Leo whispered, and sank into a chair. "It's a bloody treasure hunt."

Arthur barked out a bitter laugh. "Exactly, dear brother. I couldn't have put it better myself."

Leo stared unseeingly at the pattern of the rug as his mind raced, recalling his conversation with Elizabeth at the ball. She had questioned how to collect the reward: *I'm sure if you truly want the ring back, then you must have a system of exchange planned out.* He had stupidly told her exactly what to do. And now she had done it.

He pushed himself out of the chair. "I think I know who is involved in the ring's disappearance."

Arthur jerked his head over in surprise. "You do? Has your man learned something?"

"No." Leo shook his head. "*I've* learned something." He rubbed his face hard with both hands, then ran them through his short hair. He let out a long sigh. "The day after the theft of the ring, I met an urchin outside the palace. At the base of the very tree we are told to leave the ransom." Leo slid his hands into his pockets, a thoughtful expression on his face as he remembered the scene. "There was something suspicious about him. He was tucked into a thicket below a tree, and I had the strong impression that he was hiding something. When I told him to empty his pockets, he spooked my horse and ran away before I could question him further."

"A street urchin? What's this got to do with the ring?"

Leo held his hand up. "I'm getting to that. The boy bore a black mark on his wrist, as if he'd been branded, like a heifer up at Smithfield's Market. It was a most unusual mark—I thought perhaps he was a Gypsy." Leo stepped nearer to his brother and dropped his voice. "I would have forgotten about the incident except the mysterious Elizabeth bears the exact same mark. *That's* the reason I dropped my wineglass at the ball."

Arthur cocked his head in surprise. "Are you speaking of Wills' friend Elizabeth?"

"Yes." Leo nodded. "It was too much of a coincidence that they would both bear the same mark, so I drew the shape on a page and took it to Mamie."

Arthur let out a disbelieving laugh. "I'm wondering what type of guidance you're seeking from a woman we used to consider to be a witch."

"If you'll recall, Arthur," Leo said defensively, "you're the one who has insisted that the missing ring holds a truce with the world of Faerie." He jerked a glass off a tray and angrily poured some wine into it. "Who better than Mamie to question about that world?"

Arthur gave a slight shrug. "You have a point. So tell me, what did she say? Did Mamie recognize the mark?"

"She did." Leo drank deeply from the glass, hoping the wine would settle his ragged nerves. Though he suspected Elizabeth played a part in the ring's theft, to receive a ransom note in the exact manner he had described to her was both startling and damning at the same time.

"Mamie rattled something off in Gaelic when she saw it. Said the mark meant the faerie ring. That it was 'a mark of the fey.'" Leo reached for the decanter and refilled his glass. "I'm afraid I've been converted to a believer about the truce, Arthur. I fear there are fey in our midst who mean to do us harm."

"Because of a mark on some street urchin's wrist?" Arthur said in a disbelieving voice.

"Because the mark is evidence of a faerie connection," Leo snapped. "Because of the questions that Elizabeth, *who also bears the mark,* asked me about ransoming the ring at the ball."

"Are you sure, Leo? It seems like a bit of a leap. Can

you be positive the mark is the same? Can you be positive that Mamie knows what she's talking about?" Arthur raised his eyebrows. "You'll recall she's practically as old as time."

Leo threw up his hands in frustration. "How could Elizabeth know of the ring?"

"What did she tell you?"

"She said she overheard someone talking about it."

"Didn't you say Isabelle Cavendish asked you about the ring recently, too?"

"Well, yes . . . but—"

"Isabelle was at the party. Perhaps Wills' friend overheard her. And while we're on it, how is it that Isabelle knows anything of the ring to begin with?"

Leo wanted to explode. "But Arthur, whoever has written that ransom note"—he jabbed the page that Arthur still held with his finger—"has done exactly what I told Elizabeth to do." His shoulders sagged. "And now I'm concerned that she's involved with Wills. After everything that Wills has been through, I wonder if he has any idea who he's got himself mixed up with?"

Arthur's eyes narrowed. "Wills is the least of our worries, and I warn you, Leo—you need to be very careful before you accuse a friend of his of having an association with faeries. We'll become the laughingstock of London if that gets out." Arthur folded the note one last time, creasing the edges into crisp lines, and tossed it on the table. "Did Mamie have anything else to say?"

"Yes." Leo's concern was reflected in his expression. "She said there's a spy among us."

"A spy?" Arthur choked.

"She told me the fey are everywhere now that the ring

has gone missing, just waiting for their opportunity to strike." Leo's voice dropped. "That some could even resort to murder."

Arthur's face was unreadable. After a long moment, he spoke. "There has been a shocking increase in the number of dead bodies that the mudlarks are pulling from the river now. I'm sure you've heard. They all appear to be mutilated in the same fashion, as though they were ripped apart. As if they've been attacked by some kind of monster."

Leo nodded. "She seemed especially concerned about Mother. And Baby."

Arthur gripped the back of a chair with both hands. "And did Mamie recommend how we are to fight against something we can't even see?"

"We have to recover the ring," Leo said. "There's no other way. I'll have to deliver the money."

"You can't be serious." Arthur's normally dry tone was etched with disbelief.

"It's the only way I know to get the ring back," Leo said. His voice was insistent.

"But to go alone? At midnight? Mother would have your head."

"She won't have my head if she doesn't know." Leo raised his eyebrows at his older brother.

"It's one thing to sneak out for a little fun and mischief," Arthur replied, as though stating the obvious, "but something completely different to ride alone in response to a ransom note."

He pulled the stopper from a crystal decanter and filled a glass with amber liquid. He lifted the glass and drank deeply before continuing. "*That's* called stupidity. Not to mention the fact that the ransom is being claimed by a thief who snuck in and out without leaving a trace."

Leo moved a step closer. "Lives are hanging in the balance now. We can't take the chance of *not* paying the money. We've *got* to get that ring back." He nodded at the folded ransom note that Arthur had tossed on the table. "And there's only one way."

Chapter Twenty-two

Tiki burst through the door, her sides heaving as she tried to catch her breath. "Clara's been stolen!"

"What?" Shamus jumped to his feet. "Tiki, what're you talking about?"

"Stolen?" Fiona echoed. "Who would *steal* her?"

Toots turned from his perch at the peephole. "Why would somebody want Clara?"

Tiki's eyes fell on Rieker, who stood across from Shamus near the stove. He was scowling, the muscles in his jaw clenched, his eyes black with anger.

"What are you doing here?" she asked.

"I asked him to come talk to me," Shamus said. "Now, tell us about Clara."

"I went to visit her in hospital and she's been taken away," Tiki cried. "The nurse said some relatives had picked her up, but that's not possible." She could hear the hysteria in her voice, but she couldn't help it. She wanted to cry and scream and hit somebody all at the same time.

"When I asked what they looked like, the nurse said the woman had blond ringlets just like Clara." Her eyes shot over to Rieker's. "It's Larkin. It's just like you said. She wants the ring. That's why she took Clara."

"Slow down," Shamus said. "You think the girl who has been following you took Clara?"

Tiki's breath came out in a hiccuping gasp. "Yes. I've got an address. Up in Soho. Forty-six Oxford Street. I want to go up there and find her."

"She won't be there." Rieker's voice was flat. As one, they turned to look at him.

"She might be." Tiki's eyes held a pleading look.

Rieker shook his head. "If Larkin's got her, there's only one way to get her back."

"And what's that?" Shamus asked.

"Trade."

The silence that filled the room was deafening.

"I know a place where we can meet Larkin." Rieker scowled as he spoke. "It's a place in Hyde Park called the Ring. It's very old." He ran his hand through his hair, mussing the dark waves. "Faeries are drawn to nature, to water. They like to gather there. To this day it is still a meeting ground for the fey."

"Where is it?" Tiki asked eagerly.

Rieker's jaw was set. "It's in the northeastern part of the park surrounded by trees, not far from the Serpentine."

"And Larkin will be there?" Tiki asked.

"If we go there, she'll get word that we're looking for her." Rieker's expression was serious as he moved closer. He slid his hands along the backs of her arms, and Tiki fought the urge to throw herself against his chest and beg him to help her. "I wasn't joking when I said she would expect a trade," Rieker said. "There's one reason Larkin took Clara and only one reason. The ring. We might as well forget it if we go empty-handed. Faeries don't have emotions like humans."

"But the ring is hidden inside Buckingham." Tiki's

words came out in a rush. "And now the royals are in residence again. How will we get in to recover it?" She didn't mention the ransom note. That seemed the least of her worries right now.

"Where's it hidden?" Rieker rubbed her arms gently.

Tiki clutched her hands together. She wasn't going to reveal the ring's location to anybody. Even Rieker. Because he would only give the ring back to the royals, either to collect the reward or for safekeeping. Either way, it didn't help her get Clara back.

"It's on the main floor," she said as she pulled free. "Why? Do you have a way in?"

Rieker shrugged. "Maybe. But first I'd have to know exactly where I was going."

Shamus's head swiveled between the two of them. "Are you sure Larkin will return Clara if we give her the ring?" he asked in a quiet voice.

Tiki bit her lip until she tasted blood. She couldn't stand to think of Clara in the hands of someone like Larkin.

"She would trade anything for that ring," Rieker replied. "Mark my words, the danger will grow until we return the ring to the royals or someone who can guard it." He scowled at the floor, rubbing the back of his neck. "The fey can inflict a lot of damage when they want to. Already things are happening. There was a storm the other day that practically ripped apart the carriage I'd caught a ride on."

Rieker raised his head and looked at Tiki. "They found MacGregor's body dumped behind the World's End pub, you know. With his legs ripped off." Tiki gasped as his words hung in the room. What kind of creature could rip the legs off a man the size of MacGregor? "And it's all because the ring is unguarded."

"But the ring is our only way to get Clara back," Tiki cried. "We've got to trade with Larkin. What else can we do?"

Rieker rolled his shoulders as though to stretch the tension from his muscles. "I don't know for sure. I'll have to think on it." He turned to her. "You better decide if you're going to tell me where the ring is. Otherwise it's a waste of my time." Rieker walked to the door and without even looking through the peephole disappeared through it.

Silence filled the room after his departure, and the weight of it rested on Tiki's shoulders.

"This is all my fault," she cried, tears welling up and spilling over her cheeks. "If I hadn't stolen the ring, the fey would never have come looking. Larkin wouldn't have taken Clara."

She flopped down on her blankets, wishing she could just go to sleep and wake up to find this was all a bad dream. But she knew that wouldn't happen. She had to do something.

Tiki swiped at the tears in her eyes with the heels of her hand, feeling the scratches on her arm pull uncomfortably as she moved.

"What are you going to do, Tiki?" Shamus asked.

Tiki opened her eyes and looked across the dim room at him. Toots was back at the peephole, watching the station, casting furtive glances at her. Fiona was huddled in the corner with her blankets.

"I've got to find a way to get the ring back," Tiki said. "I've got to be able to trade for Clara."

Shamus was silent for a long time. When he spoke, it was with quiet surety.

"We don't need the reward money to survive, Teek. Things have been looking up lately. As long as we don't have to leave here"—he motioned to the small room—"we should be fine." He paused, as though searching for the right words. "I know you feel the same way, but I can't stand the thought of little Clara being harmed."

Fiona crawled from the corner and sat next to Tiki, resting her head on her shoulder.

Shamus came and sat across from them, drawing his knees up. "Maybe you should just trust Rieker and tell him where the ring is. Let him deal with this Larkin creature. I don't think being involved with the faeries is good for any of us. Maybe it would be best if they got what they want and left us alone."

For Shamus, it was quite a speech. More words put together in a row than Tiki had ever heard him speak.

She nodded. "You're right, Shamus." The words sounded heavy in her ears, but she knew she couldn't continue to fight. "I've got to trust Rieker."

Chapter Twenty-three

Tiki was out in the station early the next day, waiting for Rieker to appear. She hadn't been able to sleep for worrying about Clara, and instead of pacing in their small room, she had decided to head into the station. She sat on the same bench outside Mr. Potts's bookstore and waited, rolling a coin over her knuckles nervously.

"Better be careful who sees you do that." Tiki jerked around at the sound of his voice. "Somebody might think you're a thief."

"Rieker," she breathed, relieved and nervous at the same time. She jumped up from the bench. "I've been waiting for you."

He raised an eyebrow. "Missed me that much? Let's take a walk, then."

Tiki didn't rise to the bait of his insolence, she was so intent on setting things right between them so she could save Clara. They left Charing Cross and cut through the winding streets, passing people laden with bags full of Christmas gifts. Tiki eyed the colorful displays in the shopwindows, and a longing for the past created a pressure in her chest. What she would give to celebrate Christmas with her parents in their home. But even as she wished for it, she realized that she couldn't imagine Christmas without the others.

Tiki shot a glance at Rieker out of the corner of her eye. The weather was still cold, and she shivered, though she knew it was partly from nerves.

She blew out a big breath of air. "I think you need to understand something," she started. "Clara, Shamus, Fiona, and Toots are my family. They are all I've got now." She gave him a beseeching look. "I would give anything to keep them safe."

Rieker was silent for a moment, contemplating her words. "How did you come to live on the street?"

His question sounded sincere, and Tiki remembered Shamus's words from the night before. She had agreed to trust Rieker.

"My parents died of consumption within a week of each other." Her voice was quiet. "I was only fourteen at the time, so I was sent to live with my mother's sister and her husband. I'd only met my aunt and uncle once or twice at family gatherings." She took a deep breath. "It was like being sent to live with strangers. I found myself in a house that had never had children in it, with two people who couldn't stand each other." She paused, and to her surprise, Rieker reached over and took her hand, pulling her close.

"I'm listening," he said.

"To make matters worse," Tiki continued, "I learned in a few short weeks that my uncle liked to drink, and when he drank, he took a peculiar interest in me." The words died in her throat as old memories forced their way back into her consciousness. "He would stare at me. . . ."

"What did you do?" Rieker asked softly.

"He was so evil," Tiki whispered. "He watched my every move. I could feel his eyes on me constantly. I didn't know what he was going to do, but I couldn't stay there and just wait for it to happen."

"So you ran."

"Yes." Tiki nodded miserably. "I went to a friend of my mother's, but when I arrived at her house, I learned she had died of the fever." Tiki had to focus so her voice didn't crack. "I had nowhere else to go. So I went to King's Cross, thinking I would find a destination there. Instead, someone stole all my belongings." She forced a laugh. "There was nothing left to take from me. If Fiona hadn't taken pity on me and shown me how to pick a pocket, I probably would have starved."

"And how did you end up in Charing Cross?"

"Fiona and Shamus had discovered an abandoned clockmaker's shop. They invited me to live with them." She looked up at him. "Truly, they saved my life. Shortly after that I found Toots and then Clara." Tiki swallowed hard. "You have to understand. They're everything I have."

Rieker threaded her fingers with his own. His eyes were intent on her. "I do understand," he said softly.

They walked on in silence. Finally, Tiki mustered up her nerve again. "Do you have a plan to get into the palace?"

"Yes." Rieker squeezed her hand. "But I need a partner."

"A partner?" Tiki echoed. Her surprised expression turned to a suspicious frown. "Who?"

Rieker smiled. He looked so much different when he smiled, so much younger and carefree, that for a second it made Tiki want to smile, too. But she didn't.

"What?" she asked. "I can't imagine you needing anybody's help. Ever."

"What do you mean?" Rieker protested. "I needed help from you and Shamus out in the alley that night."

"I'm sure you could've got rid of Marcus and the others by yourself if we hadn't come out."

Rieker gave her a quizzical look. "What's that supposed to mean?"

"Just what I said." Tiki worked to modulate her voice. "So tell me, what's your plan? It sounds like they've got the palace under triple guard. I don't know how anybody could sneak in now unless they knew of a secret passageway." She peered at him out of the corners of her eyes. "You don't, do you?"

"No, unfortunately, no secret passageways for me." He sighed. "I was thinking more like the front door."

Tiki stopped. "The front door? How in bloody hell would you get in through the front door of Buckingham Palace?"

"A social call, of course." Rieker flipped his dark hair out of his face and took a deep breath. "You're not the only one who attended the masked ball."

She gave Rieker a wary look. "What are you talking about?"

"Keep walking, Tiki, our conversation is much more difficult to overhear if we're moving." Rieker took her arm. It reminded Tiki of another time, not too long ago, when he had used the same move to hold her against her will. When he had spied her birthmark. This time, however, Rieker didn't force her. He waited, his hand tucked under her elbow, until she took the first step, and then he fell in along with her.

"Do you mean *you* were at the masked ball?"

"Yes, as a matter of fact I was. And I have to admit, at

the time, I didn't for one second even consider that *you* were the breathtaking Elizabeth." He looked down at her shocked expression and smiled. "That is, until I saw the mark on your wrist. But a bath can have an amazing effect, wouldn't you agree?"

Before Tiki could gather her wits to form a reply, he added in a soft voice, "And I have to say that you were certainly the most beautiful and interesting girl at the ball. Enough so to make Leo drop his glass of wine, which I can assure you has never happened before."

Tiki's jaw dropped as her cheeks suddenly burned.

"You've given me a lot to think about this last week." Rieker turned his head away and gazed down the street. "Not always pleasant thoughts, but I suppose it was inevitable that the time would come."

Tiki noticed the difference in his speech, as though a mask had dropped away. "But how did you get into the ball? Where did you get clothes?" She hesitated before she asked the question that burned on her lips. "Did I meet you?"

Rieker sighed. "You've forced me to make a decision, Tiki. I've realized I've got to change my life, whether I'm ready or not. There's too much at stake now." He stopped and turned toward her, bending in a formal bow. "William Becker Richmond, at your service, miss."

It was as though the ground had turned to shifting sand, and Tiki swayed on her feet.

"I don't believe it," she whispered. Though the idea that she had met William Richmond somewhere before had flitted through her head, she'd convinced herself it wasn't possible. That William Richmond could be Rieker, a common thief, had never entered her mind.

Rieker watched her expression, his own face guarded. "Trust me, Tiki, I felt the same way when I realized whose hand I was kissing." His lips lifted in a half-smile. "Though after the shock wore off, it was a rather pleasant surprise, wouldn't you agree?"

Tiki didn't answer. Wills Richmond had been so handsome and so . . . so aristocratic. Tiki looked away, biting her lip to stop the tears that suddenly threatened to fall. He'd lied from the beginning about who he really was.

"Are you a blue blood?"

"No. I just had a family who owned some land. It's as simple, as lucky, as that," Rieker replied. He looked over his shoulder and surveyed the street for oncoming carriages before steering Tiki across Horse Guard Road and into the park.

"Tiki, let me ask you this." Their boots crunched on the gravel path as they walked. "If we can get into the palace"—he held up his hand to stop her question—"through whatever means we can devise, and I'm able to engage Leo and Arthur in conversation, could you get to the ring if you needed to excuse yourself?" His smoky eyes rested on her face as he waited for her answer.

"Yes." Tiki nodded.

"Leo will not have forgotten you, I'm quite sure. He seemed shocked by your birthmark. Do you have any idea why?"

Tiki hesitated. "I ran into him in the park when I was dressed like this, as a boy. He asked me about my birthmark then."

"Well, he has apparently put the two of you together. We'll have to be careful and pretend that *Elizabeth*"—he said the name with an odd emphasis—"and I have been acquainted for some time. We'll have to work out our story ahead of time, so if they ask us questions, we'll both give the same answers." Rieker gave her a sideways glance. "There's no chance he suspects you in the disappearance of the ring, is there?"

Tiki clutched her fingers together. "He seemed to suspect me of something. He asked me to empty out my pockets."

"Did you have the ring at the time?"

Tiki nodded, afraid to speak for fear her voice would break. "I was checking to make sure it was safe."

Rieker shifted his shoulders as though trying to dislodge a weight. "Well, clearly you got away. We'll just have to be very careful."

She worked to make her voice sound bright and cheerful, though she felt more alone than ever. "So, what's your plan, then?"

Rieker was quiet for a minute. "Leo has wanted to borrow a special bridle I had made for a spirited horse. I thought we could take him the gear. During our visit you could excuse yourself to powder your nose or whatever it is women do, recover the ring, and we would depart with no one the wiser. That way, you don't have to trust me with the location of the ring, but we can still work toward getting Clara back." He put his hand on her shoulder. "How does that sound?"

"That sounds good." She would get the ring. That was all she was going to concentrate on for now. Get the ring and trade it for Clara. She took a deep breath, trying not to drown in emotions she didn't understand.

"Do you think you could 'borrow' a dress again?" he

asked. Out of the corner of her eye, Tiki could see him looking at her. "We could plan a visit for Saturday."

Tiki's head snapped up. "I think we have a problem."

"What's that? No dress?" Rieker asked. He didn't sound surprised.

"No," Tiki said. "Something different."

"What is it?" Rieker seemed unconcerned as he gazed down at her.

"Isentanotefortherereward." Tiki tensed, preparing herself for Rieker's reaction.

"What?" Rieker asked. "Slow down, I can't understand a word—" Suddenly his voice dropped off and he grabbed her arm to turn her to face him. "You sent what?" His expression was horrified, his voice a mixture of disbelief and anger.

"I haven't had the advantage of a family who just happen to *own some land*," Tiki spat, suddenly angry herself. "I've had to work and scrap for every penny I can get my hands on. I sent the note before Larkin took Clara. I wasn't going to walk away from a bloody fortune." She clenched her hands into fists, prepared to fight if she had to.

Rieker glared at her, his grip tight on her wrist. Then, instead of attacking, to her great surprise he started laughing. He laughed so hard that he bent at the waist and grabbed his sides.

Tiki relaxed her stance. What was wrong with him?

"I should have known that there would be no part of this that will go according to any plan I think up," Rieker gasped, wiping tears from the corners of his eyes. "My God, girl, you can bugger up any well-thought-out scheme. It seems you have a magic for creating chaos." His laughter died away and he shook his head. "So you have served up a demand note for the reward from the royals. Did you wish them Happy Christmas at the same time?" He chuckled under his breath. "I doubt they will pay but tell me what in heaven's name you said." He started walking down the path again, and Tiki hurried to keep up.

Because of the cold, few others braved the park. They were alone as they walked, and Tiki told him the contents of the note.

"Well, it might work to our advantage," Rieker finally said. "If Leo does suspect that the boy with the mark and Elizabeth are the same, and if there's any chance he connects you to the disappearance of the ring, the last thing he'll expect is for you to pay him a visit."

Chapter Twenty-four

W ILLS!" Leo hurried into the drawing room. "I'm so glad you're here. I've been trying to track you down since the masked ball." He strode across the room to give Rieker's hand a hearty shake. "Do you remember that lovely young—"

"Leo, so good to see you," Rieker interrupted. "Surely you remember Miss Elizabeth Dunbar." He raised his hand toward the far wall. "As I recall, you danced a waltz with Miss Dunbar at the ball."

With a gasp, Leo spun around and stared at Tiki, his mouth hanging open.

Bowing her head demurely, Tiki dipped into a graceful curtsy. "I'm so pleased to make your acquaintance again, sir."

"You," Leo breathed. His eyes swept over her as though she were a mirage.

"Yes, Leo, the woman whose dress you destroyed with red wine. Surely you remember her," Arthur said in a dry drawl. "I'm quite sure she'll never forget you."

Arthur's comment snapped Leo out of his daze, and he had the grace to flush at his brother's words.

"Yes, and I do apologize again—Miss, uh, Dunbar, is it?—for my clumsiness that evening. Quite unforgivable." Leo moved forward toward Tiki, his hand reaching out to take hers. Grasping her fingers, he bowed over her left hand, then gazed intently at her face as though memorizing the contours. "I shall have to find a way to repay you."

Tiki looked into Leo's eyes and froze. His gaze was unwavering and almost steely. He suspected her. She was sure of it. She dropped her eyes, unsure how to extract her hand from his grip.

"Leo." Rieker interrupted with a loud cough. "I've brought you that bridle with the soft bit you've been asking about. How is Diablo these days? Are you getting that mad beast under control?"

It took Leo a moment to drag his eyes away from Tiki. He released her hand, but not before he cast a questioning glance at her covered wrist. His brow drew down in a frown as he contemplated Rieker. "Yes, thank you, Wills. Very kind of you. Diablo is as robust as ever. Tell me, Elizabeth"—he turned back to stare at her—"do you ride?"

"Oh," Tiki said, "I rode as a child, but not as much lately." That was all true, she thought. Rieker had told her to stick to the truth whenever she could. "Thank you." She smiled at Arthur as she accepted a hot cup of tea.

"Perhaps you would grace me with your presence on a ride some afternoon, then?" Leo asked. "Say, in St. James' Park? You like to frequent the park, don't you?"

"In this weather?" Rieker chuckled. "Leo, surely you jest. What are you trying to do to Miss Dunbar?"

"Yes, really," Arthur added, frowning at Leo. "What are you thinking? I'm sure if Miss Dunbar should choose to ride in the dead of winter, then Wills will be most accommodating with his mounts." Arthur's tone held a hint of warning.

She gave Leo her most charming smile. It wouldn't do

to insult the prince. It was clear he suspected her. "Actually, Leo, thank you for the offer. I would be honored to ride with you." Her heart was pounding so hard, she was surprised it didn't burst through her chest. They needed to get the ring and get out. Before they were arrested.

Leo flushed. "Yes, brilliant . . . lovely. We'll have to make plans, then. Soon."

"I'll look forward to it," Tiki murmured.

"Grand," Rieker said. "Now about that bridle, Leo . . ."

"Oh, yes, of course." Leo turned to Rieker. "Nice of you to bring it by, Wills."

Tiki released a slow breath as she waited for the right moment to beg their pardon to use the water closet. Before her a large fire burned, the wood crackling in the hearth. She tried not to stare at the elaborately carved figures of a man and a woman dressed in exotic garb standing on the mantel, appearing to support the thick wood trim that surrounded the ceiling. The richness of the dark paneling that covered the walls, and the plush rug under her feet, made Tiki feel as if she had plunged into one of the books she borrowed from Mr. Potts. Her father had been a barrister, they'd lived a comfortable life in a nice home, but nothing like this.

Rieker's cough brought her back to reality, and she moved over to join their conversation.

"I'm so sorry." A blush crept up her cheeks that was all too real. "I need to use your . . . facility."

Leo and Arthur both gave her a blank look before they realized her meaning.

"Certainly, my dear." Arthur stepped forward. "Allow me, I'll show you the way."

"Oh, I don't want to interrupt your conversation," Tiki

said. "If you'll just point me in the direction, I'm sure I can find it."

"I'll hear nothing of it." Arthur offered her his arm. "Any chance I get to escort a beautiful lady, I take."

"Thank you." Tiki looked down in embarrassment. She could feel both Rieker's and Leo's eyes follow her as she took Arthur's arm and let him lead her from the room.

"So, you've known Wills for a long time, have you?" Arthur asked as they made their way down the grand hallway.

"Quite a while now," Tiki replied. Dread filled her at the thought of being questioned by Arthur. "What about you? Have you known him long?"

"Oh yes, practically grew up together." Arthur laughed. "He was a wild one, even as a boy. He and Leo were particularly good chums, being the same age and all."

"I wager you have some wonderful stories to tell." Tiki's mind raced to make sense of what she had just learned. Rieker had grown up playing with the princes of England?

"Yes, many good times. I haven't seen him much the last few years, of course, and now I'm traveling with the Rifle Brigade and gone from England for long stretches, so we have even fewer occasions to get together. But it's good to see him. He looks better than he has in ages, if you know what I mean." He gave her a conspiratorial smile.

Tiki nodded. She had no idea what he meant. Did Arthur somehow know that Rieker was spending his time among pickpockets and thieves? She pushed the thought away. That was ridiculous; of course he couldn't know of Rieker's other life. He must have meant something different. Maybe he was referring to his own travels. Still, why did Rieker choose to live among those who survived by their wits on the streets of London? Somehow he had repeatedly dodged that question.

Arthur stopped before a large paneled door. "Well, here we are," he said. "Just go back down this hallway when you're finished. The drawing room is on your left." With a small nod, he turned and walked away.

Tiki's gaze followed his departing back, wishing for just a second that she could peer inside his head and know everything Arthur knew about Wills. She shook her head as she pushed through the wooden door. She had more important things to worry about than wondering about Rieker's past.

Inside the water closet, Tiki stared at the stranger in the mirror. She had changed so much since her parents had passed away. A girl she didn't recognize stared back at her. Her face was much thinner than she remembered and her cheekbones more pronounced, making her green eyes seem almost too big for her face. For a second, her eyes seemed as mismatched for her features as Marcus's almond-shaped eyes were for his. With a gasp, Tiki covered her face with her hands and jerked her head away from the mirror. She would not allow herself to even think such a thing.

After a proper amount of time had passed, Tiki peeked back out the door. The hallway was clear. She slipped out and tiptoed back toward the drawing room. Arthur had distracted her with his talk of Wills, but she recognized the small alcove where she had hidden the ring.

She slowed as she neared the half-circular area and stepped lightly into the small space. The beautiful painting hung on the wall as she remembered, the scene depicted even more dramatic in the light of day. The exquisite detail of the delicate faerie's wings made them seem to shimmer, like the reflection of sunlight on an afternoon pond. From the look on the man's face, he was besotted by the beauty of the creature before him. Yet the faerie had a look on her face that suggested she shared the man's passion.

Tiki reached forward and ran her hand along the intricate curve of the frame. She remembered exactly where she had attached the ring.

"Quite a picture, wouldn't you agree?"

Tiki let out a startled cry and whirled around. Leo stood behind her.

"Oh, you s-startled me." She clutched her hands together over her heart. "I didn't know you were there."

"I beg your pardon." Leo stepped up next to her, his hands folded behind his back. "I saw you admiring the painting." He gazed at the large picture before them. "It's one of my favorites."

"Yes," Tiki agreed, trying to still her breathing. "It is quite beautiful."

"She's a faerie, you know," Leo said in a bemused voice.

"Yes," Tiki murmured.

"Some people think she's an angel," Leo explained. He looked over at Tiki. "Tell me, Elizabeth, do you believe in faeries?"

"It's a charming thought to consider." Tiki smiled at him, but her mind raced. What did he want from her? Would he have her arrested? How she could escape?

"I'm not so sure." Leo turned back to the painting, and his eyes lingered on the figure of the winged woman. "I've heard stories that the fey like to steal things." He looked over at her with a forced smile. "I've also heard that some are marked."

"Marked?" Tiki repeated. She gave a questioning look to the young prince. "You'll have to forgive my ignorance on this topic. Have you studied the world of Faerie? What do you mean?"

"An fáinne sí." Leo's tone was as bland as though he were discussing the weather and found it quite boring. "Like this here." He pointed to a decorative circle on the woman's wrist in the painting.

Tiki had to bite her lip not to gasp out loud. Those were the words that Rieker had muttered when he'd seen her mark the first time, she was sure of it. She looked closely at the painting. During the ball, the lighting had been dim and she'd paid little attention to the details. At first glance she'd thought the mark he indicated was a bracelet. But now, she could see the same swirls and turns as adorned her own wrist. Was it possible? What did it mean? How long had these connections between faerie and man existed?

Leo turned from the canvas and faced her. "I've been told *an fáinne sí* means 'the faerie ring.' The mark is the same as the one on your wrist, I believe." His eyes dared her to deny it. "May I see it?"

Chapter Twenty-five

T HERE you two are."
  Tiki turned with relief at the sound of Rieker's voice and took a step toward him. She widened her eyes, hoping she could subtly convey her panic. Her ears rang with the words Leo had just uttered: An fáinne sí *means* "*the faerie ring.*" A terrible fear spread through her limbs, making her feel weak.

"I hate to interrupt your enjoyment of the arts, but we need to carry on," Rieker said. "I've got an appointment later this afternoon and I promised Miss Dunbar that we would return before three." He extended his arm.

Tiki could sense Leo's frustration. His eyes lingered on her with a disturbing intensity as she moved to take Rieker's arm.

"I'm sorry to see you go," Leo responded politely. "We need to spend some time catching up, Wills. There are matters we need to discuss. I feel like I don't even know you anymore."

"It's difficult with our busy schedules, isn't it?" Wills agreed in an easy tone. "Will you be heading back up to Balmoral or are you home through the holidays now?"

"Mother is quite ill and not showing improvement. Much as she'd like, I don't think she can even travel to Windsor, so we'll be here at Buckingham for now." His face was unsmiling as he stared at Rieker. "When are you available to meet?"

"Soon. Soon. I hope Her Majesty takes a turn for the better. Winter in England is never pleasant."

They stepped out into the gray light of the December afternoon and descended the steps toward the carriage that waited for them. Tiki had no idea where Rieker had come up with a carriage and a driver. He had just mumbled something about "connections" when she had asked earlier.

"Miss Dunbar . . ." Leo took her hand and bowed over her fingers. "I look forward to seeing you again soon and continuing our conversation." His gaze shifted to Rieker. "Wills, I'll be calling on you. We need to talk."

Leo suspected something, Tiki was sure of it. At the ball he had clearly recognized the mark on her wrist as being similar to the urchin's mark. Had he found reason to connect the ring's disappearance to her? Tiki's stomach roiled uncomfortably at the thought. Blast it, why had she brought up the ring to him at the ball? And then gone on and asked how stolen property could be returned. What in bloody hell had she been thinking?

Tiki fought the urge to run down the steps and get as far away from Leo as possible. She was treading on treacherous ground and needed to be very careful or it would only be a matter of time before she made a mistake and got caught. She would be no good to Clara locked away in Newgate Prison.

After what felt like an eternity, Rieker climbed in the carriage and finally shut the door. As the driver pulled away, Tiki glanced back. Leo stood on the steps, watching their departure with a frown on his face.

"You didn't get it, did you," Rieker said in a low voice.

"No," Tiki replied. Her worried eyes flicked to his. "Leo surprised me in the hallway before I could get to the spot where I'd hidden it," she said. "He practically dragged me into that alcove to admire the painting." She didn't want to give Rieker too many clues to where the ring might be hidden. "He suspects us, could you tell?"

Rieker released a long sigh. "He did seem a bit out of sorts."

Tiki glanced at him out of the corner of her eye. There were so many things she wanted to ask him, but it was like sitting next to a stranger. He was so handsome, so self-assured. Damn Rieker anyway. He pretended to be her friend, but in the end he was nothing more than a thief in search of the biggest treasure either of them had ever seen.

Rieker leaned his head back and stared at the ceiling of the coach. "Now we have a problem. I don't know how we're going to get back in there." He drummed his fingers on the arm of the seat as he thought. "I was afraid something was off. He left so abruptly after you went down the hall that I was sure he intended to intercept you." He gave Tiki a half-smile. "Luckily the prince is besotted with your beauty and charm. He didn't outright accuse you of anything."

"Beauty and charm." Tiki gave a half-laugh, remembering her distorted image in the mirror at Buckingham. "You don't make a good liar, Rieker."

"Actually, I'm quite accomplished in that area," Rieker replied lightly. "But I'm not lying. You're like a different person when you're dressed in decent clothes and actually clean." He raised an eyebrow as he smiled, somehow looking charming and rakish at the same time. "There were moments when I stood there today and wondered who the beautiful creature was flirting with Prince Leopold."

"Flirting!" Tiki exclaimed. "I did not flirt with him."

Rieker threw his head back and laughed. "'I would be honored to ride with you, *Leo*,'" he mimicked in a falsetto.

Tiki blushed. "Pardon my lack of proper etiquette. I'm not used to socializing with royalty like some people." Her temper flared as she thought of Rieker's deception. "Exactly how rich are you, *Wills*? Why do you hide among orphans and steal from rich people? Why do you need the ring if *you're* rich?" Her emotions confused her and sharpened her tongue. "If you've overspent your allowance, I'm sure your dear father will just give you more."

"I don't have an allowance." Rieker's voice was low, but his tone held a warning.

"Well, maybe you should ask for one. Don't all young men of your position have stacks of money available for their every whim?" Tiki sneered at him. "No doubt you've got lands of your own, too. Maybe you should sell some so you don't have to steal." Tiki didn't even know why she was so angry. One comment had led to another, and now she was saying things she didn't even mean. "Or maybe your mum has some jewelry you can pawn so you can keep up with the royals."

A multitude of emotions flashed across Rieker's face before a darkness settled in his eyes and his mouth thinned to an angry line. "I don't have to explain myself to you or anyone. What I choose to do with my life is my business." His words came out in a growl. He leaned forward and slid open a small window to the driver with a bang.

"Geoffrey, stop. I'm going to walk. Please deliver Miss

Dunbar to Charing Cross." Without another word, he yanked the door open.

"Rieker, wait." Tiki reached for his arm. Regret filled her. She had gone too far. "I didn't mean it like it sounded, it's just—" But Rieker yanked his arm free, slid out the door, and slammed it closed. Tiki felt the carriage jerk as the horses started moving forward again, the jingle of their reins mingling with the staccato rhythm of their hooves on the cobblestones. She pressed her face to the small rear window and could see his dark head above the others in the street. But he never glanced back toward the carriage before he disappeared into the crowd. She slumped back into her seat. Now what was she going to do?

How did it go?" Toots asked as soon as Tiki came through the back door. Shamus was whittling a swan from a piece of wood where he sat close to the stove, and Fiona sat nearby, stitching the sleeve of Rieker's jacket. They both watched her in anticipation.

Tiki shrugged, still angry and upset at her fight with Rieker. She was bothered not only by what she had said, but also by the fact that his actions mattered to her.

"Didn't work. I think Prince Leo suspects I'm connected with the disappearance of the ring. He seems especially curious about my mark."

"Connected?" Fiona said. "He can't arrest you, can he?"

"Where's Rieker?" Shamus asked.

Tiki tried not to snap her answer. "I don't know. He got out of the hansom cab and walked." She turned her back to Fiona. "Fi, can you unhook some of these buttons?"

"Walked?" Shamus repeated. He carved off several strips of wood. "Walked where? It was his carriage, wasn't it?"

"We had a fight," Tiki admitted.

Fiona's fingers froze against her back. Shamus paused in his whittling and waited.

"Well, Leo obviously suspected us," Tiki said defensively, "and I couldn't get the ring, and then Rieker was all chummy with both princes because he grew up with them and I didn't really belong there at all." She took a breath. "And then, on the way home, he was insulting me about—"

"He insulted you?" Toots interrupted.

"Yes. Well . . ." Tiki cleared her throat. "Sort of. He was teasing me in an insulting way and then I said something and he said something"—she waved her hands—"and then it was just a big fight and he got out and walked." Tiki ducked her head. "It just goes to show you that we can't rely on Rieker anyway. We've got to depend on each other, like we always do, to figure out a way to save Clara. It's the only way." Tiki held her dress in place as she jerked around to face Shamus. "We don't need Rieker. I'm going to go on my own and find Larkin."

"Slow down, Tiki," Shamus said. He spoke with his usual measured pace, but his face was creased with concern. "I don't know if that's a good idea. Rieker seems to understand these things better than we do."

"He understands how to get what he wants. I'm going to do what's best for us." Tiki stomped behind the privacy blanket and yanked the dress down over her hips. She hadn't needed Rieker's help to survive this long. She didn't need his help to save Clara, either.

Chapter Twenty-six

LEO tightened the cinch on Diablo, ignoring the snort of protest from the big horse. "You're not the only one who doesn't want to go riding at this hour," he muttered. He patted his coat pocket again, reassuring himself that the bag containing fifty £10 notes was safely stored.

"I've just asked a few men to hide around the tree in St. James' Park." Arthur's face was drawn in a worried frown. "Are you sure I shouldn't come along?" he asked again.

"No, Arthur," Leo responded with a sigh. "And I asked you not to have any men out there. The note said 'alone.' If they had wanted to do us harm, they would have gone about it in a different way, not by stealing a ring. All they want is the money." He grabbed Diablo's reins and led him from the stable. "I say let's give them what they want and be done with this mess."

"Well, I don't have anyone following you. They're just positioned to keep an eye and to see if they can catch sight of the thieves."

Leo gave him a sharp glance. "Make sure they *don't* follow me. There is no way they could remain unseen at midnight. There's bloody few people out at this hour to hide behind."

Arthur didn't reply as he walked along beside his brother.

Leo pulled Diablo to a stop and stepped into the stirrup, pulling himself effortlessly into the saddle, the leather creaking with his added weight. He looked down at Arthur. "Go have a drink, Arthur. I'll be home before you can figure out your next move on the chessboard." He threaded the leather reins through his fingers. "With the ring."

"Be careful."

The prince squeezed Diablo's sides and headed into the dark night, the horse's hoofbeats echoing across the quiet grounds. He hoped that what he'd said to Arthur was true. He wasn't at all sure what sort of wild chase he was headed for tonight. If there was any way he thought the guards could follow him without being seen, he would have been all for it. But it wasn't possible. There was, however, another way they might catch the thief.

After reading the ransom note, Arthur had predicted that the message had already been planted in the tree. A guard had checked during the dead of night and sure enough—there had been a note tucked into a rotted-out hole where a branch had once been. The instructions had said to go to the obelisk in St. George's Circus.

Now Arthur had guards at the obelisk as well as hidden around the perimeter of the elm, though they had been unable to locate a second note at the obelisk. Perhaps the thief planned to meet him there and would ultimately be caught. Leo allowed himself a small smile of satisfaction. That would teach people not to try to steal from the monarchy.

He was just leaving the palace grounds when he was intercepted by a guard.

"Sorry, sir. This was just delivered."

Leo's heart sank. "Thank you," he replied, reaching for the note. He stopped under one of the gas-lit lamps that lined the road. He unfolded the page and read the shaky writing scrawled there.

Change of plans. Look in the mouth of the lion in Trafalgar Square. Come alone.

He crumpled the note in his hand and gazed out into the quiet night around him. A grudging smile curved his lips. Perhaps he had underestimated the thief after all.

Chapter Twenty-seven

I T was just past midnight when Tiki hurried through St. James's Park. She'd slipped out of Charing Cross without telling Shamus and the others what she was planning. The instructions to deliver the reward money had been sent to the royals. What if they were willing to pay? She couldn't pass up the opportunity to try and collect the reward just because Rieker didn't think it was a good idea— could she? They needed that money.

She slipped on through the milky light of the half-moon. If there was someone following Leo, her timing was critical. She needed to get back down to the boats tied along the edge of the Serpentine and hidden before Leo followed the notes and arrived there himself. She closed her eyes and whispered a prayer that her plan worked.

T IKI lay perfectly still in the bottom of the second boat in a group of skiffs tied along the shore of the Serpentine. Her dark clothes blended with the shadows in which she hid, making her invisible.

The night was oddly still at this hour, the myriad birds that frequented the lake noticeably absent, leaving only the movement of the river as it slipped silently past. Tiki shivered in her hiding spot. Was she truly alone in the darkness? Or were unseen eyes watching her?

The far-off sound of galloping hooves caught her attention. Her heart rumbled in her chest, keeping time with the echoing hoofbeats. The horse slowed as it approached the bridge. From her vantage point, Tiki could see Leo's silhouette cross the overpass. He was the only rider out at this hour.

A guilty twinge coursed through her at the sight of him. Now that she'd met the prince—danced with him, even—could she steal from him? It was different when it was a few shillings from some bloke's pocket she didn't know. But five hundred pounds from a man with whom she'd shared tea? Her stomach twisted in a knot, making her feel sick. They needed the money so desperately and the prince wouldn't miss a single pound. But did that make it right? She shook her head, trying to shake away her confused thoughts.

Leo had made good time tonight—going from Buckingham to Trafalgar Square to Covent Garden back to Hyde Park. The best part was that she hadn't heard the beat of any other hooves that would suggest a guard was following him.

She watched as he retrieved the last note from the stone pillar at the end of the bridge where she had hidden it. From her hiding spot Tiki could see him standing under the gas lamp holding the paper out to the light to read the words. Tiki closed her eyes and envisioned what she had scrawled earlier.

Leave the bag with the reward at the base of the weeping willow tree. The ring is in Buckingham. When it is safe we will let you know where it is hidden.

"Please, just do it," she whispered under her breath. His head jerked back in surprise as he read the words. Tiki pressed her lips together. What must he think to find that the ring was at Buckingham all this time?

Tiki shivered as she remembered how close Leo had come to catching her as she'd tried to remove the ring from behind the picture. Had it only been this afternoon? It felt like ages ago. What would he have done if he'd caught her with the ring in her possession? Probably would have thrown her into prison, straightaway.

As she watched, the prince's head swiveled as though trying to locate anyone who might be watching, but his eyes never landed on where she lay hidden among the shadows of the boat. Instead, he climbed back on Diablo and turned the horse in the direction from which he had just come. Halfway across the bridge he kicked Diablo into a canter and disappeared into the night.

Tiki sat up. Her earlier concerns of stealing the money were forgotten. An eerie sensation of falling made her clutch the sides of the small boat. He hadn't left the money. Leo had ridden off without leaving the money. The royals weren't going to pay for the return of the ring.

A shudder shook her shoulders as she gasped for breath. The reward money was their ticket out of Charing Cross. They needed the money to start a new life in a home where Clara could remain healthy. Now what would they do?

It was all Tiki could do to crawl out of the boat. There was no money, the ring was back in Buckingham, and Clara was missing. She had failed.

THE fog had crept in and wrapped the City in its arms by the time Tiki arrived back at Charing Cross. Each step had been an effort. She slipped down the alleyway, wanting to avoid the night bobbies patrolling the railway station. The shadows were thick and her breath came in short, nervous gasps as she navigated the alleyway to the door to the maintenance tunnels.

A shadow rose out of a doorway and she darted away, fearful that it was Marcus or Larkin, but it was just a drunk, mumbling to himself. In the distance Big Ben chimed the three o'clock hour as she slid the panel aside and stepped into their home.

"Where have you been?" Rieker's low voice cut through the darkness like a knife, causing Tiki to jump in surprise.

"And look who's asking," she shot back in a harsh whisper. "I think you owe the first explanation." She was too tired and upset at the loss of the reward to hide her anger. Rieker would probably only remind her that he had warned her not to pursue the reward anyway.

Rieker didn't reply as he pushed back in the wooden chair, tipping the front legs off the ground, the wood creaking in protest. Tiki could feel his eyes on her as she moved across the room and sank into her pile of blankets, but she ignored him. He could stare all he wanted but she was not going to fight with him again tonight.

She counted heads, as she did every night before she went to sleep, to make sure everyone was home safe. Fiona was a huddled lump over by the stove. Toots snored softly from the corner next to Clara's empty spot. Tiki glanced toward Shamus and wasn't surprised to see his thin silhouette propped up looking at her.

"Glad to see you home safe, Teek," he said.

Would Shamus be glad if he knew what she'd done? He

hadn't thought they needed the reward money in the first place. Now, not only did they not have the reward money but they didn't have the ring, either. With a sigh, Tiki bunched several of her blankets to form a pillow and laid her head down. Where was Clara?

Chapter Twenty-eight

THE next afternoon, Tiki slipped out of their room and hurried through the alley away from Charing Cross. The others were gone, working the streets. She had pretended to be asleep hoping they would leave her alone. She wondered where Rieker was. He'd been gone when she finally got up. From the corners of her eyes, she could see what looked like strange shapes and faces watching from the darkness that surrounded the buildings. She was afraid to look directly at them for fear they would become more than just eerie shadows. Tiki raced through the wide-open plaza of Trafalgar Square, where no one paid any attention to her. She tried to convince herself she was imagining it all, but there was one moment, when she cut through Green Park, that she could've sworn she saw Marcus leaning against a tree, his black eyes following her.

Her sides ached from running. The trip back to Hyde Park seemed to take longer today. She cut over the arched bridge that stretched across the Serpentine, glancing down at the brown water flowing lazily below. Today, the air was filled with the sounds and flight of a wide variety of birds. A pair of black swans rode the current, their regal necks stretched in a graceful arch as if they owned the place. She headed for the area known as the Ring, where Rieker had told her she could find Larkin.

Surrounded by trees, the Ring was a huge oval expanse with a wide gravel trail that wound around the perimeter. Tiki cautiously entered the area. Given how cold the air was and how unpredictable the weather had been lately, she was surprised by the number of people strolling around the path. Several couples were near her, following the lane under the canopy of trees. One woman recoiled when she turned to find a young boy in dirty clothes standing so close to her.

A surge of irritation shot through Tiki. What would this woman think if she knew this same dirty orphan had shared tea with a prince of England just yesterday?

The woman's eyes narrowed and she swept Tiki from head to toe with a cold gaze.

"Scoot along now, child," her companion replied, moving his hand in a shooing motion. "We've no pennies to spare today. Go do your begging elsewhere."

Tiki moved on, scanning faces for someone who reminded her of Larkin. But she couldn't see anyone out of the ordinary. Most of the people she passed in the park avoided her eyes, fearful that she would beg for coin or bread. She continued walking and searching, checking shadows under trees, until her legs were shaking.

Exhausted, Tiki sank onto a bench. Had Rieker been wrong? Maybe he'd just said he could contact Larkin here at the Ring to make her feel better. Her mind drifted to thoughts of Rieker, of Wills, his chiseled features so clear in her mind. How easily he had joked with Prince Leo and Prince Arthur. How comfortable he had seemed in their presence. And why wouldn't he be? He'd known them since he was a child.

Images of those opulent rooms, the rich fabric of their

clothing, the easy way they discussed the horses and houses they owned, skipped through her mind. A pressure in her chest built and twisted until the truth hit her with a sinking realization.

She was jealous.

Jealous that the princes and Rieker *had* a home, a family, someone who cared for them and took care of them. *That* was the reason she had gotten so mad at Rieker in the carriage.

She wanted what he had.

The discovery was unsettling, and Tiki pushed away from the bench, feeling the need to move again. To move away from these feelings that were making her uncomfortable.

But she did have a family, she told herself. Just a different kind of family. And she needed to focus on the reason she was here. To find Clara.

Tiki pulled a biscuit from her pocket and picked nervously at the edges of the hard bread. She was hungry, but the bread tasted like sawdust in her mouth. Her stomach was jumping with nerves. Part of her just wanted to shout Larkin's name at the top of her lungs over and over.

Instead, she continued along the path, her eyes searching the shadows beginning to form under the trees as twilight settled. Should she just start asking everyone in the park? Was there a certain spot she should find? After another thirty minutes with no success, she spied a stone bench tucked away by itself under a hawthorn tree and dropped down to rest and think.

"I 'eard ye're lookin' for me."

Tiki jumped to her feet. Larkin's hair was wild and tangled together like a tuft of yellow grass, much different from the perfectly coiffed ringlets of the girl she'd seen in Charing Cross. There was something untamed about her beauty now, as though the forces of nature had collaborated to create her perfect features. But her blue green eyes reminded Tiki of the bottles containing poison in Mr. Lloyd's shop.

"Wills' been talkin', has he?"

"L-Larkin?" Tiki stuttered. "He thought you might know something about . . . about a little girl named Clara who went missing from the Great Ormond Street Hospital."

She inhaled, and the tantalizing aroma of dried summer grass mixed with the scent of earth baked hard in the heat of the sun filled her head. The smell reminded Tiki of her childhood and made her ache with longing.

"Did Wills send you?"

Tiki eyed the girl next to her. Larkin was without a coat and dressed in short sleeves as though it were summer, seemingly unaffected by the chill December air. She was a little taller than Tiki and looked several years older, but her skin was the color of fresh cream and her hair shone like a shaft of golden sunlight. She was as beautiful as any person Tiki had ever seen.

"Rieker didn't know I was coming," Tiki said.

"Ooch, ain't you the brave one," Larkin snickered. She moved with a fluid grace, as though her feet barely had to touch the ground to support her.

Tiki ignored her comment. "Do you know where Clara is?"

"Maybes I do and maybes I don't." Larkin danced a little jig next to Tiki, her long green skirts flaring with her movement, revealing her bare feet. The other girl put her face close to Tiki's, her expression suddenly serious. "Have you got the ring?"

Tiki leaned away and fought the anger that welled in her throat. "Is Clara all right?"

Larkin shrugged and danced away in front of Tiki to twirl in a full circle, her skirt dancing with her. "She's alive." For a split second, Tiki could have sworn she saw wings on the back of the girl; then the fleeting impression was gone.

"Where is she?"

"I can't tell you that," Larkin replied.

"Why not?"

"Because it's a secret." The blond girl looked over at Tiki and gave her an innocent smile that did little to hide the malice behind it.

"What do you want?" Tiki asked in frustration. She wanted to shake the other girl. "Give her back to me. She's sick, and someone needs to take care of her."

"And I already told you, guttersnipe"—the words came out as sharp as a dagger—"I want the ring." Larkin's eyes were ice cold and hard as stone. Tiki sensed the very real threat.

"Why do you think I can give you the ring?" Tiki held her hands out in supplication. "What if I don't have it?"

Larkin twirled away from her again, humming a soft tune, her wild mass of hair flying behind her, her bare arms held out to the side. She danced like a child at a summer picnic. The way Clara might, if she were well.

The blond girl stopped twirling abruptly, her skirts swinging one way and then back the other around her ankles, her eyes locked on Tiki. She snarled then, looking almost feral, her lips curled back from sharp white teeth.

"Then you better find it." In a heartbeat, Larkin's face was mere inches from Tiki's. "And tell my Wills I'm getting tired of waiting." Something in her eyes, an emotion Tiki couldn't name, smoldered. "Maybe he can help you get the ring."

"*Your* Wills?" Tiki repeated.

"Bring me the ring." Larkin twirled away and came to a stop. Her strange eyes were fixed on Tiki. "And I'll bring you the brat." Her flawless face was so beautiful that Tiki didn't want to look away.

Tiki gritted her teeth. "Fine. Then where shall I meet you?"

"Bring the ring here." Larkin's lips curled in warning. "Meet me at twilight tomorrow. And there's one last thing." Tiki stepped back from the threatening gleam in Larkin's eyes. "Don't ever forget that Wills is *mine*."

Chapter Twenty-nine

Wills *is mine*. Larkin's possessive words echoed in Tiki's ears as she sat on a bench in Charing Cross the next morning. The dangerous girl who danced outside in December in bare feet was never far from her thoughts.

Tiki's restless nerves had pushed her out of their room early. She needed to *do* something. To keep trying to find a way to negotiate with Larkin for Clara's release. But there seemed to be only one answer. Trade the queen's ring for Clara.

Now, the same question kept drumming through her head: How was she going to find a way back into the palace to get the ring? Rieker's connection to Prince Leopold seemed like the only plausible way for her to get into the narrow alcove where the ring was hidden. Despite her mixed feelings, she *needed* him right now.

As if conjured from her thoughts, a low voice spoke in her ear.

"We need to talk."

Tiki eyed the sky overhead, shivering with cold. The flat gray clouds were weighted with snow. By the cool bite of the air, there could be lots of it. She and Rieker were alone on the path along the lake in St. James's Park, the weather too harsh for most people to wander outside. Rieker had been silent as they left the railway station, and Tiki debated which questions to ask him first.

"Tell me about Larkin," she finally said. She glanced up at him. "Tell me the truth." His dark hair hung long below his collar, and he seemed more distant than usual, walking with his shoulders hunched inside his coat. "How long have you known her?"

Rieker looked down at her, his smoky eyes a strange reflection of the sky. His defined cheekbones and strong jaw made Tiki realize that neatly groomed Wills and wild, unpredictable Rieker had blended into one person in her mind. When she looked at him now, she only saw his handsome face. She understood why Larkin was in love with him.

He took a deep breath, as though gathering courage. "I have to start before Larkin." His words were low and heavy, as if they were stones and it took an effort to force each one out of his mouth.

Tiki frowned, confused.

"Our fight the other day forced me to think about things I've tried to avoid for a long time." There was something dark in his tone that made Tiki nervous, unsure of what was coming. "I shouldn't have stormed out of the carriage like I did, but your words made me angry," Rieker said. "It took a lot of walking and thinking before I realized that you couldn't possibly know what an impact they would have on me."

"Why is that?" Tiki asked in a small, guilty voice.

Rieker looked sideways at her, his eyes almost raw in their honesty. "Because you don't know the truth."

Tiki's heart skipped a beat. "The truth about what?"

He slid his hands into his pockets and stared at the

frozen ground as they walked. "My family was murdered," he said. "I have lived alone now, for over two years." His voice faltered and he lifted his gaze to the distance as he cleared his throat. "At first, I struggled just to find a reason to stay alive. Then I found a family of sorts, on the streets of London. Found a purpose again." He turned to look at her with a strange intensity that seemed to envelop her, as if he had wrapped his arms around her. "And then. . . ." He paused. "I found you."

Tiki's heart skipped with an unfamiliar rhythm.

"The first time I saw you, you were picking pockets in Charing Cross. I had heard about you. The boy with hands so quick you'd never been caught." He nodded at her surprised expression. "You have quite a name among pickpockets. I was curious, so I started watching you."

Tiki swallowed hard. "You were watching me?"

"Well, following you, really," Rieker admitted with a wry grin. "It was quite a shock when the bobby ripped your coat off in King's Cross that day and I realized that the boy with the quick hands was really a girl." He chuckled under his breath. "*That* was a surprise."

He hunched his shoulders again. "The more I watched, the more curious I became. You weren't what you appeared to be at all." They walked in silence for a minute. "You've made me look at myself in ways I've not done in years, and I've come to realize that I need to rethink my own life."

Tiki didn't know what to say. Rieker admitted that he'd been following her. This was not what she'd expected from him. "I don't know what you mean," she said quietly.

"You're not just a pickpocket with fast hands." Rieker's eyes locked on hers. "I found a girl caring for other orphans like a mother. A girl who'd befriended an old bookshop keeper who had lost his only daughter. A girl who can read and is helping others learn to read." His voice softened. "And a girl so beautiful at times, you take my breath away."

Tiki averted her eyes and hoped the dim light would shadow the blush creeping up her cheeks. "Is that why you were at the World's End that night?"

Rieker nodded. "But I wasn't the only one. Marcus was there, too." His face darkened at the memory. "I'm not sure if it was when you tried to pick MacGregor's pocket just to prove me wrong or after Marcus attacked you that I realized I had more than a passing interest in you." He looked away as though suddenly embarrassed by his revelation.

Rieker had an interest in *her*?

"And now," he continued, "I realize that I can't go on as I have. Not trusting. Not caring. It's time for me to regain my life and deal with the past." He stopped and turned to face her, his eyes dark and fathomless. "I need to be honest with you and tell you the whole truth."

Unsure of what to expect, Tiki waited, her heart drumming inside her chest as though it were a hollow kettle.

"It's taken me a long time to figure it out, but I've finally realized that things started going wrong when Larkin came into my life several years ago." Rieker put his head down and began walking again. "As you now know, I grew up in a moneyed family. We had a big house. My father owned land, and we were friends with those in power."

He gave a little shrug of his shoulders. "I took it for granted. I knew no other way of life."

He took a deep breath and raised his gaze to the distance again. "I had two younger brothers." He paused and the muscles in his jaw clenched as he fought for control. "Thomas and James."

Somehow Tiki knew that he had never spoken of this with anyone before. Without thinking, she slipped her hand up under his elbow and gave his arm a squeeze, leaving her hand to rest there. She could feel him press his arm close to his side to hold her hand in place, and they walked on in silence.

After a few moments, Rieker cleared his throat and started again. "Two years ago, my entire family drowned as we crossed the Channel on our way to Paris for the Christmas holidays." He didn't falter, yet there was a brittleness about his words, as though they might shatter and break like a dropped piece of glass. "I've been running away from that moment ever since."

"I'm so sorry," Tiki whispered. A sadness pressed down on her chest. She had been wrong to think Rieker had so much more than she.

"Save your sympathy. I've found rather than helping, sympathy complicates things. Picking one's self up and plodding through the next day is the only cure that seems to work for me." He gave her a bitter smile. "Besides, I'm sure you've seen your share of sorrow."

An image of her mother and father, always so close yet so far away, flashed before Tiki's eyes. Rieker was right. It hurt to remember the life she'd had before.

"After the . . . a-accident"—Rieker stumbled over the word—"I couldn't stay at home. Everywhere I looked, there were memories of my family. Especially my younger brothers. They were all around me, yet I was alone. So unbearably alone." He threw back his head and took a deep breath, exhaling a cloud of white smoke before he plunged ahead.

"I wasn't really old enough to take over running the estate. My father had employees who did that. There was no place I was needed. I was lost. I couldn't stay home, but I had nowhere to go. Then one day I was in London and a filthy little boy tried to pick my pocket."

Rieker's lips curved at the memory. "My first thought was that it was my brother Jimmy. It was a game we played often as children. I turned, expecting to see his grinning face, and instead found this scrawny, dirty, frightened boy dressed in rags staring at me." Rieker shrugged. "He ran, I followed and found a new life."

Tiki was afraid to interrupt for fear he would stop talking. It was hard to imagine Rieker, so tough and resilient, ever being frightened or feeling lonely.

"At first, I came and went. It was a game. Something that took me away from the pain of being home. But then I began to see the need of these children. Some of them were literally starving to death. So I came home less and less, sleeping where these children did—in railway stations, in back alleys, abandoned buildings, under bridges. Helping them find food in a way that wouldn't have them end up in jail. Sometimes I just bought the food and told them I had stolen it."

Tiki nodded, pretending not to be surprised at his generosity. She was only too aware of her own constant struggle to find enough food for herself and her family of orphans.

"That's when I met Kieran," Rieker continued. "I

thought at first that I had found him, but later I realized that he had carefully placed himself in my path to make me think that."

Tiki stumbled over a tree root in the path and clutched Rieker's sleeve. "Who is Kieran?"

"An old man. He'd been injured in a fight of some sort, and his wounds hadn't healed. I suspect now that he knew he was dying. He was living on the streets and barely able to survive. I felt sorry for him, so I helped him." Rieker paused. He gazed out across the park, lost in memories. "I think he came to warn me."

"Warn you of what?"

"Of Donegal and his dark court. Of Larkin. Of the past." Rieker's voice was bitter. "Of the future."

Tiki's pulse quickened. "What are you talking about?"

"There's a battle for control that wages within the world of the fey. Between the Seelie court and those that fell from grace and formed the UnSeelie court." His voice was low and dark. "Eridanus was a formidable king of the Seelie court, but when Eridanus was murdered, the battle intensified."

"Did you know about this war before your family . . ." Tiki's words died in her throat.

"No." Rieker shook his head. "Though in retrospect, I'd say my father knew. Some of the things he said, some of the things he did. I see now they were to protect us. But I had no idea until Kieran started explaining it to me. A lot of what he told me didn't make sense at the time, but now"—he looked down at her—"now, more of it is tying together."

Tiki pictured Larkin dancing in bare feet in the chill of December. Imagined the wild swing of emotions across the beautiful girl's face last night. "So how does Larkin fit into all of this?"

Rieker took a deep breath. "Larkin was responsible for the deaths of my family."

Chapter Thirty

THE words dropped like stones into a still pond, a wave of emotion moving like ripples across the surface of Rieker's face.

Tiki jerked to a stop. "What did you say?"

Rieker's eyes were as dead and black as a piece of coal. "Larkin is part of the UnSeelie court. The dark court. That's one of the things that Kieran was trying to tell me. Trying to warn me about. But they murdered him, too."

A wave of dread washed over Tiki as she imagined little Clara in the grasp of the beautiful girl. "But why do you suspect Larkin? I thought you said your family drowned."

"The first time I saw Larkin she had come through the woods to our estate. She told me that she lived nearby. Though there were no other houses close, as we owned hundreds of acres, she had a horse so I didn't really question it. For months, on and off, she would appear. It was always when I was outside and alone, almost as if she knew I was there." His voice became dark and bitter.

"I saw Larkin the day before we left for Paris." Rieker's words came out low and intense. "I met her in the forest that surrounds our land. Our dog had disappeared into the trees and I was trying to find him. Instead, I happened upon Larkin. She said her horse had spooked at a snake and bucked her off before running away. I didn't suspect anything. She was very pretty and . . ." His words died off, and he gave Tiki a guilty look.

"I feel foolish now," he continued, "but she wanted me to walk her back through the woods to her estate." Rieker took a deep breath. "Even though I knew there were no houses close, I probably would have if Jimmy hadn't come yelling toward the woods right then, looking for me to come home for supper. Larkin hurried away and disappeared before he reached us. I don't think he even saw her."

Rieker started walking again, and Tiki hurried to keep up with him. "We left the next day for Paris. That night"— his voice dropped again, almost to a whisper—"the night of the storm, the night of the . . ." His voice died off, as though his memories overpowered his ability to speak.

Tiki's heart pounded a little harder, and she dreaded for him to say the words.

"Our boat was taking on water," he started again. "We were all up on deck, clinging to the rails. It was so black and cold. The wind was howling, and the waves kept crashing over the side, making it impossible to see. The salt water burned my eyes. Choked me." Rieker's eyes were unfocused, and Tiki knew that he was seeing that awful night again.

"After a while, I realized I was alone. The deck became pitched at a steep angle as the boat took on more water and listed to the side. My arms and legs were so heavy, it was as though there were ropes tied to them, and someone was trying to pull me down into the water. I didn't think I could hold on any longer, and then *she* was there, on the boat with me." He gave Tiki a quick glance to see if she understood. "Larkin. She wrapped my arms around the railings and held me there. *She* kept my head above water until a rescue boat got there." His whisper died away, and he stared into the distance, seeing his memory. "I was the only survivor."

"She saved you?" Tiki asked in surprise.

"If that's what you want to call it. All I know for sure is that she was the one who kept me out of the water," Rieker replied. "When I came to, I asked about the blond girl, but nobody else had seen her. They all thought I was hallucinating from the shock."

"Could you have been?"

"No." Rieker shook his head. "She was there."

"Why did she save you, if she murdered the rest of your family?"

"Kieran said she had been ordered by Donegal to murder my family but she didn't let me drown because she had *grá do dhuine básmhar.* He said that she had been watching me for a long time."

"*Grá do* what? What does that mean?"

Rieker's lips tightened. "He said it meant love for a mortal."

Suddenly the memory of Clara's little voice when Tiki was telling them the story of Tam Lin rang clear in Tiki's ears: *Can faeries and humans fall in love?*

Tiki choked back a gasp. "A faerie is in love with you?" A sting of jealousy burned through her, but his words didn't surprise her. In truth, she already knew that Larkin was in love with him. And he knew it, too.

"I don't know." Rieker looked uncomfortable. "That's what Kieran said."

Tiki wondered at the pained expression on his face, and a new thought struck her. Was Rieker in love with Larkin?

"You must be flattered." Tiki tried to keep her voice even. "You'd better be careful, though, or she'll steal you away to her world just like the Faerie Queen stole Tam Lin."

Rieker scowled at her. "There's more to it than that. This isn't some tale out of a storybook, Tiki. She wants something from me." His words were short and clipped. "At first I didn't know what it was. But now I do. She thinks because I grew up with Leo and Arthur, because I have access to Buckingham Palace, that I can get her the ring. I suspect that's been her plan all along."

A twinge of guilt shot through Tiki. Why would she say something like that after Rieker had just told her that Larkin had murdered his family? Tiki nodded. "That's what she told me, too. That maybe you could help me get the ring."

Rieker raised his head in surprise. "When did she tell you that?"

"Last night."

Rieker grabbed Tiki's arm, forcing her to look at him. "You went out by yourself and found Larkin?"

"I wanted to know if she had Clara or not." Tiki was tempted to jerk her arm free, but she resisted. "You were the one who told me we could find her in Hyde Park. I couldn't just sit there and do nothing."

"When I told you about the Ring, I didn't think you'd be daft enough to go there by yourself." His body was rigid with disbelief.

"She is breathtaking to look at. Her beauty is mesmerizing," Tiki said. "So much so that you just want to stare at her. But there's something not quite right about her. She was barefoot and in a short-sleeve dress like she thought it was summer. She didn't seem to feel the cold."

Rieker released her arm. "Faeries aren't affected by our seasons. They don't measure the passage of time like we do. In the Otherworld it is always *now*. For those of the Seelie court, it is always as warm as summer in the space they inhabit," Rieker said. "Kieran told me that."

"One time I thought I saw wings. Beautiful, iridescent wings like a dragonfly's. But it was only for a split second while she was twirling. Then she snarled at me like a vicious animal that wanted to rip me apart." Tiki shuddered at the memory. "I think she was jealous. She called you 'my Wills.'" As she repeated the words, an uncomfortable sensation clawed at her chest.

Rieker stiffened beside her. When he spoke, his voice was so low that she had to lean close to hear him.

"I didn't pay attention to a lot of Kieran's ramblings because I thought he was delirious at the time. So much of it didn't make sense, I just let him talk to humor him." His breath came out in white puffs as he spoke. "Some of it I still don't understand."

They came to a fork in the path and stopped, standing close together under the canopy of bare limbs. Snowflakes drifted down from the sky like white feathers.

"So you were helping Kieran survive, but really he was there to help you?" Tiki pulled her coat tighter around her waist to ward off the chill air.

Rieker nodded. "I think so. I didn't realize until after the ring was stolen what some of the things Kieran told me meant. He told me that unless I had the ring, or the royals had the ring, then the fey could attack mortals. And that they would attack those that matter the most to me." His eyes fell on hers, and Tiki once again felt as though he had embraced her. "At the time, I didn't realize there would be anyone else they could take from me that would matter."

He reached up and ran a finger along her jaw, his eyes dark. "I can't bear to lose anyone else," he whispered.

Her eyes traced the contours of his face, the sculpted cheekbones, the straight nose, and the cut of his strong jaw. A few strands of his long, dark hair had been caught by the wind and blown against his face. Without thinking, she reached up and smoothed the strands away from his skin, wishing she could smooth away the pain etched there.

Rieker lowered his head toward her. Tiki leaned into him, the physical pull between them more than she could deny. She rested her hand on his chest, a sudden yearning filling her. His fingers slipped behind her head as his lips descended on hers, warm and urgent, as though he wanted to claim her before she was snatched from him.

Tiki wasn't prepared for the onslaught to her senses. The smell of his skin, the warmth of his lips, the insistent pressure of his fingers against her neck, pulling her closer. All of it sent a craving through her body that she'd never experienced before. She'd known love, but this was something different. This was desire.

"Tiki." Rieker pulled back, his eyes locked on something in the distance. His voice was suddenly tight, sending a warning chill down her spine.

"What?"

"Run as fast as you can and hide. Go back to Charing Cross." He shoved her behind him. "I'll meet you later."

"Why?" Tiki swiveled her head around to identify the unknown danger.

"Run! Now! I think that rider is Leo."

Tiki jerked in the direction he was looking and spied a lone horse and rider headed their direction at an alarming rate. "Damn." Why *now*? The prince's big black horse was recognizable, even if the prince's features weren't.

She didn't hesitate. She flew down the path, headed for the nearest tree to disappear behind, fear fueling her departure. Dressed as the street urchin that she was, Leo would certainly recognize her this time, both as Elizabeth and as the ragged boy he'd met in the park. Especially if he insisted on seeing her wrist. She feared he would arrest her straightaway.

Tiki didn't slow down until she emerged at the far end of the park and crossed over Whitehall Road. There, she mingled with the crowd, her sides heaving from the exertion, sweat beaded above cheeks made rosy from the chill air. Leo! She knew that he often rode in St. James's Park, but to be there today when there was no one else but them? What rotten luck! Had he recognized Rieker? And even more important, had the prince seen her?

Chapter Thirty-one

LEO stood up in the stirrups to stretch the muscles in his legs that were beginning to fatigue. His brain, on the other hand, felt as if it were on fire. What luck! The man walking alone on the path before him looked to be Wills. He knew his friend often walked great distances to wrestle with the ghosts of his past. Leo urged Diablo faster, not willing to let this opportunity get away.

"Wills!" Leo hailed the young man, hoping to catch his eye. The other man had turned down a fork in the path heading away, but Leo turned Diablo across the field and headed straight for him.

Hearing his name, Rieker stopped and waited as the prince approached.

"Hello, Leo, what a pleasant surprise. From a distance that beast reminded me of your devil horse."

"What luck!" Leo pulled abreast of Wills as Diablo stamped and snorted clouds of smoke into the cool air, his sides heaving. "I've just come from your town house."

"Really?" Rieker asked. "And was I there?"

"Funny." Leo threw a leg over and dismounted. He walked around Diablo's head and grabbed the reins, walking the horse to cool him down. Rieker fell in beside him. "Are you alone?" Leo glanced over his shoulder. "I thought I saw you talking with someone."

"Yes, quite alone. A street urchin was begging for spare change."

"Anyone you knew?"

Rieker eyed the prince. "What's that supposed to mean?"

Leo nodded at Rieker's clothes. "You're dressed a bit like one yourself today."

Rieker shot a glance at the sky. "Didn't see any reason to ruin perfectly good clothes walking in this weather. What are you about?"

"There's something suspicious going on, Wills. I think you need to be aware of the circumstances." Leo gazed at his friend. "Tell me what you know about Elizabeth."

"Elizabeth?"

"Yes." Leo's voice was tinged with excitement. "Elizabeth Dunbar. I want to know everything you know about her."

"Ah." Rieker slid his hands into his pockets and hunched his shoulders. "The lovely Elizabeth." He turned his dark head away and followed the path of two boys through the park. "She's an interesting creature, Leo, I'll give you that."

Leo rubbed the smooth leather of the reins between his fingers. That didn't sound good. He'd known Wills his entire life. Handsome and kind, his tall, dark-haired friend always had the girls twittering when he came around.

"What do you mean, 'creature'?" Leo asked. Did Wills have any idea of Elizabeth's double life?

Rieker laughed. "She has her moods, Leo. One minute sweet and nice, like a lovable little kitten, the next she'd give you a pop in the jaw if you say the wrong thing."

"Oh. You sound like you know her well." Leo had fallen

in and out of love several times, and rather painfully once or twice, but as far as he knew, Wills had never given his heart to another. There were times when he wondered if Wills would ever *allow* himself to fall in love. But now, to fall in love with someone who might be a thief? He had to warn his friend.

"Sometimes I think I know her as well as I know myself. We think the same way about many things," Rieker said. "Then there are other times when she's a complete mystery."

"That's it exactly. There's a mystery about that girl." Leo was unsmiling as he looked at his friend. "I'll tell you something, if you can promise to keep it to yourself. Something I think you need to know."

Rieker looked over at Leo. "Your secrets have always been safe with me, Leo. You know that."

Leo nodded. "And it's a gift I'm grateful for. Arthur can get a little monotonous in his need to always be the older brother now and give me advice."

"So what is it you want to share?"

"You've heard that one of Mother's rings was stolen, no doubt?"

"Yes, I'm aware of the ring gone missing."

"What you might not know is that the stolen ring is quite old. It's rumored to have a connection to the world of the fey." He checked Wills's reaction.

"The fey?"

"The world of Faerie." He held up his hand. "Don't laugh. I didn't believe it at first, either, but there have been *things* that are occurring . . . consequences . . . it's enough to make a person believe." Leo stopped as Diablo put his head down to pull at a tuft of grass.

"But that's not what I want to warn you of. It's *who* I think is involved in the theft of the ring that's the problem."

Rieker faced Leo. "And who might that be?"

"Elizabeth."

Rieker smiled, as if amused at the idea.

"Have you seen the mark on her arm?"

"I have, Leo. It's a birthmark, I believe."

"A birthmark that is associated with the fey." Leo paused to let his words sink in. Then he continued in a low voice, "Just like the ring. Which makes perfect sense, because the missing ring holds a truce with the faeries." Leo's voice rose with excitement. "One they'd like to destroy."

"Truce?" Rieker cocked his head to look at Leo. "Are we at war? Perhaps Elizabeth is a spy."

"I'm not joking, Wills." Leo's tone was sharp. "Elizabeth is more than what she appears to be. Shortly after the ring was stolen, I met a beggar boy here in the park. I thought I saw him with something." Leo gestured, causing his horse to jerk his head back. "It could have been Mother's ring. And listen to this: He had the same mark on his wrist as Elizabeth."

Rieker seemed unimpressed. "Do you think the boy was her brother?"

"Brother?" Leo cried. "No, I think it was *Elizabeth*. That's why I dropped my wineglass the night of the ball. I *recognized* her."

Rieker tilted his head back and laughed out loud. "That's a good one, Leo. Did it take you long to think this up? Tell me, do you think Elizabeth was disguised as a beggar or the beggar was disguised as Elizabeth?" Tears of laughter glistened in the corners of his eyes as he waited for Leo's response.

"Laugh all you want, but a ransom note was delivered for the ring. It was written in exactly the manner I had discussed with Elizabeth. We've talked of having her arrested. That's how sure we are that she's involved in this."

"Arrested?" Rieker's laughter dissolved into an angry frown. "You can't be serious. Did you pay the reward?"

"Well, no. But—"

Rieker jerked away and walked down the path, his shoulders rigid with anger. Leo pulled Diablo's head and hurried to catch up.

"I'm trying to warn you, Wills. At the ball, after I danced with Elizabeth, all she wanted to talk about was the ring. I don't even know how she knew of its existence, let alone its disappearance."

Rieker glanced over at him. "You think Elizabeth stole your mother's ring? Is that it?"

"Yes," Leo said grudgingly. "There's something suspicious about her. I can *feel* it. And that mark . . ."

Rieker snorted in disgust. "I'd like to see Elizabeth dressed like a beggar boy. She looked enchantingly feminine to me at the ball." He slid his hands into his pockets and kicked angrily at a pile of leaves. "Why didn't you pay the reward?"

Leo hesitated.

"Well?"

"The thief's note said that the ring was hidden in the palace." Leo threw his hands in the air. "They wanted us to leave the money without even giving us the ring in return."

Rieker jerked to a stop and turned to face the prince.

Leo took a step back at the scowl on his friend's face. "Let me get this straight. The ring is in the palace, yet you want to charge Elizabeth with stealing it? Are you completely mad?"

"Yes, well . . ." Leo forced a laugh. "You have a point. But I wanted you to be aware of our suspicions. I can't tell you the hours I've spent pondering the whole situation. How could two people have an identical mark as unusual as that unless they are one and the same? And by the way . . ." He turned his scrutiny to Rieker again. "Was Elizabeth your guest? I didn't see her name on the guest list."

"Yes, she came with me."

"Then why did you introduce yourself to her?"

Rieker gave Leo a stern look. "Now you'll have to keep one of my secrets. It was, shall we say, a private joke?" He smiled. "She was nervous about not knowing anyone, and I told her I would introduce her to several handsome men. So I introduced myself to her." Rieker cleared his throat. "Several times."

"Ah . . ." Leo nodded. "You do care for her. I'd recommend caution, then, until you can verify the truth."

Rieker let out a sigh of exasperation. "Leo, she is an enchanting young lady. I don't need to 'verify the truth.' I believe she is everything she says she is."

"Yes, well, be that as it may, you need to be careful, my friend."

They walked along in silence for a bit before Leo spoke again. "How are you doing? I know this is a difficult time of year for you."

Rieker exhaled. "I walk a lot and fight back the memories. Each year it's a bit easier, I think."

Leo rested his hand on the side of his black horse.

"You know, I went and saw Mamie the other day. You remember her, the woman who has tended Mother all these years?"

"Of course I remember Mamie. The witch woman."

Leo nodded. "Yes. That's the one." He looked up at Wills. "She often asks about you. Even after all these years."

"Really? Why do you suppose that is? I'm surprised she even remembers me."

"You spent a lot of time around us when we were younger. I think your family's accident came as quite a shock to her, as it did to all of us." He shook his head as though to shake the sad memories away. "She's always been particularly concerned about your welfare. Anyway, I drew a picture of the mark on Elizabeth's arm and asked her if she'd ever seen such a thing before." Leo's voice dropped to a whisper. "She recognized it immediately. Called it *fáinne* something. A Gaelic term." He snapped his fingers. "*An fáinne sí*. She told me it was the mark of the faerie ring. Supposedly comes from a line of the fey who were said to have died out centuries ago. Quite rare, apparently."

Rieker's lips wavered at the corners. "And do you believe that the mark makes Elizabeth a faerie?"

Leo didn't smile. "Well, there is quite a history to the ring that was stolen, and it's said to be linked to the faeries. I'll tell you, Wills, there is more than meets the eye to this thing. And I'm quite concerned about Mother's health. Her fever continues unabated, yet she shivers as though chilled. Her bones seem to ache without cause, and her fatigue keeps her in bed constantly. She continues to deteriorate."

"Well, I thank you for informing me of your suspicions," Rieker said, clearly ending the conversation. "I'll proceed with caution."

There was a long moment of silence.

"I hope you do," Leo replied. "I'm telling you this for your own good, Wills. I don't wish any additional heartache to come your way. You've had more than your share." He pulled a watch from inside his jacket and glanced at the time. "I need to get back. Let's keep this conversation between ourselves for now." Leo walked around Diablo and pulled himself into the saddle. "Come by tonight. Arthur and I and a few chums are playing cards. Can you join us?"

"I'll do my best to be there. What time?"

"Come at eight." Leo looked down from atop Diablo as the horse pawed at the dirt, ready to run again. "By the way, I found your cousin to be charming and exquisitely beautiful. Were she not married, I would ask your permission to call on her."

"My cousin?" Rieker gave Leo a puzzled frown.

"Of course. When I went up to your town house this morning, she was there. Beautiful girl with those golden ringlets. Nice of you to invite her to care for her sick daughter there."

Chapter Thirty-two

TIKI paced around the room again, her fingers tapping a nervous rhythm on her crossed arms. Where was Rieker? It had been hours since she'd left him in the park. She hadn't had a chance to tell him that she needed the ring by twilight *tonight*. She was so anxious, she felt as though she were going to be sick.

The information he'd shared about his past and about why he was at Charing Cross churned inside her. She couldn't escape the images of Rieker alone in the water, of his family drowning. Her chest ached at the thought of him coming home to an empty house with nothing but memories haunting the rooms like ghosts.

When her parents had died, she'd had no choice but to move, to go to her aunt and uncle's. Then she'd been forced to run from there. Her day-to-day world had been filled with survival, which had blunted the pain of her loss over her family. But Rieker . . . he'd gone back to the same life, the same home—one that would never, could never, be the same again.

She stopped and closed her eyes, imagining Rieker's lips on hers. The hunger she'd felt had been real, compelling, pulling her to him. She couldn't deny the burning desire she'd had to wrap her arms around him and hold him close. A cry of despair escaped her lips. When had she fallen in love with him?

"Calm down," Shamus said from his seat by the stove where he sat watching Tiki pace. "He'll be back. The prince won't do anything to Rieker."

Tiki shot him an uneasy glance, then resumed her pacing. They were running out of time. Larkin could harm Clara the way she'd harmed Rieker's family. She turned and paced the other direction. She needed the ring now. She would have to trust Rieker. Tiki hurried over to the peephole and peered out into the station for any sign of him. Where was he?

THE snow continued to fall as the day dragged by. Tiki was afraid to head into the station for fear she'd miss Rieker. She worked with Toots on learning his letters for a while, but as the afternoon wore on, both Toots and Fiona begged her to leave.

"You're a bit cranky," Fiona complained from her corner where she had retreated and was curled up looking at the pictures in a book Tiki had brought her from Mr. Potts's shop. "Go pick some pockets. That'll give you somethin' to do besides pace."

Their conversation was interrupted when the back door slid open and Rieker stepped into the room. The wave of relief that flooded over Tiki was so palpable, she thought her knees would sag.

"Where have you been?" she asked. His dark eyes locked on hers, but he didn't smile. His mood was very different from when they were in the park. His defenses were up again, the walls in place, and he was the Rieker of old.

"I got word of Larkin." He was wet from the snow, his

dark hair plastered to his scalp. He stepped near the warmth of the stove.

"And?" Tiki asked. She hurried toward him, wringing her hands anxiously.

Shamus sat up straighter. "What did you hear?"

Fiona put her picture book down and stared hopefully across the room.

"She's been keeping Clara in a house up in the West End. In the Mayfair area. The owner comes and goes for business. He's gone for weeks at a time, and apparently she showed up and claimed to be kin."

Tiki's shoulders sagged for a moment at his confirmation that Larkin held the child. Even though she'd known there was no place else Clara could be, she'd held a shred of hope that Larkin was bluffing. "How'd you find that out?" she asked.

"I ran into someone who had visited the house," Rieker said. "I knew it was Larkin from the description they gave. I'm going there straightaway. Larkin can't keep Clara outside overnight. It's too cold. That means she should be there tonight."

"Did they see Clara?" Tiki bit the corner of her lip, her heart pounding uncomfortably. "Is she all right?"

"I don't think they saw Clara. Just Larkin, but she said something to alert them that she was caring for a sick child." He put an arm around Tiki's shoulders and gave her a squeeze. "We'll get her home."

For a second, Tiki wanted to give in and lean against his strength. Instead, she clutched at his lapels. "I need the ring by twilight tonight." Her words were rushed. "Larkin said she would trade."

Rieker peeled her hands away from his jacket. "Sit

down, Tiki. I have a way into Buckingham tonight, but we need to talk first."

She sank into one of the rickety chairs, a nervous anticipation bubbling in her stomach. "How are you getting into the palace?" she asked.

"Leo's having a card game. I'm invited."

"You've been invited to Buckingham Palace?" Shamus asked in disbelief.

Tiki and Rieker both looked over at him as if they'd forgotten he was in the room.

"I'll explain it later, Shamus," Tiki said. She turned back to Rieker. "Go on."

"Actually, I think it's more accurate to say I've been commanded to be there." He pulled the other chair close, facing her. Shamus and Fiona hunkered down near the stove, while Toots manned his post at the peephole. But every eye in the place was on Rieker.

"Tiki, you never told me what you and Larkin talked about last night." His gaze didn't waver. "I need you to tell me now before I go talk to her."

Everyone's eyes turned to Tiki. She took a deep breath and focused on speaking calmly. "Larkin said she wanted to trade Clara for the ring, just like you said she would."

Rieker didn't seem surprised. "But the ring is still hidden in Buckingham, isn't it?" At Tiki's nod, he leaned forward to rest his elbows on his knees. "What else did she say?"

"At first, she asked where you were and I told her you didn't know I was coming. Then she asked me for the ring. When I told her I didn't have it, she said to ask you." Tiki rubbed her sweating palms along her thighs. "And that was it. She just said to bring the ring back to her in Hyde Park by twilight tonight and she would bring Clara."

Rieker stood and Tiki jumped up, too. "Why does she think you can get the ring for her?" she asked.

"I'm not sure. Hopefully, I'll find her and get some answers."

TIKI watched silently as Rieker exited through the back door. She stared blankly at the wooden panel after he'd gone. How was she possibly going to sit and wait for him to come back with news? With a start, she realized she couldn't wait. She needed to go with him. She could help Rieker negotiate with Larkin, and maybe there was a chance they could find Clara. The little girl might need her. She grabbed her coat and ran for the back door.

"I'll be back," she said over her shoulder.

"Tiki, wait . . . ," Shamus called, but she slipped through the maintenance tunnels without answering and out into the dim shadows of the alley, tucking her long braid into her coat.

She ran through the alley, dodging the garbage and debris piled up alongside the buildings. She reached the entrance to the alley and scanned the street.

There. Rieker's broad shoulders were visible heading toward the intersection. Tiki cast a quick glance around, then set off after him. He moved quickly, and she had to run to keep up. He turned on the Strand and hailed a hansom cab. As she watched, Rieker climbed into the covered sitting area of the cab and pulled the door closed.

Tiki had to sprint to catch up to the carriage. Pure adrenaline fueled her leap onto the boot. She tucked herself tight against the back of the cab and prayed that she would remain unseen.

The cab went past Trafalgar Square and the four great black statues of Nelson's lions and cut over to Haymarket. They wound around Piccadilly Circus and over to Bond Street. As they headed west, the houses and gardens became bigger and more lavish.

When they turned onto Grosvenor Square, Tiki stared at the beautiful buildings in amazement. So this was Mayfair, where London's wealthiest lived. It was like being in a different world.

The cab pulled to a stop in front of a row of immaculate town houses, their black porches a crisp accent to the white brick. Tiki stayed perfectly still as Rieker exited the cab. She debated when to reveal herself, suddenly unsure if her plan to help would please or anger him. She could hear him talking to the driver as he paid the fare.

"Get up!" the driver cried as he slapped the reins and urged the horses on their way. As the carriage rolled down the street, Tiki watched Rieker climb the steps to Number 6. She rose to a crouch and waited until they had rounded the corner of the square before she timed her jump from the moving cab.

Tiki hurried back past the lush garden that filled the square and worked her way down until she stood in the shadows of the trees across from Number 6. By the time she got back down the street, the front door was closed and there was no sign of Rieker.

Tiki paced back and forth between the trees, plotting how to get in.

Finally she threw caution to the wind. She had to do something. She ran across the street and up the steps. With a shaking hand she lifted the brass knocker, letting it fall hard twice, the metal ringing against the stop. Tiki took several deep breaths, trying to calm her nerves. It was only a few moments before the door swung open. A tall, robust man dressed in the black-and-white apparel of a butler peered down his rather large nose at her.

"Yes?"

She had to think fast. She doubted the man would let someone off the street dressed as she was into his master's affluent town home.

"Good afternoon, sir," Tiki said. "I've got a delivery for a Mrs. Arthur Emerson. Is this the right address?"

His eyes narrowed as he examined her empty hands. "What sort of delivery?"

"Oh." Tiki clapped her hands together. "I don't have it with me at the moment. See, I'm with, um, Binder's Bakery, and we have a . . . um . . . cake delivery to make tomorrow. They sent me on ahead to make sure we had the right house." She smiled up at him. "Don't want the cake to be late for the party."

Tiki tried to peer around the man's sizable girth to see into the house. If she spotted Clara or Rieker, she was going to force her way in. Somehow.

"Yes, well, how very fortunate that you checked," the butler said in a dry tone, "for you do indeed have the wrong address. This is the Richmond residence. Good day." The butler started to swing the door closed, but Tiki threw her hand out to stop him.

"The Richmond residence?" she echoed. "You mean *William* Richmond?"

"Yes. Exactly. William Becker Richmond." His eyes raked over her. "I assume you don't have a cake for him?"

Tiki swayed on her feet. For a second the butler seemed very far away, then he rushed back into focus. "No . . ."

"I thought not. Should you locate your Mrs. Emerson, you might note that she will most probably want her cake delivered to the *back* door. Good day." Then he shut the door as soundlessly as he had opened it.

Tiki reached out to grip the black iron railing to steady herself. This was *Rieker's* house? He lived here, in Mayfair, one of the poshest parts of town? She pushed herself away from the door and stared at the blank windows, hiding the secrets within. This was where Larkin was keeping Clara? It was as though someone had knocked the wind out of her. She sagged against the railing and held tight to the black handrail to hold herself up. Then a blinding rage filled her. Had he known all along? It was all she could do not to pound on the door and demand entry. Demand an explanation.

She drew a shaky breath, trying to steady her nerves. Her stomach turned with an unusual queasiness, and for a minute Tiki thought she was going to be sick. Rieker couldn't be trusted. That much was clear now. She needed a plan. She needed to outsmart him at his own game. Before it was too late.

Larkin is staying in *his* house." Tiki knew that she was bordering on hysteria as evidenced by the shrillness of her voice, but she couldn't help herself. She fought to keep her tears in check at the depth of Rieker's duplicity. "He's done it all for the bloody ring. He doesn't care about Clara or . . . or any of us." She wiped her nose on her sleeve. "He's lied about it all. He only wants one thing."

"Calm down, Teek." Shamus reached out a hand to steady her. Fiona sat next to Tiki, her face drawn and worried. Even Toots was frowning.

"He's a bloody liar," the young boy cried.

"I knew he was too good-looking to be trusted," Fiona said.

Shamus raised his hands to quiet them. "If what Tiki's said is the truth, then we just need to be one step ahead of him."

"What do you mean?" Tiki sniffed and wiped her nose along her sleeve.

"Well, the ring is in Buckingham now, isn't it?" Shamus asked.

Tiki sniffed again and nodded.

"And Rieker knows the princes. Didn't he say he was invited to a card game there tonight?"

"Yes."

"And now you know where he lives, right?"

Tiki nodded.

Shamus held his palms up. "Well, I say we let Rieker get the ring out of Buckingham for us and then we'll just steal it from him."

Tiki turned the idea over in her mind. Rieker had access to the palace. He was really their only hope of getting the ring back from the royals. Then, once it was out of the palace, she could steal the ring from him.

"It might work," Tiki said. "But Larkin told me to be back to Hyde Park by twilight tonight. Rieker probably won't even go to the palace until this evening, so the first chance we'll get to steal it will be after he plays cards and goes home. What if she doesn't wait?"

Shamus's voice was steady and sure. "Trust me, Tiki. If Larkin has been after the ring all these years, she'll wait one more day. Trading Clara is her best chance of ever seeing the queen's ring. I think one more day will be all right. What we need to focus on is getting the ring from Rieker."

Chapter Thirty-three

I T was dark when Rieker returned. Tiki and the others were huddled around the meager heat of the stove, which couldn't keep up with the cool air seeping in through the walls.

Tiki jumped to her feet when Rieker came through the door and hurried toward him. It was all she could do not to shout accusations at him.

"Did you find her?" She searched his face for answers.

His expression was guarded, and he shook his head wearily. "Larkin was already gone. She must have known that I would find out where she was staying."

Tiki looked away. Her stomach turned at the thought of Rieker using a helpless child for his own gain. "Are you sure Clara was there?"

Rieker reached inside his jacket. He pulled out a worn pink puppy that looked as though half of its stuffing had been removed.

"Doggie," Tiki cried. She reached out to take the little stuffed animal from Rieker. The toy's black button eyes were askew, but his felt mouth smiled at her. A pang of sadness welled inside her. "Clara can't sleep without Doggie," Tiki whispered. She took a deep breath against the helplessness that threatened to overwhelm her. Maybe Larkin had left Doggie behind just to taunt her.

Rieker reached out to comfort her, but she shied away, turning so he couldn't see the anger in her eyes. He dropped his hands to his sides and stared at her, sadness etched across his face. "We'll find her, Tiki. I promise."

Tiki couldn't bite back her words. "If she's still alive."

"She's alive. But we need the ring." His words were firm.

"What time are you going to the palace tonight?" Tiki watched him with wary eyes, Doggie clutched to her chest.

"Leo said to arrive by eight." Rieker stood with his arms folded across his chest, his lips pressed tight at the corners. "If I don't show up, I think Leo will hunt me down so he can drag some answers out of me. He's very suspicious of the beautiful Elizabeth."

Tiki ignored his compliment. Just another lie. "And what will you tell him?"

"At this moment, I have no idea." Rieker turned back to face her. "But this is probably my only chance to reclaim the ring to negotiate with Larkin." His smoky eyes shifted to her face. "Will you tell me where it's hidden?"

Tiki chewed on the corner of her lip. She had to tell him, to play along with the charade of trusting him, yet it was a secret she hated to share. What if Rieker and Larkin disappeared together once he had the ring? Perhaps they would never return Clara. Tiki pushed the thought from her mind. She couldn't allow herself to think of things like that. First, she had to get the ring out of Buckingham, and Rieker was going to do that for her.

"It's hidden on a piece of wire behind the painting of the faerie on the second floor." Tiki said the words quickly, before she changed her mind. Once Rieker got the ring, she would be one step closer to stealing it back.

"Sir Thomas' Folly?"

"Pardon me?" Tiki squinted at him, unsure of his meaning.

"The painting. Is it the piece of art that you and Leo were discussing when I interrupted the other day? In that alcove that looks out to the back gardens?"

"Yes."

Rieker laughed. Not just a chuckle. He laughed until his sides heaved with his exertion. Finally, he wiped a tear from the corner of his eye and heaved a deep sigh of delight.

"I'm afraid I missed the joke," Tiki said in a cold voice.

"The painting," Rieker explained, "behind which the ring of the truce is hidden is quite aptly titled *Sir Thomas' Folly*. The canvas is named after a play where a prince falls in love with a faerie and loses his kingdom to her deceptions." He eyed Tiki. "Or perhaps you already knew that and just have a vicious sense of humor."

"I had no idea that was the name of the painting," she said. "It appeared to be a good place to hide the ring where it wouldn't be found." Tiki turned away and stared at the glow of flame flickering through the vent in the box stove. How was it possible to love someone one minute and then hate him the next?

"So you and Leo stood a foot away from the very ring he has sought so desperately?" Rieker chuckled again. "Ah, if only Leo knew. He would probably laugh, too."

"Amusing, I'm sure, but do you think you can retrieve the thing without being caught?"

Rieker sobered. "Which side of the canvas is the ring on?"

"On the lower right," Tiki snapped.

He wasn't smiling now. "Yes. I can get the ring."

TIKI sat on the bench outside Mr. Potts's bookstore and nervously flipped a coin across her fingers. Rieker had been brusque when he'd left. Perhaps it was in reaction to her mood, or perhaps it was because he didn't need to pretend to care anymore.

She had desperately wanted to follow him, to keep her eyes on something, anything, that would lead her to Clara. But she had forced herself to stay seated as he'd walked out the door with the knowledge of where the ring was hidden. She had given up everything to save Clara. She prayed that it worked.

A long sigh escaped her lips. The constant worry about the little girl was draining her energy. And then there was Larkin. A jealous twinge went through Tiki as she envisioned the other girl's exquisite looks. It was no surprise that Rieker wasn't immune to her unearthly beauty.

Tiki searched the station. Even now, travelers hurried back and forth as the bellowing gusts of steam and the shrill whistles of the trains coming and going echoed through the cavernous room. Things wouldn't be the same without Clara. There was something so endearing about the frail little girl, something so compelling, that Tiki couldn't imagine life without her. For a second, she allowed herself to consider the worst: What if Larkin didn't return her? What if Clara died?

Tiki took a deep breath, trying to hold back the sob that tore from her throat.

If Clara didn't come back, it would be like losing her parents all over again. She didn't know if she could go through it another time. There was no place she could run to escape that kind of pain. Or guilt. Because this time she would be responsible. For not taking better care of Clara. For not saving her from Larkin. A crushing ache formed in Tiki's chest.

Frustrated, Tiki jumped to her feet and headed for the main part of the station. Traffic picked up as she got closer to the loading ramps. She watched the crowd as she walked, fighting the sense of desperation that threatened to engulf her. By tomorrow she would have the ring again and could make the trade with Larkin.

A voice whispered in her ear, "Your little girl is sick."

Tiki jerked around. Larkin gave her a guileless smile. The other girl's blond ringlets hung in perfect sausage curls and her beautiful face was serene, as though she were asking the time of day.

"How sick?" Tiki forced herself to remain calm.

"Well, I don't normally deal with children, but I'd say she's not doing well at all. She seems to sleep most all of the time, and she's coughing up a lot of blood." Larkin's blue green eyes gazed at Tiki without emotion. "I'd suggest you bring me the ring tonight as you promised."

"I don't have it. Yet." Tiki wanted to throttle the girl and cry at the same time. "But I'll have it tomorrow. Let me have Clara and I *promise* I'll bring it to you tomorrow." Longing tore at Tiki's heart, and she clenched her fingers so tight that she could feel her fingernails biting into the palms of her hands.

Larkin laughed, her eyes crinkling at the corners as her lips curved in a dazzling smile. "It's a terrible thing to want and long for something you can't have, isn't it?"

"Yes, but I'm concerned about a *person*. You want a *thing*," Tiki snapped. "Why do you want the ring so much? Just to destroy the truce?"

The other girl's eyes narrowed. Her voice was cold when she spoke. "I live in a world that you can't even begin to comprehend. A world of battles and oaths and passions that bind us for a thousand mortal lifetimes." For a fleeting moment, there was something in Larkin's expression that Tiki had never seen before. Bitterness? Or was it sadness? The faerie's voice came out in a whisper. "Of loss that is beyond your ability to understand."

Then Larkin's lip curled in disgust, her voice tinged with anger. "It's taken me a very long time to find the one I love. And I'm risking my own life to be with him. *Nothing* is going to stand in my way. With the ring of the truce, we'll be free of those who pursue us."

"But who is after you?" Tiki tried to think of something, anything, to keep the faerie talking. To stop her from disappearing before she could find out more about Clara.

"Donegal." Larkin spat the name out. "The high king of the UnSeelie court is displeased with me." She glared at Tiki. "The power held within the ring will buy my freedom. I've tried for a very long time to get the ring. And it's finally in reach. If Wills doesn't get it tonight, then you had better have a plan to bring me the ring tomorrow. Or your little girl is dead."

Tiki stood stunned as Larkin stepped into a group of people and disappeared into the crowded station. Larkin knew Rieker was going after the ring tonight. Had he told her? Tiki hadn't considered the ring might have value to Rieker beyond the reward. But now that she thought about it, why would he need the reward? He was already rich. He'd tricked her into revealing its hidden location so he and Larkin could run away together. The ring must offer them the power to escape.

Even now, Rieker could already have the ring. Had she just sabotaged her one chance to reclaim Clara?

Tiki ran for home. She needed to talk to the others. They needed to get in position to steal the ring from Rieker. They couldn't take any chances that he could slip away.

Tiki was breathless as she stood in the shadowed candle-light of their little room and told the others of her encounter with Larkin. "She *knows* Rieker is going to be at Buckingham tonight. She *knows* that he's going to get the ring. They've been plotting to run away together." Her words came out in a hurried rush. "We've got to make sure that we follow Rieker from the palace. We've got to make sure that he doesn't run away before we have a chance to get the ring. It's the only way we can save Clara."

"Slow down, Tiki," Shamus said in his steady voice. "It's not even seven o'clock. Rieker hasn't gone to Buckingham yet. We still have time." He stood up from where he had been whittling by the stove. "Now, what are you thinking?"

Tiki wrung her hands together, trying to calm herself. They still had time. "I think the three of you need to go to Buckingham. One at the front, one at the back, and one on the side near the Mews, so if he leaves, you can follow him. Just in case he doesn't go home." She took a deep breath. "I'll still go over and sneak into his town house in Grosvenor Square and wait for him there."

"But how are we going to follow him if he's riding a horse?" Toots asked.

"It's snowing outside. Hard," Tiki said. "It looks like it's going to snow all night. Which means he'll take a carriage to the palace tonight. If someone spots him, they can hop the boot and follow him. If he doesn't go to Grosvenor Square, then whoever is following him"—she looked around at their solemn faces—"it will be up to you to steal the ring from him. Any way you can."

Chapter Thirty-four

LEO stared at Wills over his cards. "You're in love with her, aren't you?"

The three other men at the table turned in surprise. As one, their eyes shifted from the prince over to Rieker, who stared at his cards, unruffled by the question.

"To whom are you referring, Leo?" Rieker asked as he threw two cards facedown to the side. "Two." With a sardonic half-smile on his lips, he lifted his eyes from the cards to the young man sitting across from him.

"Wills, in love?" Arthur echoed in disbelief, gazing at Rieker as if for confirmation. "You've got to be joking." The other two men guffawed along with Arthur, aware of Rieker's dislike of romantic entanglement.

"I can see it in his eyes," Leo said. Curiosity burned liked a flame in his gut. He turned to Rieker. "I can see it when you look at her, when you talk about her. But I feel compelled to stop you, Wills. There's something amiss. How well do you know her background?"

"She must be something special for Wills to fall," retorted Alfred, Duke of Edinburgh, Leo and Arthur's older brother. "What's her name? Do we know this amazing creature?"

Rieker was expressionless as he shook his head ever so

slightly, but Leo wasn't sure if it was in disbelief or in silent warning.

"Come on, Wills, it's us," Leo said. "We've never had secrets before. Tell the boys who she is."

Rieker picked up the two cards dealt to him and leaned back, sliding his cards into a stack and setting them on the table. He cocked his head as though measuring Leo's determination.

"You seem to be enjoying this more than me, Leo, and since I'm not even sure of whom you're speaking, why don't you tell them and then we'll all know. Perhaps it's your own desires to which you're referring."

The others laughed as Leo colored slightly. He should have known better than to verbally ambush Wills. The man had a tongue like a viper when he was mad, though one would never know by looking at his expressionless face.

"Why, it's Elizabeth Dunbar, of course," Leo said. He hated to admit he enjoyed the sound of her name as it rolled off his lips. "No need to be coy, Wills."

Arthur's head jerked up in surprise. "The enchantress from the masked ball? The girl you drenched with wine?"

"The enchantress," Rieker repeated with a chuckle. "So enchanting that she can steal your heart from you when you're not looking, Leo?" He grinned as he waited for Leo's response.

"Not m-me, you," Leo stuttered, suddenly aware of the four sets of eyes laughing at him.

"Hmmm, so Leo's in love, *again*." Alfred chuckled as he shuffled the cards. "And it sounds like the young miss must only have eyes for Wills." Alfred grinned over at Rieker and winked. "Not the first time that's happened, eh?"

"And hardly the last," Arthur chimed in, gazing at his

cards. "But Leo, maybe that's the hook, eh? The chase of unrequited love."

"It's not me, I tell you," Leo sputtered.

"I've noticed a pattern over the years, dear brother." Arthur grinned. "In case you haven't noticed, it's not a successful business model." They all laughed as they laid their cards down and Arthur lifted his gaze to Rieker. "And what do you say of the fair maiden, Wills? Do you find her as enchanting as Leo, or just a passing fancy?"

Rieker's lips lifted in a small half-smile as he took his turn shuffling the cards. "Arthur, you know it's not wise to speak of these matters. You can never be too careful about what you say, or be sure who is listening." He scooted back in his chair. "But I need a break from this enlightening conversation. Somebody keep him here"—he pointed at Leo—"so he can't follow me and make other outrageous accusations until I return and have the support of your voices of reason."

The others laughed as Alfred reached over and clamped a firm hand on Leo's wrist. "We shall keep him here if we have to wrestle him to the floor. Hurry up and get back, though, or the cards will go cold."

Rieker snapped off a smart salute and, with a wink at Leo, walked out of the room.

ARE you sure you don't want to stay? It's past midnight." Leo stood on the steps with Rieker as they waited for his carriage to be brought around. The snow was still falling, the ground and trees covered in a frozen layer of white that sparkled as the temperature dropped.

"I've taken your money, Leo. I hardly want to push my luck with your hospitality, too." Rieker laughed. "Besides, the snow is still falling. If I want to get home, I should go now."

"Not just my money, but everyone else's, too. Do you *ever* lose at cards?" Leo grumbled good-naturedly. "But, seriously, you do know you're always welcome here. I miss having the chance to talk with you."

"You've had all night to talk to me. What more could we talk about?"

"You're not telling me something, Wills. I can feel it. And I suspect it involves Elizabeth." Leo slid his hands into his pockets and raised his chin. "I don't know what it is, but I *will* find out."

"Well, let me know when you do. For now, I'm going home."

Leo stood on the steps, watching the coach roll away into the night. Damn Wills anyway. He didn't know any more now than when the evening had started. He crossed his arms against his chest to ward off a cold breeze and tapped his fingers as he thought. Ever since that bloody ring had gone missing, things had not been right.

Whether Wills liked it or not, he was going to get some answers.

Chapter Thirty-five

TIKI stood hidden among the trees in the center of
Grosvenor Square. She shivered again, whether from
cold or fear, she wasn't sure. The snow, which continued to
fall in a thick blanket of white, had quickly soaked through
the thin soles of her boots as she'd walked from the station. Her feet ached from the cold. It had been easy to find
Number 6 again, she'd just counted down the row, but it
was hard to believe that Rieker owned such a magnificent
home.

Across the street, the white brick town home stretched
up three stories, its imposing entrance decorated with
black columns and railings. The house looked like a for-
tress. Reluctantly, her eyes swept up to the two brick
chimneys that stood on either end of the roof. She shivered at the thought of having to climb down into that
small, dirty dark space. There had to be another way in.

The main entry was at street level, with four black
steps leading to the front door. Stables were housed in the
back of the building, and Tiki guessed that the kitchen
was located between the two. The servants probably lived
below the ground level in the basement. She eyed the second and third floors. Rieker's room must be on one of
those upper floors. That was where he would most likely
pull the ring from his pocket.

A small wrought-iron gate enclosed the front court-yard of each home, since the buildings shared common walls and were joined together in a row down the street. She couldn't just walk in the front door. She would need to go around the back and try to get in that way.

A clock chimed the hour of midnight in the distance. Rieker would surely be home soon. She needed to hurry.

A shred of doubt crept in. Maybe Rieker wouldn't come home. She pushed the thought away. She needed to find a way in to wait for him. Whether it was tonight or tomorrow, or the next day, she would be ready.

On impulse, Tiki ran across the vacant street and pushed through the short wrought-iron gate to the en-trance, the hinges protesting with a screechy groan. Her heart raced as she ran up the stairs and pressed the latch. She heard a soft *click* and leaned her shoulder into the door, giving a hard push, but it wouldn't budge. The front door was locked.

Behind the house, Tiki approached the back entry through the alley, staying in the shadows of the trees as she drew near. The big double doors to the coach house were open, presumably waiting for Rieker's return. She crouched behind a tree, watching the coach house for ac-tivity, but no one was about this time of night. Tiki took a deep breath and sneaked in through the doors. The black shadows within the stables swallowed her as she entered.

Tiki stretched her arms out and felt her way along the side of a coach parked in the garage, her boots quiet on the hay strewn across the floor. She could hear the shuffling snorts of several horses. She approached another door at the end of the large room and fumbled for the latch. With a deep breath, she turned the lever and pushed the door open a crack to peer in.

A harness room.

Leather bridles and reins in an assortment of sizes and lengths were hung neatly along the wall. The smell of tanned leather filled the air, and Tiki inhaled the fragrant scent as she eased her way through the room. She had taken riding lessons as a young girl, and she had loved every minute of it. The rich smell of the leather brought back fond memories.

She entered the town house through the back door and paused in a landing area. One doorway opened onto a pantry, another to a scullery. She tiptoed through the rooms, her boots tapping softly with each step on the hardwood floors.

"Sir, is that you?" a male voice called.

Tiki jerked through a doorway and pressed herself flat against the wall as the butler climbed the nearby steps from his apartment. She stood frozen, her eyes measuring the distance back to the door, trying to decide if she could escape should he spot her.

"Master William?" The butler's footsteps came to a stop at the top of the stairs. He held a candle high to light the way, its flame casting wavering shadows against the wall. "Is that you?" The silence seemed to shout at Tiki. She held her breath, praying he wouldn't see her dark figure hiding there.

"Bloody rats," the man mumbled as he turned and went back to his quarters.

Tiki released a sigh of relief. She pulled her boots off and tucked them inside one of the cupboards, then tiptoed from the kitchen in bare feet. When she came to the entrance of the dining room, she stopped to stare. The room was immense.

Rugs that were a full centimeter thick were positioned under a huge, ornate table that Tiki guessed would seat twenty. Carved sideboards lined the walls, with beautiful potted plants in each corner of the room. Large paned windows covered one wall and looked out to a snow-covered garden. A chandelier, hung with teardrop-shaped crystals, sparkled and winked in the candlelight as though acknowledging Tiki's presence.

Tiki stared in awe. Maybe someone who owned things this beautiful needed someone as breathtaking as Larkin to finish it off.

With a quick look over her shoulder toward the butler's stairs, Tiki moved through the dining room, letting her fingers trail along the backs of the chairs as she passed. The light of the moon reflected off the white snow that covered the trees and ground, casting a surprising amount of illumination through the windows.

She envisioned Rieker, dressed in his black vest and jacket, with the white cravat he'd worn to the masked ball, sitting at the head of the table, hosting a party. He would fit right in among these luxurious surroundings. A twinge went through her. No place for a pickpocket, though.

Tiki exited the dining room and went down several steps into an oversize hall. Rich wood paneling stretched to the ceiling, giving the room the cozy feel of a den. She could see another set of stairs, much grander than the first, with an ornate wrought-iron handrail, leading the way to the second floor.

Tiki eyed the stairs. Rieker's bedroom had to be on one of the upper floors. She hurried up the steps, her bare feet quiet on the wood floors, afraid to be caught in a spot where she couldn't hide. She turned in the landing and took the stairs two at a time. At the top of the stairs, she turned left and followed the hallway to two other rooms that appeared to be drawing rooms.

Retracing her steps, she went past the staircase and found herself in another immense room. Several crystal chandeliers sparkled from the ceiling. This room, however, was devoid of furniture with the exception of several settees that lined the walls. With a start, Tiki realized what the room was used for: It was a ballroom.

She tried not to stare at the lavishness of gilt-framed paintings and mirrors that lined the walls as she hurried through. It didn't matter how rich Rieker was. The opulence just emphasized the degree of his deceit.

A large tearoom opened off the ballroom and led to another, smaller set of stairs. Why would someone like Rieker need this much room in a house? Then, with a twinge, Tiki realized that when Rieker married he and his wife would entertain in this very ballroom. Maybe Larkin would dance barefoot here. Maybe she already had.

Tiki hurried on, annoyed at herself for letting her imagination run wild. She didn't care what Rieker did with his ballroom. She walked into the next room and knew at a glance that this suite belonged to Rieker. There was something about the rich, dark furniture, the orderly manner in which the room was arranged, that reminded her of him. Wall sconces had been lit to await his arrival, and the light cast a soft yellow glow about the room.

She had entered a large bedroom, an oversize four-poster bed to one side with a small alcove of windows beyond that. Across the room from her stood a tall chest of drawers and to her left a passageway. She crept down the passageway, glad for the sconces that had been lit in anticipation of Rieker's return.

A doorway led into a closet filled with men's clothes, hanging neatly in rows. She continued down the hall into a cozy living room. A fire burned low in the grate, the coals glowing orange.

Tiki retraced her steps to the bedroom and glanced around. A book was open on the side table next to the bed. Curious, she turned it over to read the title. She gasped as she read the words *Oliver Twist* and dropped the book back on the table with a bang.

Frightened that she had roused someone with the noise, she jerked around, looking for a place to hide. Though it was a big room, in the shape of a rectangle, she couldn't see a place where Rieker might not spot her when he entered. On impulse, she lifted the thick quilt that draped down the sides of the large bed and measured the space underneath the frame. Too tight. She wouldn't fit.

She whirled around and surveyed the room again. Long drapes were gathered on each side of the three windows in the alcove, and she eyed the dark, damask fabric. The great swaths of material were enough to hide her. She hurried around the bed and slipped behind the curtains, making sure her feet were covered. Convinced that she was in a safe hiding spot, she slid her back down the wall and wrapped her arms around her knees to wait for Rieker's return.

APPROACHING footsteps jarred Tiki awake. Rieker was home. She scrambled to her feet and readjusted the drapes to disguise her body. She pressed her back to the wall, barely daring to breathe. He walked into the room and let out a tired sigh. One by one his shoes clunked to the floor. Tiki was rigid behind the screen of fabric, straining to hear every sound. Rieker's muffled footsteps moved toward the chest of drawers. His pocketwatch and other miscellaneous items clattered as they were dropped onto the wooden surface.

"And you, my little beauty," Rieker said in a low voice, "have been a lot of work. I hope you're worth it." Tiki heard the clink of metal landing on wood. Rieker sighed again, and Tiki could picture him running his hand through his hair. Then his footsteps became fainter as he headed down the hallway toward the closet.

Now was her chance.

Tiki peeked around the edge of the curtain. Down the hallway, another door closed. She inched her way out from behind the drapes and tiptoed over to the dresser. Her heart tripped over itself. There, glowing in the subdued light of the room, was the queen's ring.

For a second, Tiki was transported back in time and she stood in the royal library again, debating whether to steal the ring for the first time. With a shaking hand, she reached out and her fingers closed over the stone. A wave of intense relief washed over her. She had it. Now she could negotiate for Clara's release.

"What a pleasant surprise." Rieker's cool, sardonic voice sliced through the room like a knife. Tiki jerked around with a gasp. He leaned against the doorjamb, his white shirt partially unbuttoned and untucked from his black trousers, a black vest slung over his arm.

"You knew I was here," Tiki said with sudden realization.

"I followed muddy footprints from the harness room. They were much too small to fit any of my staff, all of whom, with the exception of Charles, my butler, are asleep at the moment. The only other person I could think of who might have an interest in my whereabouts at this hour was you. Call it a lucky guess." His eyes narrowed. "Why are you here, Tiki? Don't you trust me?"

For a second, Tiki thought she heard disappointment in his voice.

"I need the ring, Rieker. Larkin found me at the station. Clara is *really* sick. Coughing up blood and sleeping all the time. The ring is the only chance I have of getting her back." Tiki tightened her grip on the stone. "I have to save Clara."

"And you couldn't wait until tomorrow?" Rieker hadn't moved, yet Tiki felt his anger reaching across the room toward her. Her own anger surged in return.

"How was I supposed to know if you'd really show up?" Tiki snapped. "Larkin told me that you were planning to escape together. She told me how long the two of you had been trying to get the ring." She gripped the ring tighter. "I couldn't take the chance that she wouldn't return Clara."

"Just don't know who to trust, do you?"

Tiki bit back a gasp as Larkin entered the room.

Chapter Thirty-six

"AH, Larkin, another surprise," Rieker said. "What a busy night we're having." He straightened up and moved a step closer to Tiki. "But since we're all here, I guess this might be the perfect time to discuss the negotiations."

"Wills." Larkin ran her fingers through her hair, which hung like a wild mass of tangled summer grass around her shoulders. She preened before him, a petulant expression upon her face. "There's no need to pretend anymore." Her feet were bare again, and the green dress she wore revealed shoulders browned by the sun.

Larkin was devastatingly beautiful. Tiki glanced at Rieker out of the corner of her eye and could see him staring at the other girl as if mesmerized. A stab of jealousy ripped through her chest.

"I've told her enough that she understands the situation now." Larkin moved closer to Rieker. "I don't know why you took so long to tell her I was staying here"—she glared at Tiki—"taking care of that brat."

For a second, the room reduced to a pinpoint of light before rushing back into view at an alarming rate. Tiki swayed on her feet as Larkin confirmed her suspicions. Rieker reached out a hand to steady her, but Tiki jerked away.

"Wills, we've done it," Larkin said. Her eyes caressed

Rieker's face as if she yearned to touch him. Tiki looked from one to the other and couldn't help but think what a beautiful couple they made. "After all these years, we have the ring of the truce. We can demand our freedom now." She glided forward. "Let me have it."

"Actually, Larkin"—Rieker held up his hand to stop her movement—"Tiki has the ring at the moment." His eyes shifted to Tiki. "I believe she intends to trade you for something you have of hers."

Tiki looked at Rieker. "Is it true?" she whispered. Her voice cracked. "You and Larkin . . . together?"

"Yes, it's true," Larkin snapped. "I've told you before, you dirty little thief. Wills and I are fulfilling our destiny." She smiled at Rieker. "And now, finally, we hold the key to our freedom."

Tiki knew she should be concentrating on trading the ring for Clara, but her heart felt as if it were breaking. Rieker's eyes were dark and unfathomable, his face like a wall, unyielding.

"You're running away together now that you have the ring?" Her voice faltered, and to her embarrassment she could feel hot tears brimming in her eyes. But for some perverse reason she needed to hear Rieker tell her himself.

"Ah." Rieker nodded with sudden understanding. "So that's why you attempted to steal the ring."

"Is it true?" Her words came out in a choked whisper. "You care for her?" Tiki barely took a breath. "How could you? After what she's done to your family?"

"First things first, Tiki." He turned to face the faerie. "Where's the little girl, Larkin?"

"Wills, we don't have to be bothered with this," Larkin simpered. "We don't need to return the girl. The ring is ours. Let's take it from her and leave now. Before Donegal finds that it's free from the oath of the royals."

"First, return Clara. You don't need her anymore." They stood facing each other, Rieker positioned between Tiki and Larkin. "Where is she?"

Larkin's eyes narrowed. "Why do you want to help *her*?" She glared at Tiki as she snapped her teeth. "What do you see in her, anyway?" The faerie looked her up and down with a disgusted expression. "She's nothing but a dirty guttersnipe."

"You struck a bargain, Larkin. The ring for the child." Rieker's voice was low and steady. Tiki didn't miss that he spoke with an ease that suggested an undeniable familiarity. "You can't keep her."

"Oh, all right," Larkin snapped. "I'm sick of carting the brat around with me, anyway."

"Is she alive?" Rieker asked.

"Yes." Larkin spat the word out in a tone so deadly, it could have been laced with poison.

"Then bring her here."

"No." Larkin reached toward Rieker, her hands out in supplication. "What does it matter? We've done it, Wills. We have the ring. Just take it from her or I will. We're free to do as we please now." Larkin took a step toward Rieker. "But I have to hurry. Donegal has others watching, waiting for an opportunity to capture me. They won't hesitate to attack if they find me."

"No." Rieker shook his head. "Bring the girl."

"What do you mean, no?" Larkin's voice took on a peculiarly distorted petulance.

Tiki stood frozen, sensing a battle of wills that raged between the two of them that she didn't quite understand.

The faerie's eyes narrowed. "You're a traitor, aren't you, William? Just like the rest of them." She took a menacing step toward him. "It's all been a lie."

"A lie of your own creation." Rieker returned her glare.

Larkin's eyes shone with anger as she advanced toward Rieker. "You agreed."

"I agreed to help find the ring. I never agreed to give it to you. By the blood of Eridanus that runs in my veins, I swear to protect the truce held within the ring," Rieker said. "That's the only promise I've made. Where is Clara, Larkin?"

Tiki tightened her fingers around the ring, warmth pulsing in the palm of her hand. What had he just said?

The blond faerie turned toward Tiki. "Give me that ring, you *Óinseach*."

In a lightning-fast move, Tiki flipped the ring across the backs of her fingers and made it disappear. "No, not until you give me Clara back."

In a blink, the faerie's face distorted into a vicious snarl. Larkin was just a blur as she crossed the room and locked her fingers around Tiki's wrist in a viselike grip.

"You don't know . . ." As the faerie's fingers made contact with Tiki's birthmark, her wrist burned as though she had dipped her skin into the flame of a candle. From a great distance, Tiki heard Rieker's roar of rage and saw him reach for Larkin, but like heat rising from a flat rock in the heart of summer, Rieker and the room shimmered out of view.

THE force of Larkin's attack pushed Tiki backward and she landed in a field of grass. Before she could process where she was, her survival instinct kicked in. She slammed the flat of her hand into Larkin's nose as hard as she could. Iridescent blood spurted from Larkin's face, splattering Tiki. An overwhelming scent of thyme filled the air.

Larkin loosened her grip enough for Tiki to jerk herself free from the other girl's grasp, and she rolled hard to the right, reaching for the blade hidden in the back of her trousers. Tiki yanked the iron dagger free as she spun to a crouch and pointed the knife at the blond faerie. Larkin was already on her feet, facing her.

"I'll stick this blade through your heart if you touch me again." Tiki's breath came out in heaving gasps. Her eyes darted from the faerie and back again, trying to take in their surroundings. They stood in a grassy meadow blanketed in the dying light of the day, as if the sun had just set.

In the distance, huge stones stood upright, dotting the rolling hills, and she could see several large, grass-covered mounds. To her left, a single large hawthorn tree stood in a meadow, its limbs outstretched toward the sky like giant arms.

Larkin straightened up and lifted her hem to wipe her bleeding nose, keeping a safe distance between herself and Tiki. "Why did you bring us here?"

"Me?" Tiki couldn't hide her surprise. She glanced around. The ragged silhouette of a line of trees meandered away from her toward the horizon. A few lights twinkled here and there, as if fireflies were just beginning to blink with the onset of darkness. One small part of the sky was still painted with the fading orange glow of sunset. In the distance, the eerie, piercingly sweet notes of a flute floated on the air, pulling at her. "Where are we?"

Larkin's voice dripped with malice. "We're in the Otherworld, of course."

Tiki's stomach clenched at the girl's words. Her eyes scanned the area, taking in her surroundings with disbelief. The air was warm and scented of wet dirt and fresh-mown grass, as if the skies had just poured rain and released the perfume of nature.

Tiki blinked. Had they really crossed over to the world of Faerie? She remembered the burning sensation from her birthmark when Larkin had grabbed her. Could her mark have something to do with it?

The faerie's blue green eyes snapped with anger. Larkin shifted her stance, her blond hair swinging with her movement, poised to spring. Her words were low and rushed. "Will you continue to pretend you don't know who you are?"

"I . . . I don't know what you're talking about." Tiki's eyes darted from the upright stones scattered about the field to the mounds and on to the trees in the distance.

"To whose court do you place your allegiance?" Larkin whispered. Her lips twisted in a bitter line. "Do you work for Donegal?"

"I don't have a court." Tiki took a deep breath. "Who is it that you think I am?" Her heart drummed in her chest, a strange anticipation filling her.

A flicker of surprise crossed Larkin's face before it was replaced with a calculating look. One corner of her mouth lifted in a sneer. "You pretend not to know of *an fáinne sí*. What game do you play? You must have learned something over the years. Adasara must have told someone."

For a moment, Tiki had a vision of forcing the information from Larkin with the point of the knife pushed tight to her throat. "I don't know what that means." She clenched her teeth together. "Tell me."

"*An fáinne sí* is a birthmark of Finn MacLochlan, a high king of Tara," Larkin said. "That mark on your arm practically makes you royalty."

For a moment, Tiki stopped breathing. Larkin had said her name. "A high king of *what?*" she whispered.

"Of Tara." Larkin spat the word out as she took a step closer, her face twisted with jealousy. "The ancient Irish faerie court. Where the deities of the Tuatha de Danann joined the Sidhe." She gave Tiki a derisive look. "Except MacLochlan was a renegade, so you'd be royalty in a court that no one recognizes."

"You're lying." Tiki's voice was low, disbelieving.

Larkin laughed, and a mirthless smile twisted her lips. "That's why Adasara hid you in London—"

"Stop it." Tiki cut her off. She didn't want to hear another word. "You're wrong. I don't know what you're talking about. I don't want to know." Her voice grew in volume with her frustration. "I just want to go home and never see another faerie again as long as I live." She ended in a shout. "Where is Clara?"

"Shhh," Larkin hissed. She held out her hand as if to physically stop Tiki from shouting. Her head swiveled, as though she expected the noise to have drawn attention in the empty field, before her eyes latched on Tiki again with a deadly glare. "If you didn't bring us here, then somehow you made *me* bring us over, which means I'm the only way you're going to get back.

"If you keep shouting, we'll both be captured and rot the rest of our days away in Donegal's prison. You'll never see your precious Clara again." Her lips quivered with emotion. "Trust me when I say he would pay a high price to capture someone like you."

Tiki looked around, her heart pounding. There was a strange sense of familiarity to the meadow in which she stood.

No, there wasn't. There couldn't be.

She jabbed her knife toward Larkin, forcing her to take a step back.

"How do we get out of here?" Tiki said. "Just take me back and give me Clara, then you can run and hide from Donegal or whoever it is that's after you."

Larkin's words were cold. "You've forgotten the ring."

"You can have the bloody thing," Tiki yelled. At her shout, shadows shifted in the twilight around them, and a sudden unnerving sense of being watched filled her. "You can have it when you give me Clara. How do we get back?"

"You're not leaving so soon?" A deep, familiar voice cut through the night air. A shadow shifted sideways and Marcus stood before them, clad in skintight brown trousers the color of bark. This time Tiki could clearly see the wings on his back, fragile pieces of glass spiderwebbed with black lines. Their slow flutter refracted the moonlight in a mesmerizing rhythm.

Tiki clenched the dagger tighter in her hand and pointed the blade at this new threat. "Stay away from me."

Marcus's gaze shifted from Tiki to Larkin, and his black eyes gleamed in the half-light.

"Larkin dear, we've been looking everywhere for you. I'm surprised you'd take the risk to be seen here."

"Shut up," Larkin snapped.

Marcus raised his eyebrows. "You must know that Donegal has quite a price on your head." He spoke in an overly sympathetic tone that made Tiki's skin crawl. "But of course, being the rebel that you are, you've always loved to walk on the wild side, haven't you?" He took a step closer. "Or maybe you enjoy pain and humiliation?"

Larkin snarled at him, her teeth suddenly sharper. "Stop talking, Marcus."

He shifted toward them. "Jamison has a claw inscribed with your name on it." He grinned at Larkin with ill-disguised malevolence as he feigned a shiver of horror. "Though I can't even *imagine* what it would be like to have your wings clamped in one of those barbaric things. It makes me sick to even think about that much iron being so close to me." He leaned forward and peered at her. "And whatever happened to your face? Is that blood?"

"How did you know we were here?" Larkin asked.

"Actually, I followed the two of you." He turned to Tiki. "I've been keeping a close eye on this one." He licked his lips. "Waiting for my chance."

Tiki shuddered as she looked from one to the other. It was her worst nightmare come to life. Larkin and Marcus, together. But this had a twist even she couldn't imagine, that she would be trapped with them in a place from which she didn't know how to escape.

"I'm sure no one will miss her in London except maybe Richmond," Marcus continued. "But if Donegal has his way, Richmond will be dead soon enough, anyway." The black-haired faerie made an O with his mouth and covered his lips with his fingers. "I forgot you're in love with him, aren't you?" His mouth twisted in a disgusted grimace. "A mortal, though. Really, Larkin, it's so revolting, what are you thinking?" He gave an eloquent shrug. "Donegal will never forgive you for this."

Larkin smiled at Marcus. "I'm afraid you're right about that. Though I'm not going to wait around for Jamison to catch me." She nodded at Tiki. "You wouldn't mind taking care of her for me?"

"No!" Tiki shouted. "You're not going to leave me with him. Take me back." Desperation clawed at her insides. She looked around, but there was no place to even run and try to hide.

"Stop shouting," Larkin growled. She took another step closer to Tiki. At the same moment Marcus moved forward, too, leering, his façade of pleasantness gone.

Larkin grabbed Tiki by the wrist. A burning sensation ran up Tiki's arm. The shadows surrounding them deepened and a strange sensation tugged at Tiki, as though her breath had frozen in her lungs. Marcus dove at her, his face alarmingly close, his clawlike hands reaching for her as he shimmered out of view.

Chapter Thirty-seven

I N that same heartbeat, they were back in Rieker's room. Tiki collapsed against the wood floor, her wrist still burning from Larkin's grasp. Before she could move, Larkin wrapped her hands around her neck, choking her. Tiki tried to defend herself, but Larkin threw her across the room as though she were weightless. Her head hit the wall with a resounding *thud,* and she slumped, semiconscious, in the corner between the side table and the four-poster bed.

Rieker stood on the far side of the bed, near the alcove windows. At their return, he sprang forward and faced Larkin, a long slim silver blade held in his hand.

"Don't do this, Larkin," he said. "This is not what we talked about. Give Tiki the girl."

Larkin spun toward Rieker. "There's no time, Wills. Marcus is right behind me. Give me the ring, *now.*"

"I told you, I don't have it," Rieker said.

Tiki shook her head, trying to clear the starbursts that kept exploding in front of her eyes. She blinked hard, trying to focus. The shadows in the opposite corner of the room shifted and moved to become solid.

Marcus hadn't bothered to assume his glamour when he'd crossed over. Instead his muscular chest was bare and the light winked off the iridescent finish of his wings. He snarled at Larkin, anxious to draw blood, but he hesitated when he spotted the knife in Rieker's hand. His eyes latched on Tiki in the corner, then shifted back to Larkin.

"Leave, Marcus," Larkin said in a low, threatening voice. "This is none of your concern."

"Ah, but I think it is." His black eyes glinted with an evil pleasure, shifting from her to Rieker. "All this time I thought Richmond had something to do with the ring's disappearance, but now I'm not so sure. You both seem to be a bit too interested in her." He motioned to Tiki. "A pickpocket." He smiled, revealing his sharp teeth. "Why is that? I'm starting to suspect that *she's* the key to finding the ring." He licked his lips. "And I know just the persuasion to get her to loosen up and talk."

Rieker took a step toward him, his knife held loosely in his hand. "Don't make me use this, Marcus," he warned in a low voice. "You need to leave. Now."

Marcus's nostrils flared as if picking up the scent of his prey. "Not yet."

At that moment two faeries shimmered into view, one with long silver hair, the other with long white hair. They wore glittering tunics over the same tight, barklike trousers that Marcus wore.

"You were heard when the two of you were in the valley," Marcus said to Larkin, making no attempt to hide his pleasure. "Seize her!" he yelled.

The silver-haired faerie surveyed the room, a metal device held in his hands. He went rigid when he spotted Larkin. His eyes locked on her, then at once the two newcomers leapt at her. At the same time Marcus lunged toward Tiki, and Rieker dove to intercept him.

With a cry of rage, Larkin defended herself against the two men, her teeth snapping, her fingernails arched into claws. In a semicoherent daze, Tiki struggled to make sense of the madness in front of her. Larkin seemed to flutter in the air as she tried to escape the attack of the two strangers, her cries of rage ripping through the room.

Tiki concentrated on Rieker's tall form as he grappled with Marcus. He seemed to welcome the attack, doing battle with Marcus, but the faerie's claws ripped at his flesh, tearing through his clothes, peeling back skin. Blood sprang from numerous wounds on his arms and legs.

Tiki struggled to right herself, but her limbs were sluggish and wouldn't obey her commands. There was something she was trying to remember, but it slipped away just out of reach like an elusive dream.

On the other side of the room, Larkin fought with the two men. She snarled and snapped like a wild animal, trying to tear at them with her hands and teeth. The silver-haired man was trying to hold her arms behind her back, while the other was trying to clip what looked like a metal clamp onto the faint outline of her wings.

Faerie blood, a thick, iridescent green liquid, had spilled on the floor, making it slippery. The scent of thyme was overwhelming. Suddenly Rieker let out a guttural cry as Marcus slammed Rieker's wrist into the dresser, knocking his blade away.

Tiki watched the silver dagger skitter across the floor, light reflecting helter-skelter off the moving blade. She needed to remember something. She pushed herself to her feet, her hands clenched as she took a wobbly step forward. She needed to help Rieker.

"What in bloody hell?" A shocked voice penetrated the melee within the room.

Rieker jerked his head toward Leo's familiar voice.

Out of the corner of her eye, Tiki saw Marcus make his move toward Rieker. Glistening fangs, as sharp as any blade, were exposed in his evil snarl, and in that split second she remembered.

Her dagger was still clutched in her hand.

She reacted on pure instinct. She leapt forward in front of Rieker, swinging the dagger with the momentum of her movement. The blade sank into the center of Marcus's bare chest all the way up to the hilt with frightening ease. A breath of air crossed the back of her hand as it gripped the knife, and she wasn't sure if it came from the faerie's lips or the hole in his chest.

Marcus's features twisted in agony, and his startled eyes found hers.

"Iron?" he gasped in disbelief through teeth clenched in pain. Tiki released the knife and jerked back, but she wasn't fast enough to avoid contact with his hands as he tried to pull the blade free.

Rieker yanked her away from Marcus's crumpling body, then dove for his own blade. With a lightning fast move, he swept the blade to the faerie's throat, but it wasn't necessary. Marcus's eyes rolled back in his head, and with a last gurgling sigh, he was still.

"Wills!" Larkin's shriek was laced with panic as she struggled with her captors. "Help me!" There was something so primal, so desperate, in her cry that Tiki stepped toward the three faeries. She wanted Larkin's screams to stop.

"Tiki—" Rieker grabbed her arm and stopped her. "You can't." He stood poised with his knife extended, as if debating himself whether to intervene, but in that instant the two men were able to clamp the claw onto Larkin's wings, and with a howl of pain she slumped forward, unconscious.

"Wait," Tiki cried. "Where's Clara?" She tried to pull away from Rieker's grip, but he slid his arms around her and held her tight. "I need her to tell me where Clara is."

The silver-haired faerie supported Larkin's limp frame and motioned toward Marcus's still body on the floor, now surrounded by green iridescent faerie blood. The other man scuttled over to the dead faerie's body and hefted him over his shoulder. The first faerie shifted his gaze to Rieker and Tiki.

"Clara," Tiki cried, tears running down her cheeks. He didn't acknowledge Tiki's question. Instead he stared at them for a moment as though memorizing their faces. Then the two faeries along with their prisoner and cargo shimmered out of view and were gone.

The silence was as deafening as the din before.

As the realization of what had just occurred sank in, Tiki turned to Rieker in panic. She clutched at his arm, fear contorting her face. "What just happened? Who were those men that took Larkin? Where is she?" At his wince of pain, she realized she was digging her fingernails into the wounds on his arm, but she didn't release her grip. "How will we get Clara back now?"

Before Rieker could reply, a strange choking noise came from behind them. As one they turned to see Leo, bracing himself against the door frame. His eyes were locked on the floor where the still figure of Marcus had sprawled moments ago. Green blood still marked the spot.

Leo's face was an ashen gray color. His chest heaved as he spoke, his words heavy with horror and disbelief.

"Was that a dead faerie?"

Chapter Thirty-eight

I THINK I'm going to be sick." Leo staggered from the room. Rieker returned his focus to Tiki.

He reached out and put his hands on her arms, as if to steady her. "We'll find her, Tiki," he said. "I promise you."

Tiki was unable to stop the tears pooling in her eyes. "What if Larkin took her to the Otherworld?" she whispered. "What if we can never find her again?"

"She wouldn't have done that. She was wanted in the Otherworld. It was risking her life to go there. Besides, faeries can't care for mortals. Clara was sick. She would have had to keep her here." Rieker smoothed the hair out of her face. "I'm sure of it."

"But where? Where is she?" Tiki wanted to believe him.

Rieker reached out and wrapped his arms around her, pulling her close. "I've learned that Larkin likes to hide in plain sight. She likes to take risks. It's almost a game to her—catch me if you can, I'm right under your nose."

He rubbed Tiki's back, his warm hand reassuring her. "It was that way when she pretended to live on the estate next to mine when I was a boy. Then she brazenly brought Clara here after she kidnapped her, knowing I was gone for weeks at a time." His tone became regretful. "Because she knew I would never think to look for her in my own house." He heaved a long sigh. "I think it amuses her to make people look stupid."

He gripped Tiki's shoulders and held her away from him so he could look into her face. "Clara is somewhere obvious, I'm sure of it. We just have to think like Larkin."

"But Clara must be alone now. She's so little. What if she's scared?" Tiki's voice started to rise hysterically. "What if she wanders away and we never find her?"

"Calm down, Tiki. It's the middle of the night. I would bet that Clara is asleep somewhere. Larkin intended to trade Clara for the ring. She wouldn't have left her someplace where she would get lost. It just doesn't make any sense." Rieker put his lips close to her ear. "Don't worry. I'll help you find Clara. If it's the last thing I do."

For a second, Tiki leaned against him. How she wanted to believe him. To believe *in* him. With a sob, she let her head rest on his warm chest, the steady beat of his heart echoing in her ear. "But what about you and Larkin?" she asked in a whisper.

"Tiki, there is no me and Larkin. She wanted you to believe that—to use us against each other to get the ring." Rieker shifted his position so he could look into Tiki's face. "I've talked to her several times, put up with her advances, to try and learn where she was hiding Clara." He wiped a tear from her cheek with his thumb. "But it was for one purpose and only one. To help you."

Tears flooded from Tiki's eyes again. Was it possible?

Rieker smiled at her. A gentle, warm smile, his eyes clear of the shadows that normally lurked there. "Don't cry, Tiki. Do you remember our walk in the park? When I told you what had happened to my family?"

Tiki nodded.

"And do you remember the reason I kept returning to Charing Cross? Why I was following you?"

Tiki gave another nod, smaller this time. A small bubble of hope rose in her chest.

"Everything I told you was true."

"You don't love Larkin?"

"No." Rieker shook his head. "There's only one person I love, Tiki." He made a noise that sounded like something between a laugh and a sob. "And I denied it as long as I could. But I don't want to live without you." His thumb caressed her cheek. "It's you I love. No one else."

His lips found hers then with a warmth and passion that confirmed his words. Tiki's arms slipped around his neck and pulled him close, her emotions burning through her. She'd been afraid to admit it to herself, but she had wanted him to love her so much.

He crushed her tight to his chest, his lips against her hair. "I love you, Tiki," he whispered. "Not Larkin. Never Larkin. Only you."

Tiki slid her arms around his waist and pressed her face against his bloodied white shirt, breathing in his scent. Rieker was here, with her. And they loved each other.

Someone cleared his throat. "I hate to break up this charming moment, but I need some questions answered."

Tiki and Rieker turned to find Leo, standing in the entrance to the hallway, looking thoroughly shell-shocked.

"Leo, yes, of course." Rieker strode over to him. He slid an arm over the prince's shoulders, motioning to Tiki with his head. "Let's go back to my sitting room and talk." He led Leo down the hallway, with Tiki following behind.

* * *

HALF an hour later, Tiki took a sip of her hot tea and wished again that Leo would stop staring at her.

"So, old Mamie was right," Leo repeated, setting his teacup down with a revealing clatter.

"Faeries." Rieker nodded his head in acknowledgment, looking over at Tiki with a gentle smile. He reached out and wrapped his warm fingers around hers. "We've been caught in the middle of a battle as old as time."

"Faeries," Leo repeated, but he didn't sound as though he disbelieved Rieker's answer. "Around us all the time, you think?"

Rieker nodded.

"Go on, then, why don't we see them?"

"Part of the truce that's held within the ring, Leo. They choose when we see them and when we don't. And sometimes we do and don't realize who we're looking at." Rieker leaned forward and rested his elbows on his knees. "Tonight was a bit of an exception. Just as we battle other countries for power, so do the fey. Their world is more ancient and complex than ours, as they straddle both worlds. But tonight the battle spilled over into London."

"And what was the battle for?" Leo asked.

Rieker looked over at Tiki. She reached into her pocket and pulled out her fist. Like a flower unfolding under the warmth of the sun, she slowly unfurled her fingers to reveal the queen's ring.

"Mother's ring," Leo gasped. With shaking fingers, he reached out to pluck the band from her palm. He stared at the flames embedded in the heart of the stone, still burning brightly. His brow drew down in a frown as a thousand different possibilities rushed across his face. Finally he lifted his eyes to Tiki's with an accusing stare. "You did steal this, didn't you?"

Rieker interrupted before Tiki could answer. "Now, Leo, don't jump to conclusions. We've risked our lives to keep the ring safe from the likes of Larkin and Marcus and others." He nodded at Tiki. "You should be thanking her for returning the ring safely to you."

"But if you didn't steal it, how did you end up with it?"

Rieker smiled at Tiki. "Probably best not to question everything. Leo, just be glad it's safe again."

Leo looked from Rieker to Tiki, as if debating whether to push for more information or not. His gaze dropped to Tiki's clothes. "And those clothes?" Before either of them could answer, Leo shook his head and raised his hand to stop their answers. "No, on second thought, don't tell me. It's probably better if I don't know that part, either. What's important is that we have the ring back. That's all that matters, really."

He turned to look at Tiki. "You *were* the boy I met in the park that day, I can see that now." His eyes dropped to her wrist. "I knew you and Elizabeth were the same person. You *had* to be with that mark." He hesitated a moment before shaking his head. "But what is your real name?"

Tiki flushed and smiled at Leo. "My name is Tara Kathleen." She leaned forward and whispered loud enough for Rieker to hear, "But just call me Tiki. I don't need any fancy titles among friends."

The corner of Leo's mouth turned up as she echoed the very words he had spoken to Elizabeth at the masked ball.

"Tiki," he repeated. "Tiki of the faerie ring." He said the words softly, in an almost bemused voice. He reached forward and took her hand, looking deep into her eyes. "I suspect there is much more to your story that I've yet to hear." He raised her hand to his lips, his eyes holding hers. "I look forward to learning all about you."

Tiki twisted the edge of her coat in her hands as she waited for Rieker to return from escorting Leo out. Larkin was gone. The ring had been returned to Leo. Where was Clara? Her eyes burned as she fought to keep from crying again. She had failed the little girl. After all this, she had lost Clara. She dropped her head into her hands and sobbed as though her heart had broken.

"Tiki . . ." Rieker came into the sitting room and slid his hand along her hunched back. "Tiki, don't cry." He took her into his arms, shushing her like a child, holding her close.

"But I l-love her," she sobbed. "I was supposed to take c-care of her."

"You did take care of her. You saved Clara's life. More than once." Rieker guided her over to the couch and sat next to her, an arm around her shoulders.

"E-even Larkin said she was my responsibility that day in Mr. Potts' bookstore." Tiki's breath came out in hiccuping gasps.

"Shhh . . ." He pulled Tiki against him, his hand caressing her hair. "We've got to think of someplace obvious that Larkin would have hidden her tonight. Maybe she said something that was a clue."

"I can't remember anything," Tiki sniffed.

"Think, Tiki. There's got to be *something*."

They lapsed into silence. Tiki let her mind drift back

over the events of the day: from Larkin finding her in the station to tell her Clara was sick, to the disturbing reality of the Otherworld, to watching those strange men in their silver tunics fight with Larkin and ultimately subdue her. She tried not to think of stabbing Marcus.

Suddenly she sat upright in alarm.

Where were Shamus and the others now? Were they still out in the cold at Buckingham Palace, looking for Rieker?

"I've got to go check on—" Another thought struck her. Toots, Shamus, and Fiona had gone to Buckingham Palace to watch for Rieker. She had come to Grosvenor Square. Charing Cross had been left empty. Had Larkin known?

"Rieker . . ." Tiki clutched at his arm, hope making her gasp for breath. "I think I might know where Clara is." Her words were rushed as she explained what she was thinking.

"There's only one way to find out."

THE snow was coming down hard and fast, coating everything in a sparkling blanket of purest white. The ruts that other carriages had cut into the covered roads were quickly filling in as the night wore on and the snow continued to fall.

Had it been under any other circumstances, Tiki would have laughed at the utter disbelief on the driver's face when he had been rousted from the bed he'd just crawled into and commanded to drive Rieker and some unknown street urchin to Charing Cross. But as it was, she had to press her lips together to keep from urging the man to hurry.

The ride was agonizingly slow as the horses worked to pull the carriage along the slippery streets. Tiki picked nervously at the blanket that covered her knees as she worried again where Shamus, Toots, and Fiona were. They were resourceful, she reminded herself. They had all learned to survive.

"Tiki." Rieker slid a hand over her nervous fingers. "We'll find Clara. If she's not here, she's someplace else. It's just a matter of elimination."

Tiki bit her lip, afraid that if she tried to talk, she would cry. If Clara wasn't in Charing Cross, where else could they look?

After what felt like forever, the carriage pulled up to the front of the station. Tiki jumped from the carriage step before the wheels came to a complete stop.

"Hurry." She grabbed Rieker's hand and pulled him along behind her through the alley.

"Please let her be here, please let her be here," she mumbled as she ran. They slipped through the maintenance tunnels, and Tiki pushed their back door open. For a second, she just stared at the scene before her.

Several candles were lit, giving the room a soft yellow glow. Shamus, Fiona, and Toots were sitting around a small form covered with blankets near the stove. For just a second, her heart dropped.

"Is she . . . ?"

Shamus and Fiona looked up. It was the soft smile on Shamus's face that told her everything was okay.

"She's home, Teek." There was a note of wonder in Fiona's voice. "She was here sleeping when we got back." She reached down and smoothed the blond curls. "Just like she never left."

Tiki dashed into the room and fell to her knees next to Clara. She burst into tears when she looked at the little face surrounded by tousled blond curls.

"Clara," Tiki said softly. She rested the backs of her fingers on the little girl's soft cheek.

At the sound of Tiki's voice, Clara opened sleepy eyes.

"Tiki!" With a cry of happiness, Clara sat up and threw her arms around Tiki. She hugged her tight, burying her head in Tiki's neck. Finally she gave a shuddering sigh and lifted her head. "I missed you, Tiki."

Tiki cupped Clara's face in her hands and kissed her forehead. "I've missed you, too. But you're safe now and we'll never, ever be apart again."

Clara took turns hugging Fiona and Shamus and Toots. She looked shyly at Rieker, then buried her face in Tiki's chest. With a smile, Tiki ran her hands over the blond curls and sat down cross-legged, pulling her into her lap. "How are you feeling? Are you still coughing?"

"I'm a lot better now." Clara smiled up, her blue eyes bright and healthy.

"I'm so glad," Tiki cried, hugging her tight. The joy bubbling inside was almost more than she could contain.

"You're smotherin' me, Teek," Clara cried, her voice muffled.

Tiki released her grip and gave a giddy laugh as she smiled down at her. "Sorry about that."

"You practically squeezed all my stuffin' out," Clara said with wide eyes. "Better be careful or I'm going to look like Doggie." For a minute, her little chin quivered. "But I lost Doggie. She ran away."

"No, she didn't," Fiona said. She jumped up and ran to one of the cupboards behind the stove. "Here she is."

Clara's eyes lit up and she held her arms out eagerly for the little stuffed animal.

"Doggie has missed you, too," Fiona said as Clara hugged the dog close. "She's been waiting for you to come home."

Chapter Thirty-nine

A T Rieker's insistence, they all piled into the carriage and rode back to Grosvenor Square. On the way there, Tiki told them of Larkin's capture and returning the ring to Leo. Rather than saying exactly what had happened to Marcus, she just told them that Marcus wouldn't be bothering them anymore.

Shamus explained to Tiki how Prince Leo had stood on the steps, watching Rieker's carriage pull away. There was no way they could have jumped on the boot without being seen. Unable to follow him, they had returned to Charing Cross to await Tiki's return. It was there that they had found Clara, fast asleep.

Once they arrived at Rieker's town house, Rieker brought out plates of beef, ham, and fresh French bread for them to feast on. Toots's head was nodding over his plate when Tiki said it was time for everyone to go to bed. Shamus carried Toots to a bedroom where each had his very own bed.

Clara and Fiona went to sleep in one of the bedrooms down the hall from Rieker's suite, where Tiki could easily hear and check on the child. Though she still had a small cough, the little girl seemed to be in surprisingly good shape, suffering no lasting damage from her time with

Larkin. It appeared that Larkin had lied about Clara coughing up blood.

It was a little while later when Tiki and Rieker sat down in his small living room. Rieker sat next to her on the sofa, swiveled around so he faced her. He reached for her hand, a soft smile on his face.

"Tiki, there's something I'd like to talk to you about." He cleared his throat, and for a second, Tiki got the impression that he was nervous. "I'd like you and your family to be my houseguests." His voice dropped as if he were suddenly unsure of himself. "Until we can figure out something more permanent, of course."

Tiki looked at him in amazement, at a loss for words.

"I've got my housekeeper, Mrs. Bosworth, living here," Rieker added hastily, "along with her husband and my staff. It will all be perfectly appropriate."

Tiki slowly looked around the room, as if appraising its appeal as a possible home. The fire flickered warmly from the hearth. Bookshelves covered one wall, and windows looked out to the trees outside. Beautiful oil paintings of the English countryside hung on the walls. A plush rug covered the floor, adding to the warmth in the room. "Stay here? And leave Charing Cross?" Her lips curved up in a grin as her eyes landed on him. "We'd love to."

Rieker laughed as his shoulders slumped with relief. "Good, then it's settled."

It was a short time later, after Tiki had gone and checked on Clara again, that she broached the subject uppermost on her mind.

"What did you mean when you said you were descended from Eridanus?" Tiki stared at him. "Is that true?"

Rieker nodded. "It was something that Kieran revealed to me. Of course, at first I thought he was a complete lunatic, and I didn't really pay much attention to anything he said. But then I started noticing things. Faces I could see that others didn't. Shadows that shimmered and moved and suddenly a person would be standing there."

He stood up and leaned an arm against the mantel, staring down into the fire. "After I had time to adjust to the idea that my family had been murdered, I started wondering why we would be targeted for elimination. Why us? Then some of the things my father had said started coming back to me. Hints of some new responsibility I would have when I turned sixteen."

He pushed off the mantel and turned to face Tiki, his back to the fire. "His insistence that I carry a knife with an iron blade at all times. The hushed conversations with my mum that would stop when I entered the room."

"Your parents knew, then?"

"I'm sure of it now." Rieker rolled his shoulders as if trying to ease knots of tension. "But there are still so many questions." He stared at her with shadowed eyes, his voice soft. "They encouraged, almost insisted, that I become good chums with Leo as a child. Now I wonder if they didn't have some plan in mind from the beginning for me to safeguard the ring or at least have access to it." He paced from the fireplace to the other side of the room.

Tiki shifted her position so she could follow his path. "You mean they knew this attack might be coming?"

Rieker's words were hesitant at first, his eyes focused on the far wall as he tried to remember. "I don't think they knew specifically what would happen, only that eventually, something would occur. From what Kieran said, the

Seelie court has been waiting for Donegal to make a move. I think my parents knew of the war between the faerie courts and knew that it could eventually put us at risk."

Tiki understood what Rieker was saying, about recognizing how some of the things she'd seen all of her life and not paid much attention to now took on a new meaning.

"And do you think Donegal will continue to hunt you?" she asked softly.

Rieker heaved a sigh. "I think he wants to eliminate me for the same reason he had Larkin murder the rest of my family. Because I carry the blood of Eridanus, I am a threat to him. A threat to his pursuit of the ring of the truce. I suspect he wants to finish what Larkin didn't."

A thread of fear trickled down Tiki's spine. "How will you protect yourself?"

"As Kieran tried to do, there are others who stand guard over me. I'm not in this battle alone." His hand moved so fast that it was nothing more than a blur. Before Tiki could blink, he held the iron dagger pointed at her. He chuckled with self-assurance. "Plus, there are some advantages to having the blood of a faerie king running in my veins. No matter how faint it might be." He flipped the knife around and just as quickly made the blade disappear.

"I find that I can move fast enough to disappear when I need to as well." He sobered. "Though now that the ring is guarded again by the royals, I'm not sure how that will affect Donegal's pursuit of me." He returned to stand before the fire, his elbow resting on the wooden mantel. "Especially since I plan to convince Leo that the palace has been infiltrated and to allow me to guard the ring."

* * *

THE dark night sky slowly shifted to the pink gray of dawn, yet neither of them wanted to rest, nor leave the company of the other and the truths they were sharing. There were too many things to discuss, too many unanswered questions.

"How did you know the name of my birthmark? *An fáinne sí?*" It was the first time Tiki had uttered the words out loud. They felt strangely familiar on her tongue. "Was it Kieran?"

Rieker stepped closer and slid onto the sofa next to her, their knees touching. "He told me it was only a rumor."

Tiki narrowed her eyes to shield her surprise. "A rumor of what?"

"That someone bearing the mark was hidden in London."

Suddenly every part of her was alert. *Hidden.* That's what Larkin had said, too: *That's why Adasara hid you in London.* Her breath caught in her throat at the implications. "Hidden from what?"

Rieker reached for her hand and threaded his fingers through hers. "He didn't say, Teek." His words were gentle, as if he knew what a shock the information must be. "Just that should I see someone who bore the mark, to know they were connected to the world of the fey." He hesitated and rubbed her fingers with his thumb as if to soften the impact of his words. "He said we would be drawn to each other. And that I should be very careful."

"Careful?" Tiki said. "Of me? What could I—"

Rieker shifted and slid an arm around the back of Tiki's tense shoulders, pulling her closer. "What happened with you and Larkin? You were only gone for a few minutes, but I swear it felt like hours."

Tiki lapsed into silence, seeing once again that meadow and the mounds, hearing the lilting music that pulled at her with an unnatural longing. "I was there." Her voice was soft with wonder as she recounted the memory. "In the Otherworld."

To her surprise, he nodded. "That's what I thought happened." He peered closer at her, clearly intrigued. "Do you know how you got there?"

The room was silent but for the crack and hiss of the fire. "It happened when Larkin pushed me backward. When she grabbed my wrist, it was as though she held a flame to my skin. The next thing I knew, we were in a meadow and it was twilight."

"What did you see?" His voice was hushed.

Tiki described what she remembered of the meadow, the mounds, the huge stones. Of how Marcus appeared and how he had taunted Larkin. "He mentioned the claw." Tiki closed her eyes, envisioning the dark faerie before her in the deepening shadows. "That thing they put on her wings. He knew those who hunted her were close, that they would clamp her if they caught her." She shuddered, rubbing her face with her hands as though to erase the memory. "He made it clear that he wanted her captured." She hesitated. "So he could have me."

Rieker's jaw clenched at her words, but then he shook his head. "Marcus is dead now. He won't ever bother you again."

"Larkin said something else. Before Marcus arrived." Tiki hesitated, getting the courage up to speak the words burning on the tip of her tongue. "She said *an fáinne sí* was the birthmark of Finn MacLochlan. A high king of Tara."

She looked into Rieker's eyes, seeking the truth. "Have you ever heard of him? Of such a place?"

Rieker reached forward and smoothed a strand of hair from her face, his fingers lingering on her cheek. "I know there's an ancient place in Ireland called the Hill of Tara. It has something to do with kings and faeries." His voice softened. "But that's all I know."

Tiki clasped his hand, lacing her fingers through his, her eyes imploring. "But how will *I* know? How do I find out who I really am?"

"Tiki . . ." Rieker's lips were so close, his breath caressed her face. "We'll have to find the answers together. We're bound by more than love, it would seem. Destiny seems to have plans for us as well."

Chapter Forty

TIKI stood in the regal opulence of the Blue Drawing Room in Buckingham Palace as Queen Victoria addressed Rieker.

"It is after extensive private consultation with my family and *others*"—Queen Victoria's words were measured, but she gave a significant look to Rieker—"along with my own personal contemplation of the matter, that as a reward for his participation, at great personal risk, in the safe return to the monarchy of a valuable and historic piece of jewelry, I am honored to bestow this ring upon the person of Lord William Becker Richmond. To wear and protect as long as he shall live."

Rieker stood tall and proud next to the queen, every bit as regal as the English royalty in the room around him. Tiki's heart swelled with pride and love as she watched him accept the honor. Though Victoria didn't refer to their meetings, Tiki knew that Rieker had spent hours behind closed doors with the queen, explaining what he knew of the situation, including the things he had learned from Kieran as well as his own connection to the events through his heritage.

Queen Victoria looked solemnly at Rieker as she reached for his right hand and slid the ring of the truce onto his third finger. Her lips curved in a rare smile, and she nodded at him.

"*Na síochána, aontaímid,* Sir Richmond. For the sake of peace, we agree."

Tɪᴋɪ admired the beautiful ornaments sparkling with a magical glow on the Christmas tree. She marveled at the beauty of the room around her. Tomorrow would be the first day of the new year. The first day of a new beginning. Dark wood paneling on the walls created a cozy atmosphere amid tall bookcases that lined the walls. A cheery fire blazed in the hearth in front of where she sat.

It still warmed her to think that Rieker had invited all of them, her whole "family," to stay here in the town house with him as his guests. They were warm, safe, and clean, with plenty of food for the first time in years. Happiness such as she'd never known filled her until it was difficult to draw an even breath. She wouldn't even think about the time when they would have to return to Charing Cross. She knew it was inevitable, but for now she was going to enjoy what they had.

Rieker sat in a chair across from her, a contented smile on his face. He looked more relaxed than she'd ever seen him.

"I need your help," he said.

Tiki gazed inquiringly at him.

"I've given this a lot of thought, and I think it's something my parents would be very pleased with." He chuckled. "Though I'm quite sure my brothers would get a good laugh at the idea. I've made a few inquiries and looked into the prospect. I've just now gotten the go-ahead to proceed."

"What is it?"

"I'm going to start a free school for orphans. A place where they can come to learn to read and write. To learn their numbers. I'm going to name the school after my brothers." He cleared his throat. "The Thomas James Ragged School."

"Oh, Rieker." Tiki clapped her hands together. "I think that's a marvelous idea. There are so many children in need, and what a wonderful tribute to your family."

"We can feed the children lunch," Rieker continued. "Make sure they get at least one good meal a day." His expression softened. "But I need help. I'm going to need teachers. I was hoping that you would consider teaching at the Thomas James School."

Before Tiki could answer, he continued, "I'll need Shamus to help build the desks and chairs, and maybe Fiona could mend the children's clothes or help stitch some new clothes for those in need. You could tutor Fiona on the side. Toots and Clara could be our first students." He gave her a hopeful look. "What do you think?"

For a second, Tiki was speechless. Tears rushed to her eyes, and she blinked fast to hold them back. They would all be employed. Toots and Clara could learn their letters. They would be able to afford a flat of their own. Her family could stay together and be clean and well fed. Just as they'd always planned.

"Yes," she whispered, the tears spilling over her lashes. "A thousand times, yes."

It was several hours later, and Tiki's eyes drifted around the room. Her heart was so full, she thought she might burst. Shamus was asleep in an overstuffed chair next to the fire, his open mouth emitting small snores with every contented breath. Fiona and Toots ran past her toward the stairs, giggling as they chased each other, playing yet another game of hide-and-seek. Clara was tucked into bed after having eaten a hearty meal and was fast asleep, clutching her tattered but clean Doggie. She hadn't coughed in three days.

Tiki's eyes fell on Rieker, who sat across from her by the Christmas tree, reading *Oliver Twist*.

"You know, Wills"—she smiled—"that book has a happy ending."

Rieker looked up at her. His smoky eyes were clear and warm as he took in her lavender dress and long, dark curls. He returned her smile. "That's the kind I like best."

AUTHOR'S NOTE

The places in *The Faerie Ring* are real, and if you find your-self in London, you can visit Buckingham Palace and St. James's Park and walk by the Birdkeeper's Cottage at the end of the lake. The Ring, dating from the 1600s, where Tiki goes to find Larkin, is still a favorite ride or walk within Hyde Park.

Charing Cross is an active station in the Underground, not far from Trafalgar Square. King's Cross is the busiest tube station in all of London, though I wouldn't recommend trying to pick any pockets.

Great Ormond Street Hospital, where Clara got help, is still helping children to this day and relies on charitable donations to survive. If you'd like more information, go here: http://www.ich.ucl.ac.uk/.

Finally, the World's End pub is still open for business in Camden Town.

Thank you for reading *The Faerie Ring,* and should you see a shadow move out of the corner of your eye, pay attention—it may be more than what it seems.

KIKI HAMILTON
May 19, 2010

Acknowledgments

My road to publication started with a dream that was shared with many people along the way. I'd like to offer heartfelt thanks to the following:

My brother, Dr. Thomas E. Martin (fondly known as Tommy), who has never wavered in his belief that I would become a published author. His belief fueled mine, and now look where we are!

Susan Chang, senior editor at Tor Books—not only for her willingness to take a chance on a debut author, but also for her love of Tiki, Rieker, and Clara and their story of the faerie ring. Our work together became a true collaboration, and the book you read today is much richer through her thoughtful comments and brilliant sense of story.

Seth Lerner, for creating the breathtaking and mesmerizing jacket for *The Faerie Ring*. I am so grateful.

Mark and Carly, not just for being my beta readers, but for their patience and understanding as my computer became a permanent fixture on my lap and they both learned to fall asleep to the *click-click* of the keys.

Also thanks to Doby and Gramps, Judy, Larry, and Emily for their endless encouragement.

To my überagent, Kate Schafer Testerman of kt literary, llc, for finding a home for Tiki.

I am also thankful to my many friends who have expressed interest in *The Faerie Ring* along the way, as well as the wonderful writers in my life with whom I share critiques, advice, opinions, laughter, tears, and sometimes secrets on this crazy journey to publication—without you guys I wouldn't be here: Paula MacLaughlin, Nandini Bajpai, Uma Krishnaswami, Sarah Aronson, Annette Gulati, Ellen C. Oh, Carrie Harris, the members of Uma's Alumni, WD2PR, the Enchanted Inkpot, the Elevensies, and the Class of 2k11. Finally, thank you to all my writing friends on the blueboards at VerlaKay.com who share, support, and celebrate the joy of being an author.

About the Author

Kiki Hamilton believes in faeries. And magic. Though she has a B.A. in business administration from Washington State University and has worked in a variety of management positions over the years, her first love is writing young adult stories of fantasy and adventure. Kiki lives near Seattle, Washington, where it only rains part of the time. She is a member of the Class of 2k11, the Elevensies, and the Enchanted Inkpot.

Visit Kiki's website and blog at www.kikihamilton.com.

For more information about Tiki and the faerie ring, visit www.thefaeriering.com.